To
Adele

Best wishes

Also by Derryl Flynn

The Albion

SCRAPYARD BLUES

Derryl Flynn

First published in 2014 by

Grinning Bandit Books

http://grinningbandit.webnode.com

ISBN 978-0-9575851-4-0

Cover design by Derryl Flynn

DEDICATION

For my dad.

Acknowledgements

Sincere thanks go to The Three Amigos – Terry, Frank and Roman.

Love to my wife and family. And to 'Our Kid' for being my brother.

Cover photo and design: Derryl Flynn. With special thanks to Kurt and Martyn.

"When I was young I was sure of everything;
In a few years, having been mistaken a thousand times,
I was not half so sure of most things as I was before.
At present I am hardly sure of anything but what God has re-
vealed to me."

John Wesley
Methodist preacher & theologian
1703 – 1791

"Lord have mercy on my wicked soul,
I wouldn't mistreat you baby, for my weight in gold
I said Lord have mercy on my wicked soul,
You know I wouldn't mistreat nobody, baby,
Not for my weight in gold."

Eddie James "Son House" Jnr.
Man of the blues
1902 – 1988

iv

Rendezvous In A Nightmare

'AM I IMMORTAL?'

'No, but you are eternal.'

'Yet this is not heaven.'

'Perpetuity does not guarantee divinity.'

'Who are you?'

'Who do you want me to be?'

'I want you to be God.'

'Then God I am.'

'You could be the Devil.'

'What's the difference?'

'One's for good, the other's for evil.'

'Hmm, perceptions; you'll have to define the two concepts for me.'

'I... I thought I could; now I'm not so sure –Good is doing unto others as ... as...'

'...As you would have them do unto you? Doesn't sound right all of a sudden does it, Jack? That little pearl of wisdom seems a bit blurred; somewhat fuzzy round the edges, isn't it?'

'Why are you here?'

'You asked for me.'

'I prayed to God.'

'Ahh, back to perceptions; you prayed to God and this is what you got. Are you disappointed, Jack? That young girl was. She prayed to God. She prayed to God so hard – look what *she* got.'

'All I want is to out the truth.'

'And so you pray to something that you only ever had a vague, medieval based notion of; some deity you previously had no time for, and possibly might not have believed in anyway. What sort of truth are we talking about here, Jack?'

'I didn't kill anyone is the only truth I know.'

'That, my friend, is merely *your* perception. Look around you. This is the only truth you need concern yourself with now. This is your reality. I would have thought you would have got used to it by now.'

'This isn't real. You're not real. This is just some sick mind fuck.'

'And still you pray – I admire your tenacity, Jack, I really do. Go ahead, try and open your eyes, you'll find the reality is still the same, always has been, always will be. That's the truth, the whole truth and nothing but the truth. Funny that; I seem to remember you placing your hand on some old book and saying the same thing – that *was* a long time ago, wasn't it? – Truth? ... The truth is just a crock of shit if you ask me – see you around, Jack; maybe the next time you decide to pray...'

My pleas of innocence are lost in translation as the image before me dissolves in a cloud of stinking sulphur and scorched metal, while through the ether, by rote, seeps the inevitable: a face I have known, loved and forsaken. Frozen in fear, her lips question *"why, Jack... why?"*

The mocking laughter of demons and keening banshees mirror my screams as muscle and sinew are torn apart. And in a blood spattered scene I start to go under, while someone hammers at the gates of Hell...

'Warder! – Warder...! For fuck's sake!'

The mocking laughter fractures and fades, giving way to a desperate beating of clenched flesh and bone upon steel. A light pops on to another world. My eyes open to the truth and I lie in a reservoir of dread induced sweat.

'Pipe down, yer goghorn,' I hear a screw shout at my frantic cellmate. ''Sup, Smiffy havin' a mare again is he?'

'Get me out of here – I swear to God I can't do another fuckin' night with that mad bastard.'

'Relax, son,' consoles the warder, eyeing him through the cake-hole. 'You won't have to endure him for much longer; he'll be gone in a few days...'

One

THE PRISON OFFICER walks briskly down the narrow corridor with a sense of purpose, shiny boots marching out time along polished concrete. I follow a couple of paces behind, at my own speed, not quite lethargic but almost. Inside my head I instinctively apply a twelve bar rhythm in order to mellow out the kerlunk-kerlunk regular beat that leads the way. He casts the occasional backward glance just to make sure I'm still with him. I send him a little reassuring smile in return. He frowns slightly and it's like he's a bit puzzled as to why I don't want to get this short journey over with as quickly as possible, only for me, this journey has been anything but short, and even now I can't be certain that it's at an end. After all this time, I'm in no rush.

At the end of the corridor the kerlunk-kerlunk stops abruptly, and the accompanying rhythm inside my head fades into the ether. I casually swing my bag of meagre but precious belongings over my shoulder and patiently watch the screw punch numbers into an electronic keypad on the wall. Patience is a virtue. He takes a key card, which is attached to a chain, which is, in turn, fastened to his belt, and swipes it in another machine. LED's twitch and beep, electronics click and whirr and metal bolts slide neatly back into their hollow shafts with satisfying clunks. A green light above the door flashes. He pushes it open and ushers me through.

'This is as far as I go, Smithy.' He offers me a look that says he's sad to see me leave, like we've been best mates for years, and like he's about to burst into tears and give me a hug. But the guy's a virtual stranger, hardly knows me. The walls know me better; I've been here longer, a hell of a lot longer. My eyes show the same sentiment as the walls: fucking none. He passes me my release papers with one hand and offers me his other. I shake it loosely. 'You take care now, and make sure you stay out of trouble. You hear?' He gives me a condescending slap on the back as I turn away, and for the millionth time a voice inside my head screams out in protest, because the fact is I've never done anything wrong in my life, not criminally wrong anyhow, but no one has cared to listen for these past twenty-five years. So the scream of protest stays inside my head where it can't fall on deaf ears like it has a million times before.

I cross the dry moat and look up into a clear blue sky on this January morning. Crisp, cold, my breath forms puffs of vapour as I walk. Waiting for me at the small gatehouse office is an overweight screw in an ill-fitting uniform. He takes my papers from me and we go inside where he hands them to a colleague sitting behind a desk. He checks them over briefly before looking up.

'So, the big day arrives at last, eh, Smithy?'

I look on impassively. Say nothing.

'You should've pleaded guilty mate; you'd have been long gone.'

Such sound advice, what the hell are you doing working in the prison service pal? A guy like you ought to have been a lawyer. Why on Earth did I never consider that after all this time? The misanthropist I have become wells up inside me. I grit my teeth but my features betray nothing but well-practiced asceticism. I humour the jocular fool.

'Yeah, you're right,' I nod in mock hindsight. 'I should've done.'

The officer somehow senses I'm not in the mood for farewell banter and quickly rubber stamps the official end to my incarceration.

The fat screw does the business with his key card. More electronics beep and click. I get the green light for go. The small door set into the giant gate opens and for the first time in twenty-five years I step back into society.

I stand there waiting for a sensation, a feeling that heralds a fresh start, a new beginning. It doesn't come. I pull air deep into my lungs and try to savour freedom. It tastes bitter. Taking a final backward glance I see the two officers chatting behind the glass. I can't hear what they're saying, but I can guess...

'Who was that then?' Fat Bloke asks his mate.

'That was JD Smith. Lifer. Murdered some young lass in pretty gruesome circumstances, so I'm told. Maintained his innocence throughout. He's done the full stretch. Twenty-five years.'

'Do you think he done it?'

The guy behind the desk blows air from his cheeks. 'Yeah, course he did.'

Mandatory: full tariff. No remission, no parole, not when you deny your guilt, not when you're In Denial of Murder. The system rules; the system will screw you into submission. You don't fuck with the system. Mandatory: full tariff. The words rattle around inside my head and I try to summon up some sort of defiance, try to claim a victory of sorts. I took the full weight of the law and came through, survived. But, try as I might, I feel no sense of victory, just emptiness. Resilience and defiance when all is stacked against you becomes just a survival instinct, a necessity you build into your psyche to prevent you from going under. There's no sense of achievement, no feeling of winning. The emotions of hate, of anger, frustration, loneliness, despair and injustice have all been absorbed; I've given them their head, they've all had their time and time is all I've had. I've trodden a path towards a horizon I know I'll never reach. The path might look different from today but the horizon stays as distant as ever.

Traffic roars on the streets; people getting on with their lives, coping with the daily grind, week after week, month after month, year after year. No past, no present, no future. And I'm invisible. I only exist in a parallel universe, forced to observe a world I've learned to hate, from a bubble. Through the privilege of a TV screen I've seen the results of wars and pestilence on a grand scale. I've learned new phrases like Tsunami and Nine-Eleven. I've watched politicians from all parties wringing their hands and paying lip service to an ever more frightened public in an increasingly sick world. New legislation is in the statute book. In future the likes of JD Smith will never be let out. Life must mean life. Then, over time, I've watched, sometimes with envy, other times with hope, the release of The Birmingham Six, The Guildford Four, The Bridgewater Four, and more recently the likes of Stefan Kiszko, Angela Cannings, Stephen Downing, and many more like them, all finally have their convictions quashed on appeal. I was never given right to appeal. There was never any new evidence in my case. I never had politically motivated celebrities or probing journalists fighting my corner. I'm not really a free man; I'm still a convicted murderer out on Life Licence, so the papers I'm clutching tell me. But now I have a choice. I can live out the rest of my days with this stigma attached to me, with this heavy burden weighing down my soul, knowing twenty-five years of my life have been taken from me by someone who might be still out there, and do nothing. Or I can search for the truth; dig up the past and clear my name.

A car horn sounds from the other side of the road. I light up a snout, sling my bag over my shoulder and cross. I'm almost killed at least three times before I reach the other side of the street. I'm not used to traffic like this. I open the passenger door of the car. It's an Audi or a Merc, I think; some posh German number anyhow.

'Fuckin' hell!' exclaims Digweed as I bounce onto the leather and sling my bag in the back.

'What?'

He looks at me wide eyed and gob-struck. 'Well, that would've been a waste of time, wouldn't it? All them years inside and then you come out and get flattened by a car. I thought you had a death wish or something.'

I give a shrug like I couldn't have cared less and admire the smart, state of the art interior of his motor. Cars have changed a lot since I remembered them.

'Very nice,' I purr, sinking comfy into the soft leather. 'Somebody's done all right for themselves. Very tidy.'

'Yeah, and I aim to keep it that way. No smoking, if you don't mind,' he remonstrates, looking nervously at the inch of ash that sits precariously at the end of my roll-up. I make a fruitless search of the door for a window handle. Then, as if by magic, the glass drops into the door with a soft, almost silent sshhh. Digweed notes my surprised expression, takes his finger off a button and shakes his head. I flick my smoke, sparking onto the pavement. 'Oh, by the way; what you just did constitutes a fifty pound fine these days,' he says as a matter of fact.

'Fifty fucking quid?' I exclaim disbelieving. He nods gravely. Things *have* changed. I have a lot to re-learn. 'Start your engine then, pal. Let's be off, I've hung around here long enough.'

'The engine's already running.' He smirks, puts his foot down so that I sink into the back of my seat, and expertly manoeuvres the silent beast into the manic flow of traffic. 'Where's it to then, old man? The world's your oyster.'

'I think the word is cloister. The world is my fucking cloister. You'd better take us up to Jeanie's…'

As we stop, start and crawl our way through the city towards the motorway I curiously observe the evolution of English suburban custom and culture; the bed sheet cum banner strung across a roundabout proclaiming that some poor, unsuspecting individual is 40 TODAY. While two hundred yards further down the road and at depressingly regular intervals, bunches of dead and decaying flowers and the occasional weather-beaten teddy bear lashed to a lamppost with strapping wire and duct tape, serve as sad, sodden shrines to accident victims, casualties who have fallen to the scourge of the drug fuelled joy-rider and drunk driver.

The exterior scenes of organised chaos and bizarre ritual soon begin to make me bored and irritable, so I focus my attention on the knobs and buttons on Digweed's flash dash. I press one at random and a disc silently spews forth from a thin horizontal slit. I take it from the unit and scrutinise it with interest.

'It's a CD,' says Digweed.

'I know what a fucking CD is,' I spit back at him. 'I haven't been in solitary for the past quarter of a century. Who is it?' He hands me the case. It's a compilation of rhythm & blues classics and what I remember as being rare and obscure. My eyes light up at some of the artists and titles. 'Bloody hell! Where did you get this?' I ask, impressed.

'Downloaded it,' he says like it was a stupid question.

Download, MP3, I-Pod. There's a technological revolution afoot where music is concerned. Nowadays it seems anything and everything is accessible with increasingly weird and wonderful ways in which to listen to it.

I offer the disc back into its slot and the machine impatiently snatches it from my grasp.

'Crank it up, then.'

Digweed strokes something without taking his hands off the wheel and all of a sudden the car is filled with music from heaven. Magic Slim and The Teardrops playing a live version of Goin' to Mississippi. Devil's music. But I'm in paradise as the twelve-bar-beat envelops me, wraps itself around me like a warm welcoming blanket, making the hairs on the back of my neck stand on end. And the sound is incredible, unbelievable, like I'm there in the hall three feet away from the stage and the blue neon indicator on the player says it's not even at quarter volume. Digweed flashes me a big, daft, cheesy grin, like he knows all about the sensations that are coursing through my body. I nod and grin back at him before closing my eyes, sinking back into the leather in complete and utter contentment, surrendering totally to the sound. I put my other issues on a back-burner for a while and let the blues take control.

With my eyes still shut I half-consciously sense a change in the sound of the engine as we escape the confines of inner city and finally reach motorway. Suddenly free and unfettered, Digweed gives the German made beast its head and I sink even further back into my seat. On the car hi-fi John Campbell john is screaming The World Is Crazy, doing the business with his bottleneck; gliding up and down frets, frantic and fraught, rhythm section galloping alongside, keeping it all in check.

I cock open an eye just as we cruise past Hartshead Moor

Services and I suddenly realise we're travelling along my old section. I sit up and take in the once familiar scenery as we drop down towards Brighouse before commencing what is now a four-lane incline up to Ainley Top. And I start to drift again, back to a time and place full of happy memories, when the world truly was my oyster, a different world, a different time and place, and a very different JD Smith. Thirty-six years ago, the summer of Nineteen Seventy-Two...

Two

I WAS BORN John Daniel Smith; Jack Daniel, like the bourbon from the American south; JD Smith, the likeable deputy from the sixties cowboy series The Dakotas played by craggy faced actor Jack Elam, or, as I was more commonly known amongst my mates at the time, Jack, JD, Jay, Smudge or simply Smithy. I used to be a good- looking kid. People would say I bore a striking resemblance to the late Stevie Marriott, ace singer and guitarist of The Small Faces and later, Humble Pie, and I wouldn't argue with that. Others said I was a cocky little sod, bit of an arrogant fucker. I used to call it confidence, and anyhow, I didn't give a stuff what anybody else thought.

That year I left school at Easter and got a job as a chain lad on the new motorway. The M62, freshly cut from the Pennines with its long, deep, brown scar carved through hill and rock and across country, ready to link east to west, and far removed from the two-way seething mass of commerce and commute that it is now.

I was a Mcalpine man. My section ran from here at Ainley Top through to the M1 interchange at Lofthouse. Along this stretch I spent a pleasant summer rocking my staff in the middle of fields of gently waving barley while my engineer took readings from his theodolite. And when it rained, I whiled away many an afternoon in some mobile canteen hovel listening to weathered Irish navvies sing rebel songs to the tune of

12

an old tin whistle played by a little grizzled looking leprechaun who went by the name of Johnny-The-Mole. Johnny was one of those intriguing quirks of nature. He wore full ballroom attire, satin striped strides and tailcoat, ten bob, Leeds market. He had large protruding, not so healthy looking front teeth, and a nose too big for the rest of his features, which made him kind of look like Vince, the cartoon gopher dude from Deputy Dawg. He dug holes for culverts, and legend would have it that every time he finished a hole and the concrete chamber had been put in place, he would christen it by taking a dump, before performing a ritual rain dance around his steaming deposit. Legend also had it that within an hour of his shaman like exploits the heavens would open and work would be suspended for the day.

They were good times, but it was never going to be a career; I never had any ambitions wherever work was concerned. To me it was just a means to an end. I didn't really want to work, same as at school, I had no interest, just couldn't be arsed really, especially with exams and shit. I wasn't thick, but I wasn't any kind of Einstein, either. I only went when I could be bothered, and that wasn't very often. When the Pennine winter kicked in, I moved on, but by then I'd saved enough for my first proper guitar.

I don't know exactly what it was that I had back then, but females seemed to flock to me in droves, and I never needed to resort to the old clichéd chat up lines that Fadge and Billy used whenever they were on the pull. To me it just came naturally; I loved women and they loved me. Thing is, I had this interest in the opposite sex from being a kid. I'd been sexually aware for as long as I can remember. I lost my virginity proper when I was thirteen. She was fifteen, babysitting for her auntie. By the time I was fourteen I was screwing the auntie as well. I never knew why, but older women seemed as keen as the young ones, like they wanted to mother me or something. I didn't mind, they were less clingy and possessive than birds my age, and more experienced between the sheets; taught me a trick or two I can tell you. I had a string of middle-aged and married on the go back then, fucking insatiable most of them, and I was more than happy to oblige. MILFS, I think they call 'em these days. Fadge and Billy used to say I was bleeding mad; said I was skating on thin ice. I put it down to that jealousy thing and I would laugh in their faces, but they said I'd be laughing on the other side of *my* face when a pissed off, six foot strapping merchant seaman came knocking on my door wanting to know who'd been shagging his missus while he'd been away. Yep, back then I didn't give a shit; nine times out of ten it was the women that were seducing me, not the other way round and anyway I was enjoying my growing reputation, especially as I didn't have to work at it. I would worry about the consequences as and when they transpired. At that moment in time I was untouchable, invincible. JD Smith felt on top of the world and life couldn't have been better.

It was also during that particular summer that I bumped into the dude who's sat in the driving seat next to me.

Celia's music shop in town was like my second home. Every time I stepped into that place I got that warm tingly sensation like I used to get as a kid on Christmas morning. Surrounded by hundreds of the most wonderful instruments; guitars of all makes, shapes and colours: Gibson's, Gretches, Epiphones, Fenders; it was like being in Aladdin's cave.

Me, Billy and Fadge were all learning guitar, and both of them were progressing better than I was. The weedy sound I managed to get out of my cheap Strat copy told me I was never going to be Eric Clapton, so I figured if we were going to start a band, we didn't need three guitarists. I switched to bass, did a Noel Redding and admitted defeat.

I was only a couple of pay packets away from owning the beautiful nineteen sixty-seven sunburst Fender Deluxe Precision bass that I'd fallen in love with. I'd already secured it with a deposit, and for the third time that week was down in Celia's basement putting it through its paces.

I remember trying to knock out an approximation of Badge by Cream but some twat was doing a Keith Moon, trashing a drum kit over in the percussion section and drowning out my Jack Bruce impersonation. The guy was manic, all over the kit like he was plugged into the mains or something. He showed no sign of letting up, so, with my lead snaking along behind me I took a stroll over to confront the madman.

'Yo!' I shouted and waited for a response but he was oblivious and continued to knock fuck out of the skins. I stood there watching him with a frown on my face and under his mop of wild and shaggy black hair I could tell he was only a spraffer, no more than fifteen, but he was good and certainly knew his way around a drum kit.

'Yo!!' I bawled at the top of my lungs, this time with success. The kid grabbed his cymbals into silence, propped his sticks on the snare, leant on them and gave me a look that was inquisitive but tinged with a: *'How dare you interrupt me while I'm in full flow?'* kind of attitude.

'Give it a rest, young 'un,' I pleaded, having got his attention. 'I can't hear myself play here.'

He regarded me for a moment, face full of insolence. 'Go on then,' he said finally.

'What?'

He spread his sticks wide in a visual *'Duh'*

'Play it,' he challenged. 'Go on, let's hear you.'

He slouched back on his stool, cocked his head to one side in anticipation, and all of a sudden he had me under pressure. The cheeky little pillock wanted me to perform. My hands went all sweaty, and like a dickhead I looked around nervously as if somebody might come to my rescue. He had me squirming and he knew it, sat there with a little smirk on his mush. I couldn't be seen to lose face having called the shots, so I stuttered into Badge and fucked up after only a few bars. The kid hit a crash cymbal and let out a sarcastic laugh.

'I think you're a little bit rusty on that one, Jack,' he sneered.

'How d'yer know my name's Jack?' I asked stupidly.

'Err, I didn't. That was Badge you were trying to play there, wasn't it? I was just making the connection: – Cream – Jack Bruce?'

He looked at me like I was thick and I felt it, a total fucking idiot.

'Wanna try again?' he said working his hi-hat patronisingly. 'I'll count you in – one – two…'

'Shouldn't you be at school?' I snapped, cutting him off.

'Shouldn't you?' he countered.

'I left at Easter.'

'I can't be arsed going.'

'I know the feeling,' I said sympathetically and decided it would be wiser to make peace with the clever sod. 'My name's Jack,' I offered as a token of truce.

'Yeah, I gathered that,' he said flatly, still obviously not impressed by my lack of cool. He hesitated a little; like he wasn't so sure he wanted to be acquainted with such an imbecile. Eventually he relented. 'Digweed.'

I slowly nodded his acquaintance, not entirely certain if he'd just given me his name or announced that he liked to smoke dope.

'So, what kind of music are you into then, Dickweed?'

'Digweed – the name's *Digweed.'* He fired me a look that warned me not to push it. 'Most things, as long as it's not chart crap, how about you?'

'Strictly R & B.'

Digweed shook his mop-top in approval, reminding me a bit of Jerry Shirley, Humble Pie's skin basher. We spent the next hour or so verbally sparring and testing each other's perceived knowledge of all things blues. The dude certainly knew his stuff and slowly we began to warm to each other as we wallowed in what had become a mutual passion. I suppose like a lot of kids our age we either had older brothers or knew of mates who had older brothers who had latched on to the British rhythm and blues scene of the early sixties, whose treasured vinyl collections had all these weird and wonderful artists from over the Atlantic that we secretly delved into and marvelled over; guys like Jimmy Reed, Howlin' Wolf, John Lee Hooker, Son House and Muddy Waters. These were the black musicians that influenced and spawned bands like The Yardbirds, The Stones, The Small Faces, The Who, and The Animals. Clapton, John Mayall and Peter Green dragged the sound out of the Delta and added a new dimension, and youngsters like Digweed and me fell for it totally.

We chatted and jammed till closing time, my new percussionist pal launching into a lazy syncopated jazz riff in three-four-time while I reluctantly, but lovingly, replaced the Fender back in its case, all the while realising that I'd probably just met my match in the cocky insolence stakes. What I didn't realise was that I had just formed a friendship that would bond the two of us like brothers over the next few years, a friendship that would endure all others through the dark days that lay ahead.

* * *

'You okay?'

I'm totally unaware that we've been sat outside Jeanie's for the last few minutes as Digweed snaps me back to the now.

'What? – Yeah, I'm fine.'

He looks across at me and knows I'm not. 'You can stay at mine, you know, if you're not ready for this.'

'No – no, just give me a minute or two, I'll be all right.' I instinctively reach for my baccy pouch. Fumbling I try to construct a roll up; my hands start to shake and I end up scattering swirls of tobacco all over Digweed's pristine motor. 'I'm sorry, I forgot...'

'It's okay,' he says reassuringly. 'It's due for valeting anyway. Take your time.'

He presses the invisible button that swooshes open the window letting in the cold crisp of the January day. I light my snout and try to calm down. I look over and try to say thanks but I can't, and he knows I can't; we've never said things like that, never had to. I silently curse myself for allowing my guard to drop, for letting the past flow into the chambers of my mind like that. I thought I'd prepared myself for this moment and then I go and fuck up at the first hurdle. I feel like the idiot I was at our first meeting down in Celia's basement, but it's different now, no taking the piss on this occasion. He allows me to finish my smoke in silence, knowing that there's nothing he can do or say to assuage the demons in my head. I know he's there for me if I need him, but this is a solitary battle, one I can only fight on my own. I'm not sure I'm up for it, not sure if I'll ever be. I grab my bag and flick my tab onto the pavement.

'Fifty quid,' he reminds me, and I force a smile, so much to get used to. I close the car door and lean back in through the open window. Genuine worry and concern are written on his face. 'Give us a call when you've settled in and remember: if things don't work out at Jeanie's, the offer's always open.'

I bang on the car roof a couple of times by way of thanks and head slowly up the garden path. There are no balloons, no bunting, no banner proclaiming - WELCOME HOME JACK - only returning war heroes get that treatment. I reach the house and hesitate. I turn back and Digweed gives me a nod of encouragement before swooshing up the window and gunning the motor. The immensity of the task I have set myself overwhelms me as I watch him disappear down the street. This is going to be harder than I thought. Where do I start?

Like a subliminal advert, an image of a severed finger and a white gold engagement ring pops into my head and straight back out again. I knock on the door.

Three

I WAS A YOUNG man, just twenty-five when I was wrongly convicted of murder. I'm fifty-one years old now and my take on the intervening years changes from month to month, week to week and day to day. When I look in a mirror a broken old man stares back through the glass, a stranger. A head of dry, lifeless silvery hair, that I mostly keep tied back in a band, has long since replaced my flowing flaxen mane. The spark in my once carefree eyes long extinguished. Greying stubble, often days old, hides features that time has etched with misery, which tobacco and dope have left pallid and drawn – I try not to look in mirrors. If I have to speak, along with the bitter cynicism that has grown inside me like a cancer, my words come out hoarse and chesty due to massive saltpetre ingestion. I've probably got enough potassium nitrate inside me to start a new gunpowder plot. I could toss a lighted match down my throat and suicide bomb the judiciary. Sometimes I'm overcome with a spirited defiance. It's a feeling that changes, that moves with the passing months, a feeling that has been charged with so many emotions over the years. It's something that comes from deep inside, that occasionally takes me by surprise, a defiance that at times I think I've lost, that returns when I least expect it or during those moments when I've got so low and suicidal that hope once again manifests and drags defiance back into my psyche. I don't always welcome the phenomenon, and now, whenever it comes to the fore, I pray for the feeling to be short-lived because in twenty-five long years hope never delivered. In the end, all hope did was to throw up anger and frustration, and so I learned to suppress it with a drug-induced fug before it dashed itself out on the four walls of my prison cell. Eventually I sussed how to deal with despair like I never could with hope. Skunk became my time capsule, my anaesthetic, and my sanctuary.

In the weeks leading up to my release, the nightmares returned: the mocking dark angel, the heavy metal demons, the pleading features of a tortured soul and the overwhelming, accompanying twisted sense of guilt. These dreams came in spasmodic batches throughout the course of my intern; sometimes nothing for months and then night after night for weeks on end. They would usually manifest whenever I started to show signs of that spirited defiance, seeping into the night, my alter existence reminding me that this purgatory was real, asleep or not. Misery compounded by screams in the dark, soaking wet bed sheets, and cell mates, angry or scared shitless – often both. By now my belligerence was no longer fuelled by hope, hope had long since fled; this was dissension soaked in bitterness, wrapped in the certainty of injustice without recourse, a defiance born of survival but paid for with a heavy price – a life. Not just a mere twenty-five years, but the preceding twenty-five that became a road to nowhere; like an absorbing book that you get a quarter of the way through only to find the remaining pages blank, like a dream without meaning; wasted, irrelevant. As for the future, who knows? The defiance helps paint a picture, plots revenge and redresses all the wrongdoing. But they're only paintings of a bitter mind, wild imaginings of how things are going to be put right. Reality is something quite different. How do I go about putting things right? Who am I plotting revenge against? When the defiance evaporates, the future looks like a brick wall with apathy and despair scrawled across it. This should never have happened to me; I never murdered anyone.

I lie on my bed and stare holes in the ceiling. I've been out for nearly four weeks now. The spirited defiance left me the day I knocked on Jeanie's door. I'm waiting for it to make a triumphant return but I'm not sure it will. The fact is I've become institutionalised. All I've done is swap four cell walls for four more only the paint job here is better. I only venture downstairs for my meals, and sometimes I don't even do that. Jeanie usually sends Ben up to my room with a tray if I'm feeling that way out. Jeanie is my big sister and Ben is her seventeen-year-old son. He seems a nice lad but I can tell he's not too sure about me, the estranged uncle and black sheep of the family, the guy he's only ever seen in old photographs. I think he knows what I'm supposed to have done and where I've been all his life but so far he hasn't brought the subject up, not in front of me anyhow. Maybe Jeanie's told him not to, seeing as how fragile I must appear right now.

Jeanie is a star, one of only a handful who refused to judge me. She's the only one I've ever looked square in the face and seen an unwavering belief in my innocence. Privately, I don't know what thoughts she harbours. Maybe she's been doing the big protective sister thing all these years. Maybe she has her doubts, I know others had, and still have. I've never doubted her. She's been my source of strength throughout all this, especially after Mum and Dad died. Apart from Digweed, she was the only one who made the effort to come visit when I was in Parkhurst. When she was heavily pregnant with Ben and that wanker of a husband of hers had fucked off for the first time, she somehow managed to scrimp and scrape for the train and ferry fairs. Even when she was on benefits and I had to give her permission to sell my amp and speakers in order to fund her visits, she never failed me. I even told her she could flog the Fender one time but she wouldn't hear of it. She knew how much my bass meant to me even though I hadn't seen or played it in years, nor am I ever likely to again. It's propped in its case in the corner of the room, the room that she prepared and freshly decorated for me on my release, still there where she left it. I haven't so much as given it a glance let alone taken it out of its case. Maybe it's a sibling thing but she seems to understand, and at times share the pain and crap I'm going through. She just has this knack of knowing when to leave me alone or when to be there for me; thank God I've got her.

I've only had one visitor up to now and I could have done without her. Digweed and Billy have phoned a few times but I keep making excuses and putting them off. I know they'll try and entice me out of the house and I'm not up to that yet.

My probation officer is a stiff and starchy looking woman called Patterson, similar age to myself; goes by the book, likes ticked boxes and pigeon holes, can't see beyond her peripheral vision. She reminds me of a horse wearing blinkers. Jeanie, bless her, put everything out ready for the visit before she left for work; two best cups in gleaming saucers, tea, and coffee strategically placed, little post-it stickers left all over her small but pristine kitchen for my guidance. The lounge, equally tiny but freshly dusted and vacuumed; cushions with pseudo Latin writing woven into them, plumped and perfectly positioned like she was trying to create an impression on my behalf - trouble is I stick out like a sore thumb. I don't fit into this neat little creation. I make the place look untidy. I present a dishevelled, unkempt article to Ms. Patterson in my baggy trackie bottoms and tee shirt and I don't fucking care. I haven't even bothered to shave again. I probably don't know it, but subconsciously I'm making a protest and it's because I *do* care that I'm acting like this. I've got a representative of authority sat in front of me; an officer of the state that did me wrong, and the last thing I want to show this woman is some sense of conformity and reformation. I want to make it hard for her to tick those little boxes. I want to push the conditions of my life licence as far as they will go, not that my bloody mindedness will get me anywhere with her. At the moment my resolve is in my boots, and it's merely the last acid dregs of bitterness coming to the fore as the law hangs on to my shirt tails.

'I see from my records that you haven't been in touch with the DSS yet.'

I shrug.

'Why?'

I shrug again. 'Just not got round to it.'

She sighs and writes something down, like a schoolteacher marking a piece of poor homework. 'If you don't make contact soon you could lose some of the benefit you're entitled to.' She looks up for a reaction and I give her none. She bats on, going through the motions. 'You attended resettlement and OLS courses in Wakefield. Have you contacted any of the prospective employers on the lists you were given?'

I shake my head, like I'm going to beg for a job in a DIY warehouse working alongside some brain dead spotty youth on minimum wages. I build a roll-up and switch off while Patterson asks a load of inane questions that I continue to nod or shake my head to whenever she looks up for a response. The blinkered one wades through a briefcase of bullshit and carries on with her spiel about how important it is for me to make contact with various organisations that help offenders resettle back into society. Well, for one I take offence at being labelled an offender, and two, society can go fuck itself. From the coffee table I pull up an ashtray that looks like it's never been used and settle back with my smoke while phrases like anger management, emotional control and moral reasoning sail over my head. I watch this woman scribble her notes and tick her little boxes while she pushes her glasses back up the bridge of her nose at regular intervals. I wonder what she's been doing with *her* life for these past twenty-five years. I guess she'd have been a student, no doubt studying hard for her sociology degree. I try to imagine her in her early twenties, try and clothe her in the fashion and hairstyle of the day; smelly afghan coat, loon pants, scoop-neck tee shirt, bangles and beads, but somehow it just doesn't work, can't seem to paint the picture as she sits across the room, shrew-like with the asexual haircut, her elephant breath attire and general drab civil servant demeanour. Did she ever see a live band? Did she ever swig Newky brown out of the bottle? Did she ever get stoned and let some physics undergraduate shag her stupid at the weekends? I doubt it. I see her in halls of residence swatting away, trying to get her head around Freud and Jung under the dim light of an angle poise, Simon and Garfunkel's greatest hits gently playing away in a corner of the room; mascot style teddy bears strategically placed, glass eyes staring on impassively; weekly meetings of the philately society; plate of chips in the curry house in lieu of a Vindaloo. Married? Nah, no rings. Lesbian? I scrutinise her hard through a haze of blue smoke but no image comes to mind. Nope, can't see that one either; my guess is definitely virgin spinster. Can't even imagine her naked - not that I'm trying too hard, mind. She doesn't eat meat but only mildly admonishes her cat when it torments birds and mice to their deaths, the same cat that she lets sharpen its claws on the Stag furniture that she's had since the late seventies, that she allows to curl up and purr contentedly on the bread board in the kitchen and drink out of her coffee cup while stroking its neck as she reads a Joanna Trollope novel. She takes walking weekends in The Lakes with a group of people she calls acquaintances, not friends because she can't stand half of them, especially the ones who try and outdo her in the intellectual stakes as they trudge up Helvellyn. She's a devout atheist but firmly believes in what she does righteously, religiously, almost fundamentally, as though she knows that the God of bureaucracy is looking down on her nodding in grim approval. I think about offering her a cup of tea but that's all I do. My bored gaze lands on Jeanie's neatly pleated curtains behind Patterson's head. My sister's been a sewer and seamstress since she left school and, as I look round the room admiring her skills, I feel proud of what she has managed to create through forced frugality; decor and ornaments perceptibly cheap but never kitsch or tacky; pictures and printed throws with a Celtic theme; groups of scented candles, incense and oil burners, showing testament to a youth of hippydom; colours and textures revealing an obvious flair for design; a room that, if money were to be thrown at it, would look stunning. Suddenly conscious of how my appearance must cheapen the place, I try and show a bit of respect and keep the ashtray close to my chest while my probation officer thrusts glossy pamphlets at me. The OBP's (Offending Behaviour Programmes) all have impressive sounding titles like the CSCP (Cognitive Self Change Programme) or the cleverly abbreviated Controlling Anger and Learning to Manage (CALM). I toss them all to one side and focus on the framed photos on Jeanie's mantelpiece and pine dresser. They're mostly of Ben in his various phases of growing up; the odd one with his mum on some rare but well-earned holiday, and one ancient-looking snap, that doesn't look worthy of the frame it's in, of me and the band outside some venue with all our gear stacked up behind us. I don't recall the time or the place but it must have been in the very early days judging by the youthful, fresh-faced bright-eyed bunch we seem to be. Conspicuous by their absence are any photos of Ben's dad, Barry, Garry or whatever his name was. Jeanie has obviously obliterated any trace of him from their lives. I don't blame her. I only ever saw the guy once, not to talk to, just to observe very briefly, but that was enough for me. It was at my old man's funeral. I was only ten years into my sentence, still at Parkhurst on the Isle of Wight, and was given ROTL on compassionate grounds to attend the service. I was handcuffed to an officer throughout and wasn't allowed to mix or converse with anyone afterwards, but I observed a lot and straight away I didn't take to that shifty eyed fucker. He'd already done a runner once, after he'd put her up the duff, and, stupidly, she had allowed him back into her life, given him another chance for the sake of the kid. I remember Jeanie kept her head bowed throughout most of the service; veiled and withdrawn; she barely made eye contact with me, which wasn't like her. This was our goodbye to dad and I know that she would have tried to speak to me with her eyes, with that comforting look of hers. But there was something not right about their body language. There was no supporting arm or sympathetic gesture of any kind from her man. She kept her focus firmly on the grave and, though I watched from a distance, I thought I could detect the faintest hint of swelling if not bruising around her eyes. Mam was consumed with grief that day, certain in the fact that what had happened to me reflected directly on her husband's gradual demise. Five years later the old girl succumbed to the unbearable distress and misfortune that had befallen her family. She passed away with a broken heart and I made the long journey north once again. Shortly afterwards I was transferred to Wakefield permanently – too little, too fucking late.

Although I was now closer to home, Jeanie's visits became more spasmodic. I put it down to her having become a full-time mum, but I still had a sneaky feeling it had something to do with her part-time spouse. Despite the infrequent visits, she wrote almost on a weekly basis, but never once spoke about her domestic situation or the fact that he was knocking her about regularly. She turned up one visiting session out of the blue after an absence of around four months looking as well as I'd seen her in a long time, like a weight had been lifted from her shoulders. It was then she told me the whole story and confirmed my suspicions. She told me she'd at last seen the light and had left him for good. He'd been giving her beatings throughout their relationship, more recently in front of Ben who was now a toddler. She'd stayed away because she didn't want me to see the lumps and the bruises he would leave her with after a good hiding. Although we weren't supposed to make physical contact I remember taking hold of her hands and squeezing them until they went white. She said she'd got a restraining order in place and assured me with a selfless smile that that particular chapter of her life was over. She said she'd had enough of men, and to my knowledge hasn't bothered with them since. I don't blame her; having had to sit through my trial listening to the gruesome accounts of what her younger brother had supposedly afflicted on someone of her own sex, and then endure the type of marriage she had like she did can't have endeared her to the gender. Despite all, Jeanie stuck by me, her love and faith never wavered, and for that I shall always be eternally grateful; I couldn't have done the time without her.

Unlike Jeanie, certain other people who were supposed to be close to me didn't share the faith. Liz had been my partner for a little over three years when my world fell apart. Never convinced of my innocence, she sold our house and disappeared soon after my conviction. I received a terse letter of her intentions and the name of a solicitor she had instructed to deal with my side of things. I have never seen nor heard from her to this day.

I've had a long time to contemplate the role that I've played in the lives of the women I have known. I have always loved their company but, like millions of other guys, I found it hard to commit. I was never any good at long-term relationships and admit unashamedly to having had a wandering eye. I philandered my way through my teens and early twenties and – well, that's about it. My last sexual encounter was with an itinerant squat-hopping student who gave me crabs on the weekend before I was arrested; a rather ironic end to the amorous antics of a guy who thought he had the world of women at his feet.

Liz had been wise to my unfaithfulness. During our tempestuous three years together I'd had a number of, shall we say, not too discreet liaisons. What I indulged in couldn't be called affairs; they were nearly all one night stands brought on by good looks, arrogance, booze, dope and a rampant libido. After all, I was in a rock band, for God's sake. But like I've said before, I didn't have to do much chasing, these things just sort of happened. Most of the girls I knew carnally were simply out for a good shag and I was more than happy to oblige. I loved women and would never do anything to cause anyone physical harm. Sadism and torture certainly wasn't my kink, and any mental anguish I might have created for those I loved stemmed simply from the inability to keep my eager manhood in my trousers.

Liz and I would probably never have lasted as long as we did except for one thing – we had a two-year old daughter, Maggie. I haven't seen my little girl since the day I was re-manded in custody. She'll be twenty-eight years old next month.

I have nothing to remind me of the life I helped to create; just a hazy, fragmented scene that has become a part of tor-mented dreams: a hurried kiss followed by a chirpy *"see ya, daddy"* then, with dodie firmly back in place and teddy bear purposefully tucked under an arm, off to tend to more impor-tant two-year old matters, blissfully unaware of grave adult undertakings that were cutting across her little world. Even what I think I remember is now just a notion; images that a tortured mind has rendered featureless in order to ease the pain. I don't even have a photograph.

Four

I FINALLY GET to close the door on Patterson the probation officer and trudge the stairs up to my room. Thoughts of Maggie set me back into a pit. I sink a couple of inches into my bed, close my eyes and the bed becomes my cell bunk once again. I shore up the levee, paper the cracks, and discipline my mind back into the numb zone just like I schooled it to do over the years. I wish I had some draw; weed makes the process much easier.

A knock on the bedroom door slowly sucks me from my self-imposed vacuum. I can't tell how long I've been in the twilight zone; linear time is hardly a concept for me anymore. It's dark. I'm slow to respond because the knock doesn't sound like the rap on a cell door. It opens part way and a shadowy figure peers into the gloom. I fumble for the bedside lamp. Flick the switch.

'Mum's sent you a cup o' tea up,' says Ben. 'Wasn't sure if you were asleep.'

'No – no, I'm not asleep; come in.' I sit up, take the tea off the lad and set it down on the little set of drawers at the other side of the bed. I instinctively reach for my baccy tin while Ben shuffles awkwardly from foot to foot like he wants to pee or something. I spread a line of Old Holborn into a skin and look up at him inquisitively. ''Sup son?'

'Nowt,' he says, a little nervously. 'It's just that – well, I don't know what to call you.'

'How do you mean?'

'Well, when I was a young un, Mum used to say she was going to visit Uncle Jack... you know, when you was...' Ben's head moves around in little circles as he struggles to find the right words.

'Yeah,' I nod in encouragement to try and relieve his discomfort.

'...Well, I think I'll feel a bit daft calling you Uncle Jack now.'

I nod again, understandingly this time, and run my tongue along the gum. 'Plain old Jack's fine by me.'

He stews it over but the look on his face says he's not quite sure. I reach over for my lighter and take a slurp of tea at the same time. 'When I was about your age a lot of my mates called me JD.'

'JD?'

'Yeah – Justice Denied.' Ben looks at me perplexed. 'Only joking. The D stands for Daniel.'

'JD – yeah I think I like the sound of that – JD, cool.'

'JD it is, then. Have you got a middle name, Ben?'

'Michael,' he says screwing his face up. 'It was my dad's middle name.'

'Oh,' I say and spend the next few awkward moments studying my nephew. Ben has inherited the Smith good looks but his colouring is much darker which makes him handsome in a Mediterranean way, like he could pass for a young Spaniard or an Italian, but his face betrays naivety and his manner shows a tendency towards shyness, which certainly isn't a Smith trait. He has perfectly unkempt hair; dark strands precisely gelled into semi-spiked angular positions. He just has to be a babe magnet but I have the feeling if the subject of girls

32

arose he would somehow squirm with embarrassment. I wonder if he still might be a virgin before trying to do a quick mental sum as to how many birds I'd had by the time I was his age. I shudder at the thought.

'Not seen much of you these last few weeks,' I break the silence.

'Mum said I had to keep out your way 'till you'd got settled. She said it might take some time seeing as you'd been...'

'...Away a long time?' I help him finish his sentence as the words trail away into more awkwardness. He nods his head and bows it to stare at his shuffling feet. 'Do you know why I was in prison, Ben?'

'Yeh,' he says without looking up.

'How much has she told you?'

'Not much. I know someone got killed. I've heard stuff. Mum says to take no notice of fairy stories.' He lifts his head and looks me in the eye. 'She says you were innocent.'

I sigh and blow smoke at the same time. 'She's right you know, son – I didn't do it.' I make sure my eyes meet his, wanting him to see the integrity that still lies behind the hurt. He nods slowly and I quickly change the subject as awkwardness starts to fill the space between us again. 'So, what occupies your time then?

Ben blows air through his lips. 'Supposed to be studying hard for my exams.' He relaxes a little and sits on the end of the bed.

'Ball ache, eh?'

'Ah, it's not so bad once I get myself motivated.'

'I fucking hated school; couldn't be arsed with all that exam bollocks.'

'Has to be done; can't get to Uni without my A-levels.'

'University, eh?' I try to sound impressed. 'What you hop-

33

ing to study?'

'I want to be a civil engineer.'

I involuntary let loose a laugh full of irony at that one and contemplate on what might have been. My head fills with visions of scorned opportunities and un-walked avenues. The aching notions of hindsight and regret mix with a thousand if-onlys and curdle sour in my gut. Long lost careers advice from schools of alcoholic Irishmen comes back at me through the ether and only now, thirty odd years later, sounds sage-like. I wonder if my choices sealed my fate. I went to the crossroads and paid the price, did a Robert Johnson, sold my soul to the devil. Sounds so fucking romantic; the ultimate rock 'n' roll perdition. Of course it's all bollocks. My karmic comeuppance had nothing to do with my love of the blues.

'What's so funny about that?' Ben asks looking a bit hurt.

I reassure him I'm not taking the piss out of his choice of career and tell him that, but for the grace of God and my devotion to the guitar, I could have trod a similar path.

'I had no idea.'

'Mcalpines were willing to send me to Tech. One day a week and night school; wanted me to do my City and Guilds. To be honest I was only ever gonna be a chain lad. I had no head for numbers; couldn't tell one end of a theodolite from another. All I ever wanted to do was play rhythm and blues.'

'And what about now?' Ben asks casting a glance over to the untouched guitar case in the corner of the room.

'Ah, all that belongs to another time, another life; a lot of water under the bridge and all that – besides, rock and roll's a young man's game.'

'The Stones are still doing it. Digweed and the boys are still doing it.'

'True, but my head's in a different place right now, and

anyhow the boys have a bass player.'

'He's not as good as you.'

'How do you know that?'

'Digweed says.'

'That's nice of him.'

I don't know what Billy and Digweed have been putting the kid up to but I detect some sort of covert amateur psychology going on here. Maybe they think it's a subtle way of coaxing me out of my shell; furtive flattery designed to make me feel wanted again, bringing me back to the fold. I try and steer the conversation back to the construction industry but he's having none of it. All he seems to want to talk about is music and the band. I don't have the heart to tell my nephew to fuck off and leave me in peace, after all this is the first real conversation I've ever had with him, so I smoke my smoke, sip my tea and try and make an effort. He wants me to regale him with stories about life on the road but I don't have any; all I remember is my last gig at the Melbourne on that final Friday; pretty much uneventful, but ultimately fateful, and my head doesn't need to go there right now, but he prompts me with anecdotes, tales that he's dragged out of Digweed that I fail to recollect, trying to ignite some spark of interest with fragments of a former life that will never again feel like my own. My disinterest fails to register the futility of dredging up my past like this, and all the while his eyes go back to the case in the corner like he's willing it over for some long lost reunion with its old master. I ask him what sort of music he's into and he reels off a list of bands and artists I've never heard of, reassuring me they're all rock and roll based, like he needs my approval or something. I tell him he shouldn't be so narrow-minded where music is concerned and he seems surprised when I tell him I used to listen to a lot of jazz, soul and funk.

'There's a difference to you not liking something and it being crap. When I first heard Beefheart's Trout Mask Replica I could barely stand it being on the turntable. It took me at least twenty uninspired spins before I even began to remotely like or understand what he was trying to do. Now, after all this time, I think it's probably one of the greatest albums ever made.'

'How can you tell what's crap then?'

'Well, I suppose a lot of people can't, that's why you've got pop music, I guess. Whereas good music usually has its roots in something else, something that goes way back, like the old spirituals that were sung in the churches in the Deep South. It has to have a feeling; it has to move you; doesn't matter if it comes from folk, country, jazz or the blues, the good stuff usually has history. People like Dylan understood all that. It's all about the sensation that lurches in your chest, or when the hairs on the back of your neck stand on end. It can be as subtle as a Beach Boys harmony or as in your face as a Bo Diddley riff, but good music nearly always has these qualities and they all come from the past; there's nothing new under the sun. R&B was there at the start; it's the spiritual side of rock 'n' roll. The only thing that came before was the delta blues that spawned it: Devil's music.'

'Why did they call it that?'

'Because it made you feel things inside that seemed unearthly; dark, sexy, scary.'

'But I thought you said that the blues came from the same place as gospel.'

'Well, they both speak the same language.'

'So how can it be part of the church and part of the Devil at the same time?'

'I can't answer that. That's one of its many contradictions. The blues is about the troubles of this world, it doesn't offer solutions; it's a lament. If it's from Mississippi it's about toiling in the fields, if it's from Chicago, it's about the streets. Gospel offers God as a solution, but basically it's the same thing. It's about stirring the emotions. Good music has the power to make you leap about with joy or weep your heart out with sorrow. For me, rhythm and blues didn't just tug at the heartstrings it smashed into my chest, ripped the thing out and beat me over the head with it. Music was my life, Ben; it meant everything to me. When I was sent down I had to let it go, I couldn't let it be part of the equation, couldn't allow it inside those four walls – do you understand what I'm saying?

'Yeah, but all that's behind you now; what's to stop you going back to it, why can't you pick it up again?'

I can't find the words to answer him, don't know where to look for them; don't know what they are. I drop my head and stare into my teacup. When I look up again his eyes have gone back to the guitar case.

'Go on then.' I relent.

'What?'

'Open it up.'

'What?'

'The guitar, get it out,' I say in a tone that asks him not to pretend to be stupid.

He looks at me cautiously. 'You sure?'

'Go ahead,' I nod wearily.

Ben manoeuvres the object of his attentions from its propped position in the corner of the room carefully onto the bed. He looks at me for one final nod of approval before flicking the catches and opening the case to reveal its contents. I closely watch his face, his lips parting slightly. His eyes take on that misty look and they flit up and down the guitar as it lies there snug on a bed of red felt. I guess that's how pretty much I

37

reacted the first time I clapped eyes on it all those years ago down in Celia's basement: silent but awestruck.

'Go on then, lift it out, it won't bite you,' I say, breaking the spell.

He hauls the old Fender into view and my heart leaps. My own reaction takes me by surprise and Ben gives me a look that says – *I thought you said it wouldn't bite?* – Light catches the smooth, near ebony of its outer contours that age, and being shut away for twenty-five years, has failed to dull. The ebony gives way to cherry that fades into old gold. Two humbuckers sit square in the middle of the sunburst and bittersweet memories begin to slide up my craw at the sight. Battle scars: faded lacquer, the odd ding or scuff here and there prevent to take away the sheer majesty of the old beast, and for a moment the sight leaves me speechless.

This time it's Ben's turn to break the spell.

'Hey, I didn't know you were a lefty,' he says cradling the guitar right handed and noticing that the G-string was at the top.

'I use my right for everything 'cept playing the bass,' I indicate to him with the sign of the masturbator.

He looks at me, grinning broadly.

'What?'

'You just used present tense,' he says triumphantly.

'Well, I still have the odd sly J Arthur if that's what you mean. Twenty-five years is a long time to go without, despite the efforts of the bromide boffins.'

'You know what I mean, and I'm not talking about wanking,' he says in an effort to get serious.

'Look, son, the fact that I may have used the word *use* instead of used doesn't mean I'll be strapping the bloody thing on any time in the future.'

'I was only saying...'

'Is he bothering you?' demands Jeanie entering the room with a timely interjection.

'No.' I lie.

Jeanie, in that way of hers, senses differently and jerks her head at Ben. 'Haven't you got some revising to do?' Ben gives a reluctant nod. 'Well go do it then and leave your uncle Jack in peace,' she threatens wide eyed.

Ben tuts and slowly but reverently places the guitar back on its bed of red felt. He gazes into the case like he's paying respect and then gives me a knowing, almost conspiratorial look that manages to unnerve me for a moment.

'Talk to you later, JD.' He eases himself off the bed and saunters to the door, the arse of his strides somewhere down by the back of his knees. I'm certain the kid isn't gay but why he'd want to walk around with some other guy's name stamped across the elastic of his trollies for the entire world to see is beyond me.

'Sorry about that; was he being a pest?' Jeanie asks after he leaves.

'No, not really; just naturally curious about my past, I suppose.'

'Didn't ask too many awkward questions I hope?'

'To be honest he was interested in the band more than anything else – and the old guitar.' I nod to the instrument at the end of the bed.

A smile slowly spreads across Jeanie's face. 'So, he finally gets to see it at last.'

I give her an inquisitive look.

'Oh, you've no idea,' she says shaking her head. 'Talk about childhood curiosity... that thing, or what was inside it, has fascinated him since he began to walk and talk – *"When can I see Uncle Jack's guitar?"* – It's all I ever got from age five to fifteen. Looking back, I suppose not allowing him to touch let alone look inside must have fed his obsession. I remember one time finding him fiddling with the catches trying to sneak a look inside. He must have only been about nine...' Jeanie's voice tails off and the smile is replaced with a sad, wistful look. '...I don't know what came over me; I just flipped. It's the only time I've ever hit him. The backs of his little legs were red; you could see the hand marks. I think I shocked us both. I remember hugging him so tight afterwards and we cried our eyes out together...' She pauses again, lost inside her memory. I watch in silence as my sister allows the guilt of that time to well up in her eyes. Her sockets fill with moisture but stoically she refuses to let the tears form and fall down her face. She sits on the bed and gazes at the Fender, stroking a thumb across the open edge of the case while slowly shaking her head. '...Get rid of everything, including the guitar, you said one time. Do you remember? I knew I'd have gotten more for this than much of the other stuff. I couldn't let it go; it was a part of you, it was all I had left of you... it was you. 'She sniffs, blinks hard and looks directly at me. 'They weren't good times for any of us you know...'

I know that, I fucking know that.

'...Barry was gone, Dad was gone; Mum was still there physically but her spirit had gone. All I had was Ben and the bloody guitar.' She lets out a laugh that's trying hard not to sound bitter. 'It became... I dunno, some sort of symbol of hope, I suppose. I didn't know if you would survive all those years. You seemed so... so young, so vulnerable...'

Inwardly I shrivel and squirm – *tell me about it.*

'...I think I must have allowed it to become a shrine. I used to spend hours gazing at it, lost in thought: what had become of us all; why us? How did I ever become involved with such an arsehole like Barry? How could I have denied to myself and everybody that nothing was wrong; accepting the kicks and the punches, convinced it was all my fault; it must be me, it has to be me; we're a bad lot, us Smiths. But mostly I thought about you, what you were doing, how you were coping; tying myself in knots. I never opened the case to look inside, I don't know why. I think I was too scared, of what, I've no idea; the thing had become kind of sacred for some reason. I don't know; maybe it was paranoia, maybe it was the pills. I must have thought all your pain and suffering were locked up inside and if I opened it, it would be like opening Pandora's box. I think that must be why I lashed out at Ben that time. Stupid, irrational I know, but they were irrational times... weren't they?' She pulls a tissue from the sleeve of her cardigan and dabs at her nose. I don't know if she wants me to respond and if she does, I don't know how, so I just lie there, propped against my pillows, waiting for her to compose herself. Say nothing. 'You've got to start again, Jack,' she says eventually, this time her tone is assiduous. Her eyes hold mine, daring them to avert. 'It's been nearly a month now; you've got to make the effort to start again.'

I should have known this was coming. She's been walking on eggshells for long enough, wrapping me in cotton wool, cosseting my moods, stroking my psyche. Fact is, even if I had the will, I wouldn't have the remotest idea of how to start again. Start again as what? I barely feel fucking human. She holds me in a Gorgon-like stare that I wish would turn me to stone, knowing that I'm betraying that hopeless little-boy-lost look, and I start to feel like a prick, propped up on the bed, looking up at my big sister, not knowing what face to pull, not knowing what to say. And she just sits there, giving me time;

patient but determined. I resist the urge to look away, curl up and cocoon; I just stare blankly at those careworn yet still beautiful slate blue eyes that transport me back in time again. We were certainly lookers in our day, me and sis; she'd turn heads and attract wolf whistles everywhere she went; her golden blond hair shaped in a feather-cut bouncing off her shoulders like some model in a Sunsilk ad as she walked down the street. She could have had any bloke she wanted and she ended up with a prat like Barry. How? Why? We must have asked it of ourselves a million times. Were we such bad bastards in past lives to be cursed so? Styled in a middle aged, shoulder length bob now, Jeanie's hair is still blond but it's out of a bottle, I can see the grey roots growing through; a consequence of the shape of our lives that has made us old before our time or simply a family trait, I'll never know. What I do know is we're both good at hiding things; with her it's domestic violence and a premature ageing process; me? Well I suppose I hide everything, it's called conditioning, I do it to keep the pain at bay, I've got good at it over the years. Now, Jeanie wants me to open up and I simply don't know how.

She reaches across for one of my nicotine-stained hands. I let her take it without resistance. 'Jack...Jack, what we gonna do, eh?' Her voice soft, her touch gentle, and her tone passive: the patience of a fucking saint. She waits for me to respond, her features pleading for something, anything. I search for words that are spinning on the Ferris wheel inside my head. I want to thank her for all she's done and all she continues to do, for always being there, for being waited on hand and foot. I long to throw off the slurry of self-pity, to say sorry for using my long incarceration as an excuse for my petty belligerence and stupid mood swings. Even a small show of gratitude is hard to express; it's all there in my head but I can't seem to unlock it; can't form the thoughts into words, and when I do they stick in my throat and lock-jaw sets in. Desperately, I resort to telepathy, hurling all my thoughts and emotions between us on invisible waves, hoping she'll understand, smile in that knowing way of hers and leave the room like she's done a dozen times before; but not this time. As I try and avert my eyes she drags them back to hers and locks them in place. I see her willing me back to her; not this lump of uselessness laying on the bed but her cocksure, carefree little brother, her Stevie Marriott lookalike – her Jack. I want him back too but he doesn't exist anymore, and keeping an old piece of lacquered wood and metal strings as a symbol of something lost won't bring him back either.

And then she plays her ace.

'I think I might know where Maggie is.'

I freeze, but inside a pressure cooker full of emotion starts to rattle and spit steam. The barren dry riverbeds that have been my eye sockets suddenly become moisture-laden reservoirs ready to spill forth a million issues. Feelings I've kept suppressed for so long come to the fore and scare the shit out of me. Jeanie bites her lip in pain as I involuntary crush her hand turning her knuckles white. I look up at my sister in choking bewilderment at what her revelation has just done to me. I swallow hard trying to keep it all in check, but the pressure cooker's already blown its lid, the levee breaks and the locked up emotions of a quarter of a century start to cascade over tired, red rims, coursing down my face into a forest of salt and pepper grey brush. Jeanie pulls me to her and I fall unconditionally into her embrace. I bury my face into her bottle blond hair while the whole of my body shudders under tons of sobs. We both cling to each other for dear life.

'Let it all out, Jack love – let it all out.'

Five

OF MY SISTER'S chance encounter with my daughter, I wrought every last detail.

'It was one of those arty-farty shops in Hebden Bridge, full of *objet d'art*. I only went in for some tea-lights, but you know I'm a sucker for anything with a hippy slant. I was picking out some joss-sticks, when I overheard the girl behind the counter mention to someone on the phone that her name was Maggie Hudson.'

'So what did you do?'

'A massive double-take, and almost dropped the bottle of patchouli oil I had in my hand. Like you, I hadn't seen her since she was two, but I could tell it was our Maggie straight away.'

'What was she like?'

Jeanie smiled at the memory. 'Very pretty; shapely slim; long sandy blond hair; healthy all-year-round tanned complexion; piercing sexy blue eyes, not too much make up, no need for it; minimal jewellery; tiny nose stud and slender gold necklace.'

'How can you have been so sure it was her?'

'Instinct. It was definitely our Maggie,' she said with unconcealed pride, 'No doubt about that.'

'And?'

'I waited till she came off the phone, and then took my purchases up to the counter. I knew what Liz had done to obliterate the Smiths from her memory and that of her daughter's. I had no idea what she'd told her of us, of you. So I knew I had to tread carefully. We exchanged pleasantries. I apologised in advance for my curiosity but said I couldn't help but overhear her mention her name and enquired as if by any chance her Mum's name might be Elizabeth. She confirmed that it was, so I told her we were old school friends and said the resemblance to her mum was striking. She smiled at that, the old Smith smile. I couldn't take my eyes off her, but I daren't say anything else. She said that she didn't see her mum too often these days, she was busy working for outreach organisations and charities that looked after homeless and abandoned children in the north of India.'

'That sounds like Liz all right. She'd often talked about wanting to do that sort of thing when we were together. I knew deep down she had wanderlust and I always had the feeling she resented it when she got pregnant...' Ever so briefly, I ponder the past. '...I hope she's happy now.'

'I was dying to ask her more. I wanted to tell her that I was her auntie, throw my arms around her and give her a big hug, but I didn't know what the consequences would be. I did the right thing didn't I?'

I nod slowly. 'I suppose.'

'I was in a quandary. I wasn't sure how you'd react if I told you at the time. I knew you'd be out in three months. I decided to tell you when I thought the time was right. At least we've found her, Jack. It's up to you now.'

'So, how did you leave it?'

'She asked me my name, said she'd remember me to her mum when she next spoke to her. I had to think on my feet. I caught a glance of the bottle of perfume in my bag. I said I didn't think for one minute her mum would remember me after all this time. I told her I was Elenor... Elenor Rubenstein.'

* * *

I catch the number forty-seven bus into town, my first tentative steps out into a world now alien. Faces cast glances at me forming faint shapes of recognition – or is it my imagination? I find a seat and wish myself invisible. I'd have bought a newspaper to bury my head in while trying to quell the growing sense of paranoia, but I was too scared to enter the newsagents in case someone had a memory for a ghost from the past.

Having the boys round hadn't been as bad as I'd feared. It had been Jeanie's idea, and, with reservations, I'd agreed. It felt a little strange at first, three out of the original four of us all in the same room again. To begin with, there had been a whiff of tension in the air. Topics of conversation were picked at carefully. Jeanie's offer of tea and coffee were politely refused but within the hour Ben had been dispatched to the off-licence and pretty soon we were all more relaxed, swapping jokes, sipping beer and generally having a laugh. I'd be lying if I said it was just like the old days, because of course that could never be, but once again, with no small thanks to Jeanie, I felt I'd crossed a bridge just by having that little soiree.

It's funny how certain images stay stuck in time. Did I really expect to see some slender hipped kid, head bowed, knife-sharp shoulder length hair swaying to the dynamite riff he was wrenching from his Les Paul, instead of the shiny domed gnarly looking dude sat opposite nursing a Bud on his paunch? Billy was a doubter; he had to be. He only came to see me once the whole time I was inside. He wrote the occasional letter but forever avoided the question of guilt and innocence. I always got the feeling that he blamed me for leaving the band in the lurch, like I was the selfish one for getting myself sent down like that and leaving them with the almighty inconvenience of having to find a succession of replacement bass players. It puzzled me over the years, but now I guess it was his way of dealing with the possibility of me actually having done what I was sent down for. I don't blame him for that; there were plenty of others who thought the same way.

I could feel Billy's eyes on me, wanting to check me out every now and then, and I was doing exactly the same to him. The physical results of time manifest; our thoughts mutual, like looking in a mirror: *what the fuck happened to this guy?* Old rock 'n' rollers don't die, they just grow ugly. Physicality aside, the old traits came to the fore as the beer flowed; Digweed still as argumentative, vaunty and off-the-wall as ever; Billy, quiet, unassuming, occasionally interjecting the conversation with some wry observation or dry caustic quip. Me? – Well, I don't know what the others thought, but I still felt like the alien, a stranger in my own body. I made an effort of sorts but I knew while ever I had unspoken, unresolved issues hanging like a storm cloud over my head, I would never find myself again.

I'd heard about Jed through Digweed's letters and occasional visits but I'd obviously never met the guy. Jed was the vocalist, harp player and sometime rhythm guitarist who replaced Fadge shortly after I was sent down. The boys spoke of him in glowing terms, and the fact that he'd been with the band for over twenty years now meant that he had to be good.

'Think of Wolf, Beefheart and Sonny Boy all rolled into one,' said Digweed enthusiastically.

'And he's a pretty mean harp player,' added Billy with a serious nod of the head.

I knew what was going on, I knew it would happen. They were weaving a blues tapestry for me, trying to rekindle the old spark, hoping to revive the passion in as subtle a way as they knew how. There were lines being cast all over the place, and although I do admit I enjoyed the craic, I wasn't about to take the bait, even when – especially when Ben, the crafty little bugger, let slip that Fergus, the band's current bass player was taking a sabbatical in the summer to tour Europe with Tony T.S. McPhee. I mean, Tony McPhee? *The* Tony McPhee? Groundhogs fame Tony McPhee? I knew that the guys were good, I mean Christ we were good even when I was around, but now they had a bass player who was about to tour with a British R&B legend, and there was certainly no way I was about to take the hook so they could reel me in as his replacement.

I suppose the value of ambition hits home when you're confined and have no outlet for that ambition, I guess that's one of the reasons I tried hard to shut out the music while I was inside. But I can't understand why Billy and Digweed didn't turn pro; they were both certainly good enough. Digweed could have flourished playing in the musical genre of his choice, he was that versatile, and Billy got so proficient in such a small space of time. He was a natural and when he played he made you sick with envy. He even took to sleeping with his Les Paul in the early days, just like Hendrix did with his Strat when he served with the elite paratroopers, The Screaming Eagles. Dedication or just some sick perversion? Maybe a touch of both. They could have toured with some of the greats and seen the world, of that I'm sure, but instead they chose to stay close to home and work the pub circuit; such a waste. I sat there and wondered at the pair of Marsden lads perched opposite, demolishing the Buds, seemingly content with their lot. I might be wrong, but somehow I got the feeling that they both had stuck around for me, biding their time, waiting to bring me back into the fold. Blizzard: they'd even kept the band's name after all these years. It sounds a bit naff to me now, but that's who we were and that's who they are, named after one of our early jam sessions when it had all started to come together; a fifteen minute version of Rattlesnake Shake, with Billy in his element emulating his hero Pete Green in fine style and at the end someone had exclaimed, *"Wow, that was storming."* And Digweed had added, *"Yeah, like a fuckin' blizzard!"* Somehow it stuck and from there on in we became a proper band.

While we'd been on the subject of band members past and present, I'd cautiously asked about Fadge. No, they didn't know of his whereabouts or what he was up to. The last anyone heard he was playing the cruise ships, churning out MOR covers for the undiscerning ear. There was no more elaboration; it had been a conversation stopper. There were awkward silences and blank stares at the progress of bubbles as they carbonated up bottles of beer. I had brought the past into the room and it had frozen everything on contact. Icicles briefly hung in the air until Jeanie came to the rescue and thawed out the scene with a change of topic.

It was just as I had feared. Taboo was still taboo and I wasn't sure if I had the strength or resolve to make it otherwise.

Nick Fadgely was once a mate and a band member. He and Lauren had been engaged. Lauren was the girl I was supposed to have murdered. And what convicted me were the gruesome items that were found in my possession: a white gold engagement ring that was still attached to a bloody severed finger, the same ring that Fadge had placed on that very finger barely two weeks previous. This tiny token of betrothal and the dismembered digit of my ex-girlfriend became the objects of my never-ending nightmares, and, to this day I still don't know how they came by me. I've had a long time to work on the who, how and why's, to nurture theories during those bitter days and the cry-myself-to-sleep nights, but after all this time theories are still all I have. I had visions. When I got out, I would be on the front page of every newspaper, be on every news bulletin, screaming injustice from every rooftop. I would be out for everybody; those who wouldn't listen, those who put me away and the scheming, murdering bastard who set me up. But time stepped in and did its thing again. Time doesn't heal; time erodes, takes away your resolve. Tolerate the term – comply. See out your stretch – comply. Be on your way and fade away – comply. And I almost did.

It was Jeanie's revelation about my little girl that filled me with a new found purpose – *little girl* – I can't help it, it's that time thing again, the past; it's all I have, all I know. It was her birthday last Thursday; she'll be twenty-eight now.

Six

I WIPE CONDENSATION from the cold wet window of the bus and peer beyond the angled rain patterns as they streak across glass, watching the soaked and windswept landscape of Marsden streets and houses flash by in monochrome. Nothing appears to have changed much in this, my old hometown in the last twenty-five years, least the weather, wild as ever, pretty much like its inhabitants, as John Wesley described them back in 1746. Two and a half centuries later the Theologian and Methodist preacher spins in his grave. *"Nothing changes"* I hear him lament, neither the elements, the social conditions nor the three throwback descendant sons of this bleak Pennine place; wild in nature, even wilder in appearance, who appropriated a holy place of worship, a chapel erected after his name, in order to dance and play to the tune of the Devil, and amongst their number one murderous scoundrel who would have hung from a gibbet at Leeds assizes back in his day.

Nothing changes? I rub hard at the condensation on the bus window to make sure my eyes aren't deceiving me. Sure enough, the garish neon sign confirms. The old Wesleyan chapel that used to be the home and rehearsal space for the Third Marsden Scouts and a wannabee rock and roll outfit respectively is now a Kebab Ranch.

I get that twinge in the chest again. Not like a stab to the heart, there are no painful memories here. It's not even nostalgia; it's just these short, sharp reminders of my past that I keep stumbling across; little pockets of time waiting for me around every corner: Milestones, millstones; as real and as solid as they ever were but not the same as we remember them. Old John Wesley turns once again, and, as reluctant as I am, I find myself falling into retroactive mode. I rest my temple against cold glass. The drone from the engine of the number forty-seven into town lulls my senses, while scenes from long ago slip into my head as easy as wet soap...

* * *

Digweed had recently discovered The Mothers' Over-nite Sensation, and, as with all things musical, had played it to death while assigning every lyric to memory before regurgitating it endlessly to all present, ad nauseam. Billy, who had been breaking strings on piecework, was already in a bad mood and was fast losing patience with Digweed and his irksome Frank Zappa renditions.

'I bet we could learn that,' piped up Fadge who, for the past half hour had been sat in a corner of the old chapel under the large, draped marching banner that belonged to the Third Marsden Scouts, quietly engrossed in a keyboard catalogue. 'Add a bit of synth. Some of the babies in here can replicate a whole orchestra,' he said, waving his pamphlet in the air. Billy and I exchanged looks. I raised my eyes to the old church rafters, but the moody guitarist's tether had come to its end. He put down his axe and stormed across the ancient wood floor, his angry footsteps echoing up and bouncing off the equally ancient stone walls. He snatched the brochure from Fadge's grasp and flung it skitting across the floor.

'What the fuck did you do that for, you mad bastard?'

Fadge asked, both shocked and appalled.

'As much as I admire Zappa as a somewhat twisted genius and guitar virtuoso, I'm not about to try and play his bloody music – we're a sodding rhythm and blues outfit, remember?'

Fadge took the force of Billy's rant full in the face and looked across at Digweed and me for a bit of support. We both smirked back at him.

'It was only a suggestion,' he whined with a hurt tone in his voice. 'I thought keyboards might add another dimension to the sound, that's all. What do you think, Digweed?'

Digweed perched himself behind his kit. 'Yippy-Ty-O-Ty-Ay,' he said non-committal while gesturing a shrug with his sticks.

'JD?'

Fuck – now he was dragging me into the argument. I tried my hand at diplomacy. 'I don't mind the sound of a Hammond, you know, a touch of the old Booker T's, but that's something I think we should only mess about with if we ever got into a studio. And as for a Moog, I think we should leave that particular sound to the likes of Mr. Wakeman and his ilk.' I launched into the Green Onions riff that Digweed immediately picked up on and joined in with. We both looked over at Billy, who had grouched back to his guitar, to see if a Steve Cropper interpretation was in the offing but he just glowered at us and continued to fiddle with his strings.

We'd all begun to get a bit worried about Fadge of late. He'd started to lose sight of the vision, was drifting away from the common cause. Because he took care of most of the vocals he liked to think of himself as unelected leader of the band, which was bollocks, we were a collective, we didn't have leaders. He fancied himself as a bit of a songwriter too, which was okay as most of the stuff we played was old R&B standards anyway. And he was fine when he stuck to the script. We loved it when he had his - *lemon squeezed 'til the juice ran down his leg,* - or when his muse claimed: - *you got your needle in me baby.* - You couldn't beat the old tried and tested formula, okay, I know it all sounded a bit clichéd, but that's what we were all about and we were happy with that. It was when he was seen walking the streets with a pile of King Crimson and Gong albums tucked under his arm and started to pen twaddle like: - *Don your blizzard season coat as night unfolds her sable cloak, scattered with diamonds light years afar, awake your love this distant star,* - that we had started to fret. The bugger even had the cheek to use the band's name in his potty prog lyrics. We hadn't been together all that long but Fadge had already begun to pull in a different musical direction. The rest of us never really said anything, but we all knew what each of us was thinking. Our rhythm guitarist cum harp player cum songwriter-vocalist was fast becoming surplus to requirements. We'd have been okay as a trio, ala Baker, Bruce, Clapton. Billy was honing his craft so quickly and so well, Fadge's Telecaster had become merely filler, and I suppose the only reason we hadn't already given him the boot was because he was a mate, and, because we didn't have a manager, he tended to be the one who did all the leg work to find us gigs and do the promoting – plus the fact that despite Digweed's Moon-like delusional claims to the contrary, the rest of us couldn't sing to save our lives.

Green Onions morphed into a Ten Years After style version of Sonny Boy Williamson's Help Me. We hit the refrain time and again, building the tempo. Bass and drums working the twelve bars in an almost telepathic legato fashion until Billy couldn't take it anymore. He bent a soaring C vibrato up into the old church rafters while me and the drummer grinned from ear to ear. All at once Billy became Alvin Lee, chopping the chords guillotine like on the four, advancing the rhythm subliminally. Finally cottoning on, Fadge bounded up the tiny wooden stage and crooned into the mike.

For the next twelve minutes we forgave Fadge his musical meanderings as we created a blues canvas for Billy to paint on. He ascended the scale in arcs and swoops, bittersweet and blue before returning to the melody stroke and finally back into the rhythm, modally perfect alongside Fadge's Telecaster chops, then building another solo starting in a low-register geechie stutter that wound its way snake-like around the twelve bar pattern culminating in a series of high end bends on the run out, his eyes shut tight and his features as contorted as his new strings that didn't look as if they'd survive the session by the way he was making them scream. This was where we came together; this was where we were as one, where grouch and foul moods evaporated and we began to become aware of the increasing tightness of our sound, the stipend for hours of endless jamming. We were getting good at what we did and we knew it.

'You seeing that Irish chick again, Friday?' Fadge asked casually over my shoulder as I coiled away my leads.

'Dunno,' I shrugged. 'I suppose; depends what transpires.'

'You ever been in love, JD?' he asked out of the blue.

I straightened up to turn and frown at him. 'Christ, I dunno. What sort of a question is that?'

'She seems like a nice lass – Lauren, I mean.'

'Yeah, so, what's your point?'

'It'll all come back at you one day, you know,' he said cryptically.

'What will? What the fuck are you on about?'

'The way you treat women. One day you'll fall in love for

real, they'll do the dirty on you and then you'll know what it's like to have your heart broken. It's called karma.'

I looked into his sanctimonious mush which was beginning to annoy and wondered where all this shit is coming from. 'Bollocks,' was all I could think of as a suitable reply.

'You mark my words,' he said waving his rolled up organ pamphlet at me like he was a fucking schoolteacher or something. 'I've seen you operate. You treat your birds like shit. You need to beware of something called cause and effect, my friend.'

I swung my amp out in front of me so that Fadge had to step back or risk having his kneecaps levied. 'Thanks for the advice, *my friend*, and not that it's any of your business, but for one, my complaints file is empty, and two; how can I put this?' I said setting my combi down so it just missed his toes. 'Oh, I know, how about – fuck you!'

I humped my gear out to the van annoyed at Fadge having soured the mood again. What the hell was all that about? Had my racking up the conquests gotten to him? Hadn't he been getting any? It wasn't as if we were in a league or anything. I could have put Fadge down as a lot of things but jealous hadn't been one of them up to now. In the end I shrugged it off and soon forget all about his little lecture, as in the coming months I would be too wrapped up in myself and the music to read between the lines as to what was going down.

* * *

The air-brakes on the bus release like Digweed riding his crash cymbal, dragging me back to reality with a jolt. The Monday morning traffic crawls forward in its rain-drenched misery and as the window slowly re-mists itself with the heat and breath from the clutch of reluctant commuters, Kebab Ranch settles into its space in time waiting for the next soul to come along and hang a memory from the stone and mortar of its many manifestations.

I step off the bus into cold winter drizzle, and even on a miserable mid-Monday morning such as this, I'm surprised at the amount of folk there are on the streets. What used to be the main drag through the town centre is now a long precinct devoid of traffic but full of bustling bodies going God knows where. Is there no work for these people? In a mood as cynical as the weather I seek out what used to be the Dole office. The giant vibrant green and yellow sign that now declares itself as *jobcentreplus* fails to lift my spirit. I sigh and venture inside.

After an hour or so of waiting and form filling, I emerge eager to get on with what I really came into town for. I check my soggy note that has the all-important name and address scrawled on it. It's my note of hope that doesn't look too hopeful now that the ink has started to run. I try and familiarise myself with places that aren't too familiar anymore. The bulldozers and the demo men had already started to move into this town around the time I was sent down. The old Victorian edifices that managed to survive the modernisation look tired and neglected and oddly out of time and place, sitting randomly amongst the poor architecture of the seventies; nondescript, thoughtless structures that already appear way past their sell-by date, like *jobcentreplus* where I'd just been to sign on, with its tarted-up exterior of brightly coloured plastic and neon, betraying its soul-destroying interior.

The building I'm looking for is on a street that had managed to escape the ravages of the developer. Stone-built Victorian; nestled between a bank and an estate agents. I check out the shiny, inscribed brass plate near the entrance: Knapton &

Dupree Solicitors 1st Floor. I try the door, eager to escape the rain. It resists my attentions. Then I notice the keypad and intercom buttons on the wall. I find the right one and buzz. After a short pause, the speaker crackles into life.

'Knapton and Dupree, can I help you?' the bright female voice roller coasters.

'Er, yeah – I'm here to see Mr. Dupree.' I stoop and stutter into the wall while heavy raindrops from the carved Victorian stone lintel above my head form and fall bomb-like onto my back.

'Do you have an appointment?' The brightness in the voice begins to fade.

'No, I don't.'

'I'm sorry, did you say *Mr.* Dupree?'

'Yeah.'

'Mr. *Stephen* Dupree?'

'Yeah, that's right.' There's a pause. A long pause, and I wonder if the woman has decided to take a bog break at this juncture, when finally the speaker crackles back to life.

'I'm very sorry, but Mr. Dupree passed away quite some time ago.' The bright voice is now a solemn one and it's my turn for the long pause. I eventually become aware that someone behind me wants to get into the building and I'm blocking the way. I mutter an apology and step back. The figure under the umbrella says thanks and swiftly punches numbers into the keypad on the wall, just like the screws used to do in Wakefield. The door buzzes and opens with a click. From under the umbrella appears a woman and she is stunning. She holds open the door for me with a twenty dollar magazine cover smile and I stumble in out of the rain while the woman on the intercom crackles: 'Hello...*Hello?*'

'You look a bit lost, can I help you?' says the smiling lady, flashing her perfect teeth that are framed by a mouth that lures me in and leaves me gawping like a fool. She shakes her brolly free of rain and smoothes a hand over her tied back ebony hair even though there isn't a whisper out of place. She has unbelievable cheekbones that are accentuated by the continued smile. She smiles with her eyes as well as her mouth. I like that. They are as dark as her hair, and with just the right amount of mascara. The smile betrays faint lines that fan whisper like towards her temples, which, at a guess would place her around the forty mark. I'm not entirely sure if this is all to do with me not being around females for so long, but this woman has me spellbound, and I suddenly become aware that I'm staring like a slavering simpleton, dripping from head to foot, creating a puddle in the foyer; my hair plastered to my head – and I fucking hate myself.

'I'm not sure you can,' I concede. 'I've come to make an appointment with my solicitor, but I've just been told that he's dead.'

'Oh, and who was your solicitor?'

'Mr. Dupree.'

She loses the smile; her forehead furrows slightly but she still looks gorgeous.

'My father passed away six years ago,' she says wistfully, but a resigned smile quickly returns. 'My name's Caroline Dupree,' she says offering a long, slender and beautifully manicured hand. Again, my eyes are drawn magnet-like to the highly glossed red nails and a million testosterone induced thoughts flash through my head. I pray that the thoughts are natural but I can't help feeling like some seedy old perv, certain of the fact that I must appear like one.

'So, you must be...'

'...His daughter, yes. I run his side of the practice now.'

I continue to stare; she continues to smile. I feel electricity. She cuts off the power. 'So, how can I help?' She tilts her head to one side. Every little move she makes gets me going. This is silly; it's like I'm besotted or something. 'You said you wanted to make an appointment.'

'Er, yeah. Your dad – your father, represented me a long time ago. I've erm... just got out of prison...' And before I get any further, this vision of beauty stops me in my tracks again. This time it's with a look of total revelation. Those dark mysterious pools that are her eyes open wide as does that delicious, sensuous mouth.

She slowly raises one of those slender, painted fingers and levels it at me. You're Jack, Jack Smith, aren't you?

'Er... yeah, I er...how did you...?'

'Oh, my God,' she cuts me off again. 'Oh, my God,' she repeats almost in a whisper. This time it's her turn to stare while I stand there nonplussed. Eventually, what I assume to be professional detachment takes over; she snaps back to reality and checks out the time on her Gucci wristwatch. 'Look, I have to be in court in an hour,' she says with what I detect to be a little excitement in her voice. 'Why don't we nip upstairs and get Elaine to check out my diary? We'll have to take the stairs I'm afraid, the lift is out of order.' And without waiting for a response from me she's off, leading the way, jabbering on about schedules and how there never seems to be enough time in the day. But I'm not really listening as I closely follow this apparition, eyeing the dark denier seam that runs down the back of each shapely calf. *My God, she's wearing stockings.* The bulk of her raincoat hides the rest of her shape, but my imagination helps out as I watch the swing of her hips with every step. I've no idea of what help this woman can be to me now that the man I came to see is no longer around, but I climb the stairs

60

after her anyway, like a drowned rat following a pied piper.

I can't quite decide how my first real encounter with day-to-day reality went. Was it normal? How can you tell when you're not really sure what normal is any more? It certainly didn't feel how I expected normal to be, but then again, what were my expectations? It was all a bit too surreal for my liking, as though somehow I was removed from myself, watching it all unfold from a distance. Perhaps I analyse things too much these days, like every move, every step, every utterance has to have some underlying meaning or some hidden context. Maybe this is who I am now; maybe this is how it's to be for the rest of what life I have left.

I trudge back to the station to embark on the second task I have set myself for the day. Whenever I look up I see people beneath hoods and umbrellas juggling their survival kits: phones pressed to ears while clutching cardboard cups of coffee with plastic lids as if life depended. Strange.

I seek out the bus that will take me to Hebden Bridge, with the enchanting image of Caroline Dupree swimming around inside my fuddled head. It's still raining.

◆

Seven

I GINGERLY SNIFF the bottle of aftershave Digweed hands me, reluctant, like he's offering me a turd. 'What the hell do I need this for, I don't even shave?'

'Go on; dip yer bread, it'll make you irresistible.'

'I don't wanna be irresistible, I keep telling you, it's not a date.'

'I thought you said she was a stunner.'

'She is, but I'm seeing her in a professional capacity, I'm not trying to get her into bed.'

'You know, that just doesn't sound right coming from you.'

'Yeah, well, I'm not me – I mean I'm not him – I mean... look, she's my solicitor now; this is purely business, okay?'

'Yeah, right; what solicitor invites a client up to their apartment and offers to cook them a meal?'

'Look, she's in court a lot, her diary's full. She could have passed me on to a junior partner, but because her old man was my brief she feels responsible; she's being as helpful and accommodating as she can, that's all.' I turn the bottle of smelly in my hand and see the dude's name that Ben has on display around the top of his underpants.

Digweed looks at me sideways. 'Go on, slap it on,' he dares. 'What harm can it do?'

I take up his dare and spread a little over my freshly cropped whiskers. I haven't been clean- shaven for years;

don't ask me why, I think it has something to do with feeling vulnerable. 'How do I look?' I ask nervously.

Digweed looks me up and down. He sees *his* jacket, *his* shirt, *his* pants, and *his* shoes. 'You'll pass. You have had a bath and changed your skiddies I hope, you know – just in case.'

For some reason everyone still sees the old Jack in me; Digweed does; JD the kid Casanova philandering his way around the rock 'n' roll circuit. *"Just in case."* He thinks I won't be able to resist working the legendary Smith charm after all those years of prison pornography and the old knuckle shuffle, but he doesn't understand, and I can't really expect him to. I content myself with the notion that God granted me my lifetime's quota of women before I was twenty-five, and having one now isn't anywhere near the top of my agenda, in fact it isn't even on the map. I admit that the thought of having dinner with a beautiful lawyer this evening is making me nervous but it has nothing to do with the unlikely scenario that Digweed has swimming around in his head. It has to do with fear; fear of failing in the two most important quests I have set myself, and in the pursuit of one of those quests I have already stumbled at the first fence.

Maggie wasn't at the shop in Hebden Bridge. She doesn't even work there. She had merely been helping out on the day that Jeanie saw her. It turns out she's a buyer-cum-agent, travelling to Africa and Asia for Fair Trade organisations, purchasing locally made goods that end up adorning western living rooms. Jeanie had caught her on a rare visit home where she'd been touching base, listing stock requirements and collecting her commissions.

The proprietor tried to be as helpful as she could when I made my enquiries, but was understandably cautious about giving too much information to a total stranger, and she refused point blank to give me a mobile number. By now Maggie would be swanning her way across the sub-continent, and the shop owner said her first port of call would be in the Goan capital of Panjim, in India. She conceded to giving me a list of likely contacts; wholesalers and exporters who were on her route and who she usually did business with, but I didn't know what much good they'd do me.

I caught the bus back, in the cold and the rain, and with a heavy heart. I'd dared to be optimistic and should have known better; what the hell had optimism ever done for me? It was coming dark by the time I got back to Marsden, not that it had got bright at any time during the day. Lights peered out of the gloom all along the Salter Hebble valley, and I reached Jeanie's door feeling as abandoned and alone as I ever did inside.

I press the illuminated pad that says Dupree on it and step back to take in the exterior splendour of these luxury apartments while Digweed breaks the thick calm of this dank evening by shouting some stupid innuendo from the open window of his motor. *'Thanks for the lift pal, but please fuck off now,'* I say under my breath. As if I'm not nervous enough.

'Hiya Jack – Come on up.' The voice is warm, bright and surprisingly familiar; so much so that it unnerves me even more, but oddly excites me at the same time. The door buzzes and clicks and Digweed drives away laughing his head off.

'Look, I'm ever so sorry for having to cancel on you at the last minute like that,' says Caroline Dupree while busying herself around a spectacular open plan kitchen that is all polished granite and stainless steel. I stand rooted to the spot and offer a pathetic shrug, feeling embarrassed because of the space I'm occupying while my eyes dart furtively around her posh pad.

'A new case came up and I had to be in court. We're very busy at the moment.' She drops something into a pan that steams and sizzles and I catch a pleasant whiff of garlic and aniseed. She looks up at my lack of response and senses my awkwardness. 'Here, let me take your jacket.' She wipes her hands down her Ricard apron and I hand her Digweed's coat. She smiles without parting those sensuous lips and she reminds me a bit of that celebrity chef, the one whose dad used to be a politician. Losing the jacket hasn't made me feel any less awkward and I stand there like a spare prick in a brothel until she returns and invites me to sit. I glance over to the black leather suite and the thick-pile, light coloured carpet beneath it and hesitate.

I point to my shoes. 'Should I...?' I ask unsure.

'If you like,' she says casually and heads back to her culinary endeavours. 'I can't cook without a drink,' she says waving a third empty bottle of Merlot at me. 'Would you care to join me or do you prefer something else?'

'Wine's fine,' I say, sinking into soft leather but failing to relax, despite the lounge lizard jazz-funk vibe that Becker and Fagen are laying down on the Hi-Fi in the background. I gingerly accept the wine, praying to God that none of it leaves the glass before it reaches my lips. I take a sip and carefully set it down on a coaster next to a legal profession periodical that sits on the coffee table in front of me. I resist the urge to watch her walk back to the kitchen and by the time temptation gets the better of me she's disappeared back behind her granite island, so I lean across the leather and peruse the CD rack. They say a person's music collection can tell you a lot about them. Straight away I'm pleasantly surprised; plenty of Miles Davies; from Kind Of Blue to Bitches Brew. Ornette Coleman, Monk, and even Coltrane's A Love Supreme. She's a jazzer.

I'm impressed.

'I'm impressed,' I say, cutting her off mid flow from some small talk that I wasn't really listening to.

'Sorry?'

'Your sounds – I'm impressed. You've got very good taste.'

She stops cooking, and with spatula in hand looks at me as if no one has ever paid her a compliment before. 'Why, thank you,' she says as if the sentiment really means something. She cocks her head slightly to one side and smiles that smile and I melt into the leather. 'It's all my father's fault, I'm afraid,' she says, briefly turning back to her pans. 'There wasn't much telly in our house. It was all jazz: Basie, Dizzy, Bird. He listened to all the greats. It was his passion. It helped him relax after a hard day in court. I didn't really have much choice. It was either love it or hate it. By the time I was old enough to get into pop it was too late. All the stuff my mates at school were listening to sounded - I dunno, cheesy in comparison, somehow. Do you know what I mean?' She turns to me and tilts her head again. *Oh my God, woman, what are you doing to me? Of course I know what you mean. I know exactly what you mean.*

'Yes, I do,' I say. We exchange smiles.

Caroline Dupree takes a black grape from amongst the remnants of the continental offerings of the cheeseboard, wraps her lips around it and bites: a pure sexual act – in my eyes it is, anyway. Everything she does, every move, every gesture is accomplished in a smooth sophisticated, sensual manner and I get the feeling it's not done entirely for effect, this lady is simply class and she oozes it.

The meal is delicious and I tell her so. She smiles and looks at me in that modest, self-effacing yet totally endearing way, as if looking for signs in my face that say I must be taking the piss. Since she lost the apron and throughout dinner, I've been doing that naughty schoolboy thing. Her blouse is unbuttoned to a degree that it reveals tantalising glimpses of cleavage and I've been casting surreptitious glances towards her chest throughout, totally enchanted by pure white silk over black lace against voluptuous flesh. Digweed's inside my head, laughing his cock off, there's another empty bottle of wine on the table and we've hardly broached the subject of why I'm here.

'I am sorry to hear about your dad; I really did appreciate all he tried to do for me. Did you say it was a heart attack?'

'Yes, he survived two previous to having his by-pass, but a massive coronary got him in the end – I blamed the work.'

'Yet you chose to follow in his footsteps?'

She nods quietly in thought for a moment. 'I've never told anyone this before, and you probably won't believe what I'm about to say, but *you* are the real reason I chose to be a lawyer.'

I let out a nervous laugh at that little revelation but her gorgeous eyes hold me in serious suspension. I go silent and wait for her to continue.

'I knew that my father was involved in a high profile murder case at the time, but being as young as I was, I hadn't really taken much notice apart from being aware that it was a stressful period for him. I remember him shutting himself away for hours on end poring over case notes while the rest of us walked around the house on tiptoes, speaking in whispers. Then, one day I saw your photo in the paper, and I fell madly in love with you. I was fifteen years old...'

Shit, I didn't see that coming – straight between the eyes, or what? I don't really know how to react, but it doesn't matter because I can see she's ready to tell it how it was, how it is, without a hint of shame or embarrassment.

'...From that moment on I followed every day of the trial, every development, every twist and turn. I cut out and kept every press cutting; anything that carried your image. I even started to pester Father, so much so, near the end when things didn't look good for you, and I remember going up and screaming at him to do more. I'll never forget that look on his face as mum pulled me away and he shut the study door behind him. It was a look of defeat. I knew he'd done his best, but his best this time wasn't good enough. He took it bad when they delivered the verdict. He was never the same man after that. It made him ill. He really believed in your innocence, and he took his failure to deliver to the grave.'

I find myself in that awkward zone again, where adequate words of response fail to formulate amongst the jumble of thoughts in my head, but I give it my best shot.

'My barrister was a wanker.'

'Knowing what I do now, I have to admit that the council for the defence wasn't the best, but we had very few bullets to fire with. All the evidence, everything, stacked up against you.'

'How do you know all this, you were just a kid?'

'I studied your case notes long and hard. I used them as points of law in my exams before I qualified. I highlighted the flaws and the mistakes in the way the defence presented itself. A lot of it was hindsight. I'm not saying that Father, for his part could have done any more than he did, but the learned Mr. Mcginley certainly didn't cover himself in glory in the way he delivered the brief. Anyway, my case study earned me a first, so, thanks for that.' She raises her glass.

'My pleasure,' I say reciprocating the gesture to the sound of chinking crystal. We both drain our glasses and I continue to gaze at this woman, this childless divorcee of four years, who had a schoolgirl crush on a soon-to-be convicted murderer, and wonder as she returns my gaze, what she's thinking now. What is she making of this old lifer, this unlucky soul whose mere mug-shot had the ability to scramble the hormones of adolescent girls? Why has she really invited me here tonight? Curiosity? Digweed was right, it wasn't exactly a professional way of going about things, but I have to admit I'm not sorry she did. She can't surely still have those silly schoolgirl feelings inside her after twenty-five years, especially after our encounter in her office foyer with me standing in my own little puddle, dripping from head to toe like a drowned rat – can she?

As if sensing my slight unease she slips seamlessly into lawyer mode and starts to talk shop. 'It isn't going to be easy, you know, Jack.'

'What isn't?'

She sighs and plays with her empty glass, endlessly twirling the stem between thumb and forefinger. 'What would you have expected Dad to do if he were still alive, if he'd have been sat behind his desk when you called the other day?'

'I don't know; maybe there was something he overlooked.'

'Like?'

'Something in a statement maybe; not everyone who made one got called to the stand.'

'I've been through them with a fine toothcomb; there's nothing there. You failed two appeal applications because there was nothing there.'

'Failure to provide evidence of my alibi, along with a ring and a body part found on me, were the only things that got me sent down, nothing else. The police couldn't even find the person I spent that Saturday night with; how hard could it have been?'

'Where you said you were that night was an abandoned

squat. You didn't know the girl's name. Your description of her was at best sketchy. You admitted yourself you were off your face at the time. Appeals were made Jack; seems like whoever it was you screwed that evening was just too scared to come forward.'

The word *screwed* leaves those lovely lips with what I detect to be a hint of venom. Did I just see a flash of green? Is that old schoolgirl crush still lurking after all this time?

'You'd have made a good prosecutor.'

'I'm simply trying to show you how easy it was for them and how hard it was for us. Evidence, Jack; they had some, we didn't. And unless you've got something new to tell me, there's nothing in your case amongst what I've read time and again that's going to clear your name.'

'The only evidence they had was a ring attached to a severed finger.'

'It's all they needed. You couldn't tell them how they ended up in the pocket of your donkey jacket.'

'Still can't.'

Caroline sends me a long look of pity mixed with understanding, like she knows how I must feel, but the look also says that I have to face up to the hard facts, and she's right. She starts to clear the table while I stare into my empty glass and muse over the mystery that has tormented my every waking moment for the last quarter of a century – the finger and the ring...

Eight

PADDY RELEASED HIS grab and the load of RSJ's fell into the open mouth of the giant shear with a deafening metallic clatter. The ground around me and my control room shuddered and shook. He slewed the boom of the yellow Hi-mac away and tracked off in search of another load. I leant on a lever that sent half a dozen gleaming hydraulic pistons into action. The jaws of the Henschell slowly closed around the metal beams and I patiently waited for the green light, taking time to take a slurp of tea and a couple of tugs on a roll-up. I set the cut at sixty centimetres and sat back as the powerful hydraulic ram and tungsten blade automatically did the rest, slicing the joists like a knife through butter. I kept my eye on the first pieces, checking the size as they dropped, neatly severed, onto the already chopped metal mountain pile with a satisfying clung. And that was it for the next twenty minutes; time for feet up, time to check out the latest batch of porno mags that Mick, one of the wagon drivers, had so kindly dropped off for my perusal, or simply time to watch the endless procession of wagons, scrap dealers, car dismantlers, tatters, and travellers, all queuing to tip their loads. It was a busy time and this was a big, modern reclamation and processing plant, not your back street Steptoe and Son cowboy outfit. Scrap prices were good and the yard was buzzing. All the old Victorian city centres and mills were coming down and the demo men were having a birthday.

I laughed to myself as I watched Dennis the yard foreman arguing with a bunch of ronkers who had tried to hide a concrete grass roller underneath their load of old fridges, washing machines, bike frames and general old tat. It all looked to be getting a bit heated down there, and the guy from Wiggy's Autos, waiting to unload his lorry full of scrap cars, was tooting his horn, impatient at the hold up.

I'd been working at Sutherland's for almost three years. I'd really fallen on my feet with that little number in so far as I was sat on my arse for most of the time. Up there in my cosy crow's nest I was more or less my own boss and nobody bothered me much. I was supposed to muck in when the shear blades needed changing, but the mechanics knew I wasn't too keen on getting my hands dirty. I wasn't much use to them on that front, so most of the time they'd tell me to fuck off out of the way and I'd be more than happy to oblige. Up there I could also recover from the late night gigs and the debauched weekends. Like I said, the job was cushy and life sweet as long as I kept the thirty-two tonners filled with short steel scrap, rolling in and out on their regular trips to the steel mills in Rotherham and Sheffield.

Of debauched weekends, there'd been quite a few of them around that time, and the one just gone, particularly so. Don't ask me about it, I can barely remember a thing. It's all predictably hazy, but judging by the chemical fluttering that was taking place deep inside my gut on that Monday it must have been a spectacular scene of excess. I know Liz wasn't too pleased when I rolled home sometime during the course of Sunday. And I knew she was only sticking with me for the sake of our daughter. She just about tolerated the lifestyle that I'd tried half-heartedly to change without too much conviction in the promises I kept making to her. I knew I didn't deserve her, and I couldn't have really blamed her if she'd upped and left me. Even the threat of taking Maggie away from me couldn't seem to cure my indulgences. Jack Smith was still the selfish, arrogant, love rat he always was, and nothing, it seemed would ever change that. It had been just another wasted weekend and another nail in the coffin of a relationship that looked doomed to fail unless I started to get my act together.

The Melbourne had become a regular gig for us over the years; almost our spiritual home, you might say, with a cosmopolitan audience made up of students from the Poly and the Uni, interspersed with most of the town's punks. We'd introduced a couple of Dr. Feelgood numbers into our set and that seemed enough to maintain the status quo and keep everyone happy.

I don't really have a clue how that particular Saturday night's gig went down. I have a feeling it wasn't one of our best. Lauren was at her flirtiest; flaunting herself in front of Fadge with a succession of guys, winding him up to distraction, making him forget the lyrics half way through Walking the Dog. I was getting eyeballed from a spiky blonde stood at the bar with pneumatic tits and arse to match. Concentration levels weren't what they should have been and around eight or nine bottles of Pils later I couldn't give a fuck. After the gig, me and the spiky blonde got better acquainted. A couple of joints was all it took before she was all over me like a rash, finishing off a French kiss with a flourish by deftly flicking the tab of acid she had concealed in her mouth with her tongue, sending it sailing down the back of my throat. That's where the evening started to get a bit fuzzy around the edges.

A caste system operated in the scrap-yard canteen; little hierarchical enclaves that started with the foremen and machine operators at the top, that descended through crane drivers, grease monkeys and burners, to the much ostracised pickers at the bottom. In actuality it worked something like, the dirtier the job, the lower you were.

Me, Vinnie and Dennis were sat at one end of the canteen observing the bunch of lowly pickers at the other end of the room. We were all waiting in silent anticipation for Ronnie to take a bite of his bacon and fried egg sarnie and the inevitable eruption of golden yolk that would explode, like it always did, over his grimy whiskers, down his blackened hands and the surrounding vicinity. And, right on cue, he delivered with his usual cry of *"Bastard!"* The double-decker ejaculated its contents and Vinnie nearly choked on his tea.

I suppose you could say we were all a bit sad, us using those poor guys as our source of entertainment at snap time, but that's what we were like. And to be fair, we operated in a hard and nasty environment, and the pickers were easy targets seeing as most of them didn't have an ounce of brain cell between them. Well, let's face it, you'd have to be brain-dead to work in the picking shed in the first place; I mean, who in their right minds would accept those kind of conditions; ten hour shifts stood in front of a near-shattering vibrating belt, sifting through a constant moving mess of fragmentised automobile, picking out bits of non-ferrous metal amongst the stinking river of poisonous waste that mammoth of a plant created.

I watched the bunch of grimy specimens, with their ear defenders and their flimsy paper masks hanging loosely around their dirt engrained throats, and wondered just what amount of protection that basic equipment afforded them against the barely tolerable decibel levels and the airborne carcinogens. They took their forty-five minute reprieve, slaked their thirsts, gathered their sustenance in a blank, toxin induced stupor, oblivious to the scorn, derision and daily round of micky-taking the rest of us subjected them to. We felt no pity; we were just a bunch of twats.

Dennis and I looked sideways in amusement at Vinnie who was still choking on his tea, and yes, I suppose we must have been a sad set of fucks to think that Ronnie's daily bacon and egg routine could still do that to us. Although Vinnie belonged to our group, the rest of us were in agreement: none of us would have relished his job. He operated the fragmentizer; the biggest and most powerful piece of kit in the yard; an awesome machine that devoured cars whole, and at the end of an apocalyptic process, spat them out as pieces of metal the size of a fist, dropping them into waiting train wagons that, in turn, would deliver the payload to British Steel Cooperation smelting plants in Aldwarke and Tinsley. The six thousand kilowatt beast drew power from its own sub-station; it had giant metal hammers that spun on a rotor at eight hundred r.p.m., and had the capacity to handle over a hundred cars an hour. The noise, vibration and sheer savagery experienced on a visit to his control room at the top of the belt where the cars were fed to the thing, made you want to go scurrying back to wherever it was you came from. Although my Henschell was a powerful tool in its own right, Vinnie's fragmentizer made it sound and feel like a mere toy in comparison, and I was always glad to get back to the relative calm of its enclave after a visit to Vinnie's.

There were guys on the ground whose job it was to check all the scrap cars that came into the yard for combustible or potentially explosive material such as gas cylinders and the like. They were supposed to take an axe to the petrol tanks of vehicles and drain them of any fuel, but on the odd occasion and especially at busy periods, one might get missed. The resulting explosion, as the fragger took the car apart, was like a bomb going off. The ground shook and the force of the blast invariably took out all the windows of any building on site and those of the mill across the railway sidings opposite, resulting in a hefty claim for compensation from the owners. I always thought Vinnie must have had nerves of steel and a constant supply of clean underwear to do what he did, but as I watched him recovering red faced from his choking fit, I could have sworn his hair used to be dark when I first came to work there and not the shock of grey-white it had become.

I sat in my little cabin, idly leafing through a well-used mag with half the pages stuck together, thinking how best I might be able to start building bridges with Liz. I worked out scenarios in my head where whatever I said to her wouldn't come out sounding all insincere and pathetic like it usually did, trying to avoid a situation where she shakes her head at me in disgust and walks out the room, slamming the door behind her as she goes.

I didn't take much notice of the siren at first; there was no explosion, no smoke or flame coming from the direction of Vinnie's vantage; probably just a motor got stuck on the chute or something. I tossed the mag to one side and picked up another from my pile of porn, barely looking up as some of the yard lads started to run around and shout at each other. The siren went dead but then started up again almost immediately. There was more commotion in the yard, but I was still in weekend recovery mode and couldn't be bothered to get off my arse to see what's going on. Paddy came to see me with a handful of his own mags and we did a swapsy.

'What transpires out there, then?' I asked while casually scanning the new batch of filth.

'Dennis thinks some bastard has put a dog in the boot of a car again,' he said while making his selection from my pile.

'He says there's blood and guts everywhere; pickers are going mental.'

'There are some sick fuckers about,' I remarked, becoming slightly bored with all the female genitalia on show.

Half an hour later, the yard had come to a complete standstill. People were still running around like headless chickens and a couple of police cars had appeared at the top of the yard, blue lights flashing.

'Bit over the top this for a dead dog, innit?' I shouted from the top of my gantry to Dennis who'd just emerged from the shower block looking all agitated.

'Ain't a dog...' he yelled back without stopping to exchange pleasantries. He headed towards the weighbridge offices at a canter. '...It's a fuckin' person!'

I lifted my donkey jacket from its peg in the locker. Nearby, stood in a mist of steam, were a uniformed policeman and a guy from forensics dressed in a white paper suit and green wellies. They were having a heated argument because someone had allowed the pickers to have showers. I left them to it, put my jacket on, and headed for the non-ferrous shed where the rest of the workforce had been told to muster. Inside was a hubbub of noise. Speculation and Chinese whispers abounded. I sought out my mate, Paddy, to get the lowdown on the latest. He related a horrific scene of blood, guts and mashed and dismembered body parts. Three of the pickers saw their lunch again, Ronnie amongst them, and one of the guys had passed out and split his head open, adding a minor sideshow to the grisly spectacle. Then, as if on cue, a copper appeared from the offices, supporting a bloke whose face looked as white as the heavy bandage around his head. They walked slowly, unsteadily past us, and all chatter fell silent as we watched them pass. It was Bernard, poor old Bernard. All of a sudden around fifteen or so hypocrites, myself included, started to feel sorry for the much derided species that was the picker as they nervously tugged on ciggies, taking shaky sips of tea and coffee, while reliving the gruesome experience via a statement.

Dennis came down and told us all to be prepared for a long afternoon. The yard had been declared a murder scene and we'd all have to be searched and interviewed, which prompted audible moans and groans from most of the blokes.

I perched myself as comfy as I could on an old copper boiler, built a roll up and continued to formulate my grovel strategy for when I had to face Liz.

'Your turn, Jack,' shouted Vinnie, emerging from the office that had become a makeshift interview room. 'See you all later; I'm outta here,' was his parting shot delivered with great relief.

I glanced at my watch and headed for the office; it was already ten-to-five.

'Place all your valuables in here, please sir,' said the bobby pointing to a tray on a desk. As well as my watch I dug out my baccy, my lighter, and my skins, a few bob in change, my house door key and my comb. He motioned me to raise my arms and proceeded to give me a pat down. He felt inside the collar of my donkey jacket, and then patted that down too.

'*All* your valuables, sir,' he said pointing at my donkey pocket.

I had a fish about and came across something cold and clammy. What I brought into daylight was a bloodied severed finger. Around it was what appeared to be a white gold engagement ring.

The officer stopped and stared in shock and bewilderment, and I did exactly the same. I continued to stare uncomprehending while the copper started to back away like the thing was radioactive. In delayed horror I dropped it to the floor. I looked from the gruesome digit to the copper and back again. One of us needed to say something. He managed it first.

'Sarge! – Sergeant…'

Nine

'JACK – JACK...'

I look up into Caroline's face and realise I've been gone for a bit.

'...Are you okay? I thought you were about to spill your wine; you seemed miles away.'

I look around and see I've made the move from dining table back to couch but I don't remember doing it. And my glass is full; she must have opened another bottle. She slowly leans in and gently relieves me of it before I have an accident. She turns back to me but doesn't move away. Her outstretched arm sinks into the back of the couch just over my left shoulder and she leans in further, unashamedly studying my features, making me feel not exactly uncomfortable but slightly apprehensive.

'What were you thinking about?'

'The past – it's all I seem to ever think about, although I try not to.'

She sighs and the scrutiny becomes intense.

'Those eyes...' she says softly. '...That look; that same look from all those years ago; from the newspapers – you still have it... haunted.'

I shrug apologetically.

'Haunted, yet enchanting – magnetic.'

I raise my eyebrows and see if I can reach my wine, but she

bars my way; trapped divine.

'I can't believe you're here, Jack, after all this time.'

'I'm not the same guy you saw in those newspapers, I can assure you.'

'Yes, you are.'

'Look, you never knew me back then and you certainly don't know me now.'

'True, but it's not too late, is it? – To get to know you, I mean?'

I shake my head and look into the beautiful features of this crazy woman asking myself why?

'I'm a silver haired fifty-one year old geezer out of prison on life licence; you'll forgive me for questioning your motives here.'

'Don't put yourself down, Jack,' she laughs. 'We all get old sooner or later. Age isn't an issue with me, and your background certainly isn't. Anyway, an eleven year age gap at our time of life means absolutely nothing.'

Caroline Dupree has me intrigued. I want to ask her a million things; why her marriage didn't work out, why she never had kids, why she doesn't have a current fella. But this closeness, this intimacy - Charlie Byrd and his guitar taking his turn at setting the mood on the Hi-Fi and too much wine is making me glow inside. Here is someone trying to make me feel good about myself for some reason, and I don't feel like letting it go at this moment in time, so the questions can wait – all but one.

'Miss Dupree, if I take you on as my solicitor, or should I say if you take me on as your client; do you think all this is a good idea?'

She smiles naughty, sexy. Volts tear through my body, still can't get to the wine.

'Is what a good idea...?'

Smiles – hovers – teases – *Oh, my God!*

'...You mean this?' She leans in, slowly. Senses dormant for an age come alive. Her scent, her hair, her warm breath; all transpire to make me dizzy. Her breasts meet my chest and yield. Her lips meet mine and they yield too, ever so briefly. Then, like the moon turning the tide she withdraws with that teasing smile and waits for an answer. Jesus H Christ, she's good, I thought she was being rhetorical.

'Yes,' I reply, not wanting to play the game any longer.

She tosses her hair back off her face and places a hand on my thigh. 'Rest assured, whatever takes place here tonight will in no way cloud my professional judgement.'

'And how much is all this professional judgement going to cost me?'

'Nothing.'

'I'm being serious; the only money I have is what my sister invested for me when my ex-partner sold the house, and it isn't a fortune.'

'Jack,' she says, squeezing my leg reassuringly. 'I'll be doing this because I want to. We both know it isn't going to be easy. There's going to be a lot of the past dragged up, but if that's what you want, if you think you can go through with it then I'm prepared to do my best for you. Anyway, we solicitors work on a thing called no-win-no-fee these days.' She smiles; the hand continues to work my thigh. 'Do you still want me to represent you?'

'Yes,' I say without hesitation.

'Before I agree, I need you to tell me one thing, and I need you to tell me the truth...' *Bloody hell, she even teases when she talks shop*'...Did you do it?'

I sigh and look straight into those fuck-me eyes. 'No.'

'Okay,' she says with a satisfied smile, 'that's the business side of the evening over with. Would you like to continue with the social part?'

'Yes,' I say, once again without hesitation. She smiles. Our lips slowly come together, the wine on the coffee table forgotten for now.

Caroline leads me siren like towards the bedroom, my head a little fuzzy with alcohol, and in amongst the fuzz, a drummer with a dirty laugh.

The bedroom is modern but not minimalist; cosy contemporary and the carpet a few inches thick. Down-lighters are set to low, aided by the pearly light of two bedside lamps and a third on a dresser that sends our shadows soft, distorted across wall and ceiling. Ankle deep in shag pile I stand nervy, anxious, and expectant, like a total fucking amateur. I take a gulp of wine, not that I need any more Dutch courage than I've already had; it's simply an apprehensive reflex. Caroline relieves me of the prop and sets the glass down beside hers on the dresser. She begins to remove her jewellery in that slow, deliberate sensuous way of hers and my head starts to communicate with my loins. She turns away and begins to fiddle with the clasp on her necklace. With her arms raised I take in the shape of her body; the curves, the contours. She catches my lustful gaze through the mirror, smiles; reads my thoughts; a look that dares me to do something about it. I oblige. My hands reach to her waist and I lean into her behind. I take in the scent of her hair, nuzzling through its silky depth until my mouth finds the soft and tender nape of her neck. She moans, tilting her head sideways to allow me better access. I take advantage, venturing upwards, breathing gently behind an ear, provoking more moans and a tangible shudder. Her breath comes shorter, sharper, harder. A hand reaches around my head and holds onto my hair. She turns her face into mine, searching for my mouth.

Our lips lock into place and tongues begin to explore. I turn her fully to face me. My hands leave her waist; one goes south to her arse, the other up behind her head and we meld as if one. My hand does a frantic tour of her backside, stroking, squeezing, kneading. Her moan goes up an octave. Her eyes widen before rolling up into her head in ecstasy. Her reactions amaze me and I keep my own eyes open just to watch them. I begin to wonder which one of us hasn't had it for so long – Jesus! Was I ever this good? And this was just the overture. What did the first act have in store? Eager to find out, my hand moves over her curves, up the small of her back until I locate the buttons on her skirt. I flick them without any trouble and glide the zip all the way down. Caroline performs a little wiggle and the skirt falls to the floor. I let out a husky growl of achievement. I still have the touch. The old JD is making a comeback. Then I catch sight in the mirror and the growl almost becomes a howl: sheer denier tracing curve of calf and thigh a hundred stories high. Buckle and strap break over soft, English Rose flesh. Shadowy casts form deep contours as light bends soft up to her sex, clad sweet in satin lace noir. And Stan Getz, or some other cool cat fucker, pipes invisible into the room, moaning into his horn. Sheer class; John Alton couldn't have set it up better.

I didn't want this; I really didn't, so I keep telling myself. But – and at the risk of sounding slightly crude – when the old cock-o'-the north gets an opportunity to come out of retirement, what can you do? It's out of one's hands, so to speak. Of course, the setting and the lady in question are having a big say here, not to mention the fantastic stroking of the old ego. I mean, it's not as if I'm about to start banging some old slag off the estate, or some crab-infested, STD-addled tart. This woman wants me – why? I've no fucking idea, something to do with the eyes – who cares? My old body is telling me it's glad of the attention right now. Digweed is shouting bravo from somewhere up in the Gods. Act One is about to begin and JD Smith is about to put in a BAFTA winning performance.

I'm not sure at what point the Heavy Metal Demon entered the room, never felt the Banshees, silent for once, slide across the walls and slip chameleon like into the shapes and shadows, lost as I was in my ecstasy. I've always been strong enough in my waking hours to keep them at bay; my thoughts controlled, trained and disciplined, and when I didn't feel strong I usually had my stash of weed to fall back on. Didn't think for one minute they could manifest here, now. Not now. The thought never entered my head, but it didn't need to, it was already there, and like a fool I'd forgotten...

I'm sprawled amongst satin and silk, still warm from her body that writhes, arching and clutching as my mouth explores, as my tongue teases, tastes and delves. In a lithesome tangle of passion she manoeuvres me onto my back and reciprocates, when I first think I hear it.

My eyes spring open; teeth and jaw unclench. I watch the rhythmic shadow of her head on the wall as she pleasures me: *up and down, up and down.* I close my eyes only to hear it again; whispered, distressed *'Why Jack, why?'* My heart skips a beat. I suddenly become conscious of my sweat that has begun to turn cold. I strain my ears at the piped jazz, desperate to pin it on a vocal, but it's an instrumental, no voice here. I stare at the tangle of dark hair that is spread all over my loins. Caroline has her mouth full, oblivious. My eyes flit around the room. The whole of my body tenses, but it's no longer sexual tension. I've heard that voice before, many times before. And the scene begins to crackle with a familiar foreboding as the shadows on the walls slowly come alive. I try hard to shut it out, to focus on the pleasure, to concentrate on the sensations that are fading fast. My hand goes to her head, to guide, to force, to keep it real. My hips buck in mounting desperation. My moans of desire turn into groans of fear. I watch the head shadow on the wall bob and writhe. I hear her gag as I plunge too deep, but I still hold her there, until the choking becomes a banshee cackle and the head shadow on the wall morphs into that mop top of Joan Jett black hair I knew so well that was now howling at the ceiling.

I recoil. My hand flies away from the back of her head. Caroline, shocked, turns to look up at me and mouths something, only it isn't Caroline any more, it's Lauren Feeney, the feisty Irish girl who got put naked in the boot of a car, whose body was torn asunder by a fragmentizer, Nick Fadgley's fiancé – my ex-girlfriend.

She looks up at me with wild, terrified eyes that sear into my soul. I see her Joan Jett hair, her punk stud earrings, saliva running down her chin, and as the blood retreats from my now flaccid penis, she appeals to me for the millionth time – *'Why Jack, why?'*

I teeter on the edge of the well, the bottomless well where the tormented Irish lilt echoes amongst the banshees' wail, drawing me into its dark depth, swirling, keening, pleading. Evil beckons, casting its lure. Head swims and I lean into the abyss, surrender to the inevitable, succumb to the inescapable: a maelstrom of eternal misery that I had been promised no reprise...

...Angels wings enfold me and pull me back from the brink; a sheath of warmth, of love and pure light. All of a sudden I feel like I'm back in the womb. The wails of torment and pain fade, retreating in an ever-diminishing spiral, back to the dark depths of hell.

I have a saviour. Caroline wraps her arms around my

clammy, shaking naked body, and for the first time ever some-one is there to break the curse.

'I... I'm sorry,' I utter emerging slowly from my live night-mare. 'I don't think any of this was such a good idea.'

'It's okay, it's okay,' she whispers soft, cradling me in her arms and rocking me like a child. I nestle into her breasts and submerge myself in her scent, allowing her comfort to wash over me. Like before with Jeanie, I desperately want to ex-plain, to show her the visions, describe the torment, but I can't. This is for me alone to deal with and as usual I'm not doing a very good job of it.

We hug in silence until, eventually, Caroline lays me down, pulling silk over us both and we embrace ourselves into a wine induced slumber.

In a fitful sleep I manage to keep the demons out, but talk-ing about the case after such a long time has opened up portals in my brain, and in fractured scenes I revisit nightmares.

Caroline gently shakes me awake. I'm surprised to find that I'm cocooned in a white cotton bed sheet.

'Oh, I'm sorry about that,' she says placing a cup of coffee at the side of the bed. 'I had to wrap you in it last night, you were sweating so much.'

I slowly untangle myself and sit up feeling like shit. I look up at the apparition stood over me and can't believe I'm not still dreaming. She looks fantastic; showered, made up and groomed to perfection, and seemingly none-the-worse for wear after the excesses of last night, which makes me feel even more like shit. She sits on the bed and takes my hand in hers. 'You okay?' she asks in a tone full of sympathy and concern. 'I think you had a few bad dreams last night.'

'I've had worse,' I reassure her with a croaky voice. She passes me the mug of coffee and sits gazing into my eyes, her features full of intrigue, and I take tentative sips, conscious of the curiosity I provoke in this woman, wishing I had my baccy and papers to hand, but not daring to ask if it's okay to smoke in her bed.

I don't try too hard to remember the events of the previous evening; especially the dreams that have already started to dissolve beyond recall.

'About last night...' I begin to say.

'It's okay, it's okay,' she reassures.

'I'm sorry; I shouldn't have let things go so far. It wasn't a good idea.'

'No, it's me that should apologise. I came on a bit too strong. I was being totally selfish.'

'I think we both got carried away a bit,' I smile.

I can't begin to explain to her the complexities of my psychosis; I couldn't even explain them to myself, so I decide to tell her about Maggie. I use my long lost daughter as an excuse for my frailties, my insecurities and inadequacies.

'It's not that I don't like you, Caroline; I do; you're an amazing woman. It's just that all this is a bit too soon for me; I'm not ready for any of this yet; as lovely and as sexy as you are, I'm just not ready.'

'I understand,' she says, buying the flattery. 'I think you're amazing too.' She leans in and kisses me, not just a peck, but a full-on heartfelt snog.

'You smell wonderful,' I continue the adulation. 'I must stink like an old tramp.'

She laughs and glances at her watch. 'Feel free to take a shower. I've left a clean towel out for you. There's stuff in the fridge if you fancy breakfast. I'd make you some myself but I'm already running late. I've got another court session this morning.' She puts on a dark suit jacket over her crisp white blouse and applies another fresh coat of lippy in front of the mirror. I watch her with a mixture of yearning and regret, reluctantly accepting to myself that what happened last night couldn't be allowed to happen again.

'I'll start work on your case this afternoon,' she says picking up her briefcase.

'What will you do?'

'Get in touch with the Home Office.'

I raise my eyebrows.

'First things first,' Caroline Dupree says in a business-like fashion. 'You've got to find your daughter, and we need to get you a passport...

Ten

I TOUCH DOWN on Indian soil early one morning in late April. Caroline had somehow performed minor miracles in her dealings with the Home Office and, after a lot of legal diplomacy and the inevitable slow workings of the bureaucratic machine they finally granted me a passport.

This is my first ever trip abroad. I haven't stepped a foot outside England in nearly fifty-two long years, unless you count my extended vacation in Parkhurst on The Isle of Wight. It feels strange, not least because I've been canned on a charter flight feeling totally out of place amongst three-hundred or so happy holiday makers all eagerly tripping out for two weeks of cut-price-package sun. The nearest I ever got to being a tourist was the trip Liz and I were planning to Majorca once Maggie had turned three. Maggie – I try and recover those fragmented images of my daughter as that little girl I once knew as my own, the same images that I'd desperately kept locked away for so long in order to keep my sanity. Now, as I shuffle along the sparse halls of Dabolim Airport, lost in thought amongst the excitable chatter of the late deal throng and the rubber stamping of visas, I try and paint a picture of her as a young woman, hanging on Jeanie's description of her. Her hair, her features, thinking how the Smith confidence and the Hudson philanthropy might have formed her character, how growing up without her father, not knowing who or where her father was could have shaped her outlook on life; has it made her into someone she shouldn't have become; sad, bitter? Or did she carry strengths that allowed her to deal with life without a dad and move on? Maybe some other bloke came into her life, someone she came to know as dad. These are all possibilities I shall have to discover and come to terms with if and when they ever arise. And now that I'm here, the already staggering odds against that happening seem to have lengthened. If she's in this place, just how am I going to find her? If somehow, accidentally, coincidentally, fatefully, miraculously our paths cross, will I know her? Will I recognise her as my own flesh and blood after all this time? I always knew this was going to be a long shot, so little to go on, just the few names and business contacts given to me by the lady from the new-age shop in Hebden Bridge. It's the last few weeks of the holiday season over here. The monsoons aren't that far away. Maybe she's already started making her way north up to Kathmandu and into the remote regions of Nepal.

It was Caroline who insisted I should do this. She said it was a pilgrimage I needed to make, even though the pessimist in me knew it was doomed to failure. *"You've no time for procrastination, you have to do it now or you never will."* I only had a vague idea of what the word meant but I understood her. She said I owed it to myself and to Maggie, even if the journey ended up being a fruitless one. She said any effort I made in a quest borne out of love would be a part exorcism for me, and I had to believe her. As she handed over the all-important maroon document I drew an inner strength from the look she gave me with those eyes that tended to jelly my legs whenever I looked into them, and I knew I had to come and search for my girl. But now, all of a sudden I'm not so sure.

There are a lot of dour looking faces in khaki uniforms taking an age to process visas and match faces to passports in this glorified tin shed excuse for Arrivals. It's hot, it's humid, and as I painfully inch my way towards passport control I catch the eye of a guard, a policeman, a security officer, or whatever he is, as he passively watches the shuffling procession. I look away and start to perspire more than is just down to the heat. I curse inwardly at my reaction, like I must still have *Guilty* written through me like a stick of Blackpool rock.

A uniformed woman relieves me of my clammy passport, her face void of expression. She casually opens it then idly chats to a uniformed colleague sitting beside her. Uniforms: everywhere, everyone dressed in uniform. I fucking hate uniforms. This isn't what I pictured. I expected to see smiling, graceful young women in saris, hands pressed together in greeting: *'Welcome to India'* There goes my first illusion. Was this such a good idea? I suddenly realise that I haven't even thought beyond the process of actually finding Maggie. In my own selfish way I've never even considered how she might react; never deliberated the notion of rejection, resentment; hate? Even if she knows I exist, she may have no wish to set eyes on her father let alone listen to his story. Who could blame her? Who am I to come charging half way across the world, crashing into her life out of the blue, without warning? - *'Hi, I'm your dad; guess where I've been all your life?'*

With every passing minute the folly of starting out on this crazy escapade grows. Amongst the chaotic carnage that is the baggage hall I fight my way through the mad melee of Brits battling for their cases. I start to panic. I need to get out of here fast. I shake off the little Goan kid who's trying to wrestle my rucksack from me while demanding a pound for the privilege. My eyes dart around the arrivals hall looking for a sign that says Departures. This is insanity; I never should have come. I turn in agitated circles like a mad dog chasing its tail. I'm just about ready to go off my head when another uniform steps out of the chaos and whips my passport from my grasp. He impatiently ushers me through a security screen, and all of a sudden I'm back in Wakefield. I obey, head down; compliant; the fucking uniform again.

Before I know it I find myself outside, on the concourse, in the stifling heat being swarmed by dozens of jabbering locals all trying to relieve me of my luggage, while a platoon of placards with names on them are being waved in my face. I try and make sense of them, God knows why I do this; there's no one waiting for me, but still I look, like there might just be one that says: '*Hi, I'm Maggie; welcome to Goa.*'

A hand in a crisp white shirt catches my arm.

'Taxi, sir?'

With my head spinning I allow the skinny bloke to lead me through the riotous assembly to the relative sanctuary of his little white cab where my beleaguered luggage and I collapse onto the back seat. An ivory smile beams at me through the rear view mirror. 'Where to, sir?'

'Panjim,' I say, committing myself but regretting it as soon as the words leave my lips.

'First time in Goa, sir?'

'Yeah,' I nod. 'First time anywhere, mate,' I add under my breath.

'Holiday, sir?'

'No, not holiday.'

'Not business, I think.'

'No.' I shake my head.

My driver momentarily interrupts his questioning to join in with the battery of car horns that are sounding, as buses, taxis and tuk-tuks fight desperately for road space out of the airport.

'Maybe you are coming for the dentist, yes?' The crisp white smile shines through the mirror. His question leaves me perplexed. 'Dentist in England very much expensive. Dentist in Goa, very cheap. People come, sit in sun, go and see dentist. English people have very bad teeth, yes?'

'Dunno mate, The Queen and the state used to look after mine.'

This time it's his turn to look perplexed. 'You no pay for treatment? You have good insurance policy, yes?'

'Yeah,' I laugh, 'something like that.'

'You maybe here looking for young girl?'

'Yeah,' I say, surprised. 'How did you know that?'

'Many people come here now on plane to look for poor Indian girl or boy for the pleasure, sir.'

Penny drops; I'm a dickhead, the guy thinks I'm a paedophile. 'No, no,' I lean forward in my seat, shaking a finger. 'Not for sex. I'm looking for *my* girl - my daughter.

'Ah, your daughter.'

'Yes.' I sit back, allowing myself a smile at the misunderstanding. 'You think I look like a pervert?'

'No, sir. Not meaning to offending, but many people come to Goa.' He rolls his head, neither a shake nor a nod. 'Who know what pervert looks like?'

My driver merrily chit-chats his way through the forty minute drive to the Goan capital, and by the time we arrive at this centre of vehicular chaos by the side of the Mandovi river, Geoffrey has offered to be my personal driver and guide during my stay, guaranteeing the cheapest rates anywhere in the state. Along with his unbelievable charm and friendliness the guy seems genuine and I condescend to let him show me the ropes, at least until I get used to the surroundings and local customs, reasoning that he might be a valuable aid in my formidable quest. I show him the piece of paper on which is written the name of my first tenuous contact. He takes in the address and does the roll of the head thing again. Geoffrey guns the cab along the stifling air-polluted roads using his horn as often as he sees fit, which is quite often, in fact he uses the horn more than he doesn't use the horn.

We enter the heart of the city, into the stinking guts of this Old Portuguese colony, meandering maze-like through the labyrinth of narrow streets and my head starts to swim again. My tee shirt is stuck both to my back, and to the seat, and I don't know which is worse, having the window open, exposed to toxic traffic fumes and open road-side sewers, or winding it up to suffocate. As I neck the last of my warm bottle of Vitelle Geoffrey stops dead in the middle of the street, grins and points. The battery of car horns behind us builds to a crescendo.

'Kerala,' he shouts pointing triumphantly at the piece of paper, then back out to the street side. I look out the window and see some sort of emporium sandwiched between a leather goods shop and what looks like a cab driver's cafe. – *Kerala-Carvings &Crafts-Importers-Exporters* – says the sign above the pokey looking establishment.

'You sure this is it?' I ask dubiously.

'Kerala,' he gestures excitedly.

'You wait here,' I say. 'Ten – fifteen minutes?'

He dismisses me with a roll of the head that I take to mean, no problem. I step out the cab to a braying symphony of horns just as a scooter nips up the inside and almost does for me. I leap the sewer gully on to the pavement and straight into the shop. Inside is quiet and cooler. Two giant ceiling fans lazily beat the air that is heavy with the scent of exotic wood. The place is chock full of beautifully carved artefacts. Herds of elephants of all shapes and sizes fill the two front windows. Inside are more pachyderms, intricately detailed turtles, coiled cobras, giraffes, little sets of monkeys of the see no, hear no, speak no variety; fruit bowls, candle holders, spice jars, photo frames; everything the self-respecting, ethnic themed Western home would want. I venture deeper into this Tardis of ebony and mahogany and the merchandise becomes surprisingly grander and even more ornate, from spiralled jardinières to the most grand dressers and wardrobes. As I marvel at the crafts-manship a smart Indian gentleman appears as if from nowhere and offers a welcoming smile.

'You like this piece?' he says in a gentle voice while run-ning his hand over the item I'd been admiring.

'It's beautiful,' I say. 'A bit out of my price range I guess.'

'You'd be surprised; this isn't England you know – I as-sume you are from England?'

'Yes, I am but I'm not here to shop I'm afraid. I've come to see a Mr. Salwar.'

'There are many Mr. Salwars,' he smiles doing the head roll thing. 'I am Xavie Salwar, second eldest son and business partner. How can I be of assistance?' he says in a soft, charm-ing manner.

'I'm looking for a young woman; an English woman who I believe is a business acquaintance of yours...' The head rolls again and I take it as a cue to continue. '...Her name is Maggie, Maggie Smith, although I think she might use her mother's surname - Hudson.'

Mr. Salwar gives nothing away but smiles his polite smile.

'And what, may I ask, is the reason for your enquiry?'

'I'm her father and I've come to Goa to look for her.'

'She's not in trouble or anything, I hope.'

'Oh, no – nothing like that. It's just that we haven't seen

96

each other in such a very long time, and – well, it's a long story, but it's time we were reconciled, so I've made the journey to find her and I was hoping you might be able to help me.'

He looks me up and down, naturally cautious. He sees a hint of desperation in my eyes and the look is genuine. Mr. Salwar flicks imaginary specks of dust from the piece of furniture he was hoping to sell me and asks how I came to him. I explain about the shop in Hebden Bridge and when I name drop the owner he relaxes.

'Yes, Maggie was here a few weeks ago, but only paid me the one visit. I haven't seen her since. She didn't purchase too much this time and I couldn't tempt her with the new stock. She is a very good business woman; drives a hard bargain, but a very nice girl to deal with; very charming, always smiling...'

My heart soars.

'...I tell her, I'll never be a rich man while she is around, but joking of course – lovely girl, lovely girl...'

'You don't know where she might be now? Did she leave a forwarding address or anything?

'No, I'm sorry. I only deal with her on a purely business level. She makes her purchases, signs the forms; I ready them for export and they go. Invoices always paid on time. Like I say, very good to do business with, but she should buy more. I know she spends time with friends and acquaintances a little further north in Goa, then maybe goes on to Mumbai where she has other business, but I don't know where she stays; always on the move – like a butterfly. I'm sorry I can't help you further.'

I thank him for his help, as much as it was. He asks if I would like tea and maybe purchase a small item to take home. I politely decline, and tell him I have a taxi waiting. I shake his hand and leave him rolling his head, out of the relative cool of the shop, into the heat and the noise, slightly disappointed at having drawn a blank. But Xavie Salwar has given me some-thing; just a small sketch of my girl, the charming, carefree woman with wanderlust, and a head for business, to keep me focused on my sojourn. I've hit the trail, trodden in her foot-steps, and that, at least offers me a small crumb of consolation.

Eleven

WE CROSS THE Mandovi Bridge out of Panjim. Underneath us, barges laden with iron ore slowly make their way down the Mandovi delta, out to sea where giant ships await to take the raw material to the steel makers of Japan. We're heading north and are soon met with narrow road and track cut through lush Goan jungle. Basilicas, churches, cathedrals and temples periodically spring out of clearings. Dilapidated palm and bamboo shacks masquerading as restaurants sit haphazardly on roadsides. Swarms of scooters, mopeds and bikes impossibly laden with all manner of animal, vegetable and mineral cut and carve their way in and around us as we head into Apora towards Anjuna. Bright yellow and black bumble-bee tuk-tuks expertly but precariously manoeuvre their oversized tourist fares past wandering bullock and goat. We flash past the occasional sad looking, gaudily decorated, money making, photo opportunity roadside elephant, and the odd acre of reclaimed scrub marshland trying its best to resemble a football or cricket pitch. Bright red signs endorsing Kingfisher beer seem to adorn every other shop and shack, while mauve and cerise bougainvillea and jacaranda add colour to the thick green backdrop, juxtaposing the discarded rubbish and man-made junk strewn along the derelict and the half built that indicates progress in this part of the world. The mark of Hindu and past colonial Portugal is evident on every village corner and crossroads in a strange but fascinating contradiction of indigenous and empire. Amidst the integrated places of worship are small, well-attended shrines adorned with garland flowers, Christian crosses and inverted swastikas.

Geoffrey does his personal guide thing as we pass points of interest or sights that have a worthwhile tale attached to them. In a little over an hour I've learned more about History and Geography from the back of a Goan taxi than I ever did in school.

We hit gridlock behind a bus in a bustling hamlet. Horns play a discordant symphony. Geoffrey takes the opportunity to check the location of my next destination with a local who seems to be carrying his entire family on an old Royal Enfield motorbike, just like the one my Uncle Jimmy used to have, while a woman cradling a sari-swaddled baby comes begging for Rupees at my window. The child has its tiny palm out-stretched; its first ever human gesture copied and cloned from its pathetic mother. Before I know it we're off again. I fumble for money in my pocket and fling a note through the open window. I watch sadly as the creature scrambles around for it in the swirling dust.

We bob and weave; filling any bit of road space that comes available. We manoeuvre, falter, turn, and twist until we find ourselves bouncing down a rough, dusty, red clay track and I see a sign nailed to a palm tree. – *Chakras- Ayuvedic and Holistic Healing Centre* – We stumble down this bumpy way, past bent and leaning palms and endless piles of two-foot by one-foot red clay bricks that have littered the wayside in scattered but uniform piles since we entered Apora. Dug out of the rich Goan soil by hand and left to bake hard in the sun, these are the staple building block of Goa, but not once on my journey here have I seen anyone building with them.

After two hundred metres the dusty track ends and the centre appears in front of us; a solid looking building painted light cream, or maybe it's just a tired looking white. It has a low, red slate roof and verandas off two sides in the style of a villa. Geoffrey slews the cab to a halt in a swirl of orange dust and turns to me grinning. Before he has a chance to do the thing with his head, I slide open the door and get out.

'Thanks mate; don't know how long I'll be here.'

'No problem,' he grins.

I take a quick look around before climbing the few steps to the entrance, above which hangs a bigger version of the sign that was nailed to the tree on the way in. It's bookended by a painted ying-yang sign and a yogic looking Buddha. The air hangs heavy with jasmine and other incense-like aromas that seem to be emanating from inside the building. Through the scattered palms, to one side of the place stands a magnificent, gnarled, ancient yet majestic looking Banyan tree. The entrance itself is framed by turquoise bougainvillea. Pots and urns filled with pungent herbs and spices adorn the veranda. I enter and set in motion a deep peal of harmonic metal chimes. As they jangle and fade into silence, the soft, floaty, pipe-driven tones of ambient music drift in out of nowhere. I assume I'm in some sort of reception area; small, clean, white and cosmically calm. The walls are full of posters and flyers hailing all manner of weird and wonderful treatments, therapies and rejuvenations, from colonic irrigation to levitation and astral travel classes. Terracotta Buddha's placed with feng-sui type precision sit lotus-fashion deep in meditation, smiling benignly. The scent from a hundred musky-sweet smelling joss sticks permeates the air while an abundance of Moroccan style cushions and rugs completes the welcoming vibe. I've entered hippy heaven, and for that reason I'm thrown back to the sixties. I see Jimi, John Sebastian and David Crosby waving to me from the corner of the room through a fug of the finest Nepalese Hashish smoke. Despite being surrounded by testaments for what seem like incredible crackpot cures, an ordered calmness seems to have gathered inside me. I like this place.

A beaded curtain parts with a jingly swish and a woman loosely swathed in a lime and lemon swirly patterned halter-type sarong thingy stands before me. She has sun bleached, sandy dread swirls of hair tied up high on her head pineapple fashion. Coffee skinned; healthy features, but not without lines, place her mid to late forties. As she approaches, piercing slate blue eyes spear me. Her greeting suits the tone of her skin: husky and warm.

'Hi,' she says.

'Hi,' I say back, and then time seems suspended, like she's doing the suspending, analysing me in microdot. It seems like hours before we speak again, but it must only be the briefest of seconds. I oddly become aware of my travel-weary appearance. I feel so tired all of a sudden and the battery of inviting, plump patterned cushions behind her seem to beckon seductively. I detect a faint smile on her lips, like she knows all that's going on in my head. I quickly gather myself and say my piece. I glance down at my sweaty list of contacts and make sure I've got the name right. 'Hi,' I say again. 'I'm looking for Kerin?' She smiles and nods. I raise my eyebrows. She smiles and nods again. I tell her how I came by her name, and, in a speech that I awkwardly punctuate with um's and er's, explain who I am and why I'm here. She listens in silence, acknowledging me with what now have become familiar nods of the head whenever I start to sound a bit hesitant and flustered, because for me, all this has gotten slightly unreal, surreal and embarrassing. The heavy pungent aromas are making my head swim, and when she invites me to sit on one of the lush lounges when I get to the end of my spiel I do so gratefully. She moves to the beaded curtain and shouts something to someone beyond it; a command in what I take to be the native Konkani. She comes over and sits unnervingly close to me, curling her legs up under her while rearranging her sarong. Her eyes pierce me again and I unconsciously pull my head back under her scrutiny.

'I know many Maggies, Margarets, Megs, Mags, and some Peggies,' she says in her smoky voice.

'Mine's just Maggie,' I say.

'Yes,' she nods again. 'I think I know your Maggie.'

Kerin doesn't pry, doesn't want to know the reason for my search, never asks the why's or how come's. It's almost as though she already knows. As we talk she skips around the most obvious questions, putting me under no pressure whatsoever, just the piercing of the eyes, sucking out my innermost thoughts.

A swarthy looking dude with pony-tailed jet black gimped hair, loose white cheesecloth top and calf length shorts enters with two drinks on a tray. He places them down in front of us. Kerin talks to him in the foreign tongue she used earlier. He glances at me and replies. She talks some more, like she's issuing orders. He gives me a withering look before disappearing back behind the beads.

'Papaya juice,' she says. 'Drink, you look as though you need it.'

I eagerly heed her instruction. The cool Papaya slips down my parched throat. It feels so good I almost drain the glass in one go. I wipe my mouth and then my sticky brow with the accompanying serviette. Her eyes never leave mine. She smiles as though she enjoyed it as much as I did.

'You're right,' I concur. 'I needed that.'

'The last time I saw Maggie was three Sundays ago...' She takes the tiniest sip of her drink. '... At Venta'

'Venta?'

'Yeah, it's a watering hole, a place where all the hippies get together every Sunday for a jam. Some of the guys bring guitars, get up and play; have a groove, y'know. It's a good night. We sometimes go when I'm not working.'

'Is it near here?'

'Yeah, near Baga, only about six kilometres away.'

'You don't know where she could be staying?'

'No. I don't think she has a fixed place. From what I know of her she tends to move around a lot; definitely a free spirit, that one.'

'What about work?'

'Well, she's been known to waitress in some of the beach bar shacks up and down the coast. Sometimes she helps out on the stalls at Anjuna Market and Engel's Bazaar. Anjuna Market is on a Wednesday, that's tomorrow; you might try there, but like I say, she doesn't tend to stay in one place too long; she could be anywhere, might even have moved up North by now – but I have a feeling she hasn't just yet,' Kerin adds optimistically at seeing the disappointment register on my face. I ask her to list some of the likely beaches and the markets on my raggy bit of paper, and as I hand over my pathetic scrap of hope she pauses and sighs. 'How did you get here?'

'Taxi,' I reply. 'He's waiting outside.'

'Where will you go now?'

I shrug casually. 'Find some place to stay for the night, I guess; start my search tomorrow.'

She gives me a look that mothers sometimes give irresponsible children. 'Have you eaten?'

'Not yet,' I say. 'Don't worry; my man Geoffrey will look after me; he's showing me the ropes.'

'Have you paid him anything yet?'

'No.'

'Come with me,' she orders assertively. I follow her obediently.

Geoffrey is sprawled across the front seats of his taxi with his bare feet propped on the dashboard, toes wagging in time to an Enrique Iglesias CD. Kerin marches up and immediately launches into a torrent of fluent Konkani making my driver sit bolt upright. There follows a good five minutes of heated discussion that looks like turning into argument, and I stand in the background, bemused and embarrassed, wondering what the hell is going on.

'Give me five hundred,' she turns to me and barks.

'What?'

'Five-hundred rupees.' She snaps her fingers impatiently.

I duly comply, fumbling in my pockets for the bunch of Indian notes Geoffrey changed for me in Panjim. I peel off a blue coloured one. Ghandi smiles up at me. I hand him over. Kerin throws the note into the cab with unconcealed contempt and orders Geoffrey off her property immediately. He obeys; slowly, reluctantly; gunning his motor and casting me a sour look in the process. I shrug my shoulders at him and he drives away, back up the track in a swirling cloud of red dust that the late afternoon sun illuminates in the still, dry air.

'What did you do that for?' I protest.

'To stop you getting ripped off,' she says.

'What the hell am I supposed to do now?' I protest some more as she turns on her heels and heads back inside. 'He was my driver.'

'You were his cash cow. He'd already clocked you for a

thousand rupees. Those are tourist rates, not Goan rates. No one pays tourist rates while under my roof.'

'But I'm not under your roof.'

'You are now, at least for a couple of days, or until you've found your daughter.'

I'm quickly learning that this bohemian matriarch is a force to be reckoned with as she dismisses my feeble protestations with a casual backward sweep of the hand.

'I can't just come along and impose on you like this; I don't even know you.'

'You say you're Maggie's Father, and if you are who you say you are... and I know that you are because you have the same eyes, then I already know you and therefore there is no argument. I am inviting you to stay as my guest, and I think it would be most rude of you to refuse, now wouldn't it?

'Well, seeing as you put it like that...'

'Good, that's settled then. Off with those clothes and into the shower with you. I'll get Ramon to prepare some food...'

Before the sinking sun has cast the last of its shimmering rays through the ancient twisted branches of the Banyan tree, I am showered and changed refreshed, sitting be-cushioned on one of the heavily scented verandas, surrounded by flickering candles, facing the most amazing meal I shall ever eat in my life. Talk about bloody whirlwind.

The Great Momos is a traditional Tibetan dish consisting of little parcel shaped steamed dumplings filled with meat and veg and accompanied by the most subtle but amazing tasting clear soup.

'You have a fantastic cook,' I remark, tucking in with ravenous zeal. 'This is superb.'

Kerin laughs, a husky chuckle. 'Ramon isn't my cook,' she explains, amused at my assumption. 'He's my partner.'

I raise my eyebrows and almost choke on my soup. I would have put the wiry, slightly diminutive, subservient-acting dude at least fifteen years her junior, and I mean, the way she orders him about... 'Oh,' I say. 'I'm sorry – I thought...'

'It's okay,' she smiles. 'Ramon is indeed a cook; in fact he is actually a master chef. We've been together for almost six years now....'

And, as if on cue, Ramon glides in with his meal and slides up to the low table, nimbly positioning himself, straight backed and cross legged. I congratulate him on the food, heaping on the accolades. He nods demurely, allowing himself a reserved but polite smile, seemingly humbled by my compliments.

During the course of the meal it's Kerin who does most of the talking, her fella only contributing to the conversation when invited to. Ramon is half Nepalese, half Portuguese which explains his small yet lithesome stature. A slight, wispy Manchurian growth on his upper lip and chin compliments his thick, long, kinked black mane. The guy oozes inner calm and peace and his gentle nature shines out of him like a beacon, but there is also a half hidden resigned melancholy about his persona that makes me feel a bit sorry for him.

After The Great Momos we eat a simple but equally delicious fresh fruit salad with yoghurt; again, I've never tasted anything like it. Kerin explains that Ramon is renowned for his culinary expertise and is in great demand. He works the cruises, and the Caribbean is where he will be heading for a six-month stint once the monsoons kick in over here.

When we've eaten we drink Honeybee Brandy and I'm invited to smoke some delightful ganja through a bong filled with minted iced water. It's the first smoke I've had since my last days in Wakefield, and is most welcome.

The drag of the ten and a half hour flight from England slowly dissipates and the dope and Honeybee combination soon begins to make me feel chilled – and still she doesn't pry. Despite my looseness and the relaxed vacancy in my eyes that must be starting to resemble piss-holes in the snow, Kerin keeps the conversation light and unobtrusive and is more than happy to fill me in on her own story.

The mysterious bohemian, Kerin, is in fact Karen Bickerstaff, a pig farmers' daughter from Lincolnshire who'd followed the hippy trail out here during her late youth. Her travels had taken her deep into the Himalayas where an old Tibetan monk named Mingyar had told her she had the gift to heal and that it was her karmic duty to fulfil that muse. Now, she is skilled in almost every alternative therapy under the sun and her old man lent her the money to build the Ayuverdic centre that she's been running here for almost ten years.

Kerin, as she now likes to be known, isn't beautiful or even good looking in the traditional sense. Her features, especially when her hair is tied up in that pineapple style, are almost androgynous. But there is something that draws you to her; a spiritual beauty that centres around the eyes; intriguing, mystery shrouded, and along with the figure-clinging halter-sarong creations she wore, under which moves a silky-smooth, cosmically tuned willowy body that tends to make her appear to glide in a lithesome fashion across the floor when she walks, puts her in the sexy category, in a perverse kind of way.

At the end of the evening she shows me to a room that is sparse but spotless. A single ceiling fan lazily beats the musk-filled air above a small bed made up in crisp white linen. I turn to thank her once again for her hospitality to find her only inches away from my face, smiling Mona Lisa like; those javelin eyes making the connection. She commands time to stand still, just like she did on our first meet. Only the chirping of nightlife and the drone-hum rhythm of the fan appear outside her spell. The disturbed air above and around us wafts her patchouli oil scent over me. It wraps us, binds us; lifts me off the ground and suspends me there. I'm having my soul searched and there's nothing I can do, or would want to do about it. The slightest of touches, her hand over mine, like brushing against a cobweb, releases me and I slowly float back to earth. Her smile broadens a little, revealing nothing to me except a sense that she knows. What, or how much she knows, I'm not sure – but she definitely knows.

'Try and get some sleep,' she says, as if even she knows I'll find that difficult. 'I'll see you in the morning.'

I watch her glide out of the room and try to convince myself that what I've just experienced is down to the dope and the brandy, though I'm not so sure.

In the morning we breakfast on porridge, bananas and honey, washed down with fresh cranberry juice. I'd slept in fits and starts, woken by fractured dreams that, thankfully, the THC from the marijuana had helped to annul from memory.

Poor old Ramon is looking as glum and being as uncommunicative as ever, no doubt exacerbated by the frequent Konkani based bollockings he is receiving from Kerin. I get the feeling that despite their spiritual surroundings, Kerin and Ramon's Yin and Yang are not in harmony and nirvana type status in their relationship is a long way off.

After breakfast I jump on the back of Kerin's Royal Enfield Bullet and we set off to Anjuna Market. She expertly weaves her way amongst the caravanserai of hawkers, peddlers, punters and artisans who are all making their way to the old hippy trading post. This is the place where Western travellers used to gather to flog the last of their possessions in order to raise enough loot for a flight home. Over the years it has flourished into a gigantic, sprawling open market where traders from all over India, and as far away as Tibet, gather to sell their colourful, exotic and often bizarre wares.

As we near the site, the roads snarl to a hot, dusty, slow-crawling scrum of man and animal. Kerin cuts and carves her way through with thumb pressed permanently to the horn and the sea of chaos parts before her – Moses on a Royal Enfield.

Kerin has already given me the low-down; briefing me on the dos and don'ts, warning me of the cons and distractions.

'Beware of people wanting to poke wire into your ear and demanding fifty rupees for the privilege,' she lectured.

'I will,' I said, wondering why the hell I would allow anyone to do something like that anyway.

I soon begin to realise why she deemed it necessary to lecture me like a kid on its first day at school. The thing is vast, like a crowd scene from a John Huston epic. The colour and pageantry set against a clear blue Goan sky unfolds before me and I can see that this is going to be far from easy.

'Don't waste your time with any of the Indian stalls,' she says. 'Head for the hippy sector near the beach. If Maggie's going to be anywhere, that's where she'll be. I won't be able to pick you back up,' she shouts above the din of horns and humanity as I ease my sweaty arse off the pillion. 'I've got clients to see this afternoon.'

'That's okay,' I shout. 'I'll get a taxi back.'

'Good luck,' she grins, while revving the Bullet's engine aggressively at the crowd that has gathered round me, waving cheap trinkets in my face. I watch Kerin depart in a deep-throated thunder of four-stroke acceleration and a string of oaths in Konkani.

I take a slug of water and begin to wade my way through a

soup of traders and beggars, all desperate to demented distraction to relieve me of some rupees. I put my single-minded head on and try and stay blinkered as I struggle into the guts of the market, but it's hard when some annoying fucker is following your every move and persistently blowing a battered old Raj era brass bugle in your ear, like it's a must-buy item, and with the conviction that at some point I will relent and throw money at him; or when pity invoking but Kamikaze like limbless specimens of humanity on tiny wooden four-wheeled trolleys appear around every twist and turn and smash into your legs.

Nearly an hour passes before I reach the first of the hippy type stalls and shake off the last of the more persistent, limpet-style hawkers. I draw a blank with the first dozen or so pitches. They don't know my Maggie or simply aren't interested when they suss I'm not buying. One stallholder guides me to another, who guides me to another. Eventually, a skinny, bearded dude selling leather and jewellery and who sounds Scandinavian, informs me that he knows Maggie but hasn't seen her for a while. I'm passed on to another four traders, all hippies, who know my girl. Two are pretty certain she's headed North, Mumbai, likely. One guy, a Belgian named Paul tells me she did a six-week stint on his stall last year but that he hasn't seen her around this season. He calls over to a dark -skinned girl on the next stall. She sports the same kind of dread pineapple hairdo as Kerin and is sat cross-legged, munching on a dish of lentils with an array of multi-coloured tie-dyed saris hung on display behind her. They have a conversation in some foreign language. She speaks in rapid-fire sentences in between mouthfuls of her lentil lunch. I watch the discourse fascinated as the large pointy-sharp jewelled piercing below her bottom lip works with her mouth ten to the dozen.

Paul turns to me and smiles. 'You're in luck, my friend.

Miriam says she's working at Souza's on Ashram beach.'

My heart leaps. 'Where's that?' I ask, trying to keep my excitement in check. 'How far?'

'About eight or nine k north of here.'

I ask him to jot the details on my scrap of paper. I select a piece of amber hung from a leather necklace from amongst his items as way of thanks while he writes. I hang it round my neck, kiss the stone for luck and walk away clutching the all-important info with renewed vigour and an extra spring in my step.

I ditch the taxi idea following the Geoffrey escapade and go for the quickest and most popular mode of transport around here - I hire an old bullet. No licence asked for, no insurance offered. No helmet required; fill her up with what looks like old chip oil and off you go.

I escape the heat and confines of Anjuna and pretty soon I'm on the coastal tracks of North Goa with the wind in my hair, I-pod, courtesy of Jeanie & Ben, firmly in place filled with an eclectic mix of tuneage *ala* Digweed download. The twenty-five year vacuum in my life compresses everything like all I ever knew or cared about happened just yesterday, and my youthful musings of yesteryear appear as fresh as ever on hearing all this stuff again. Digweed, playing the amateur psychologist knew what would re-float my boat, the devious bugger. He was right, and I *put-put-put* along like a youthful Denis Hopper with a face that doesn't feel like my own; it has a big grin on it.

Twelve

'TITILY?'

'No, Maggie,' I say to the middle aged Indian woman as she distributes an over-laden tray of food and drink around the tourist table. 'Maggie,' I try and explain. 'She's an English girl; she works here – yeh?'

The woman finishes her waitress duties at her own precise and leisurely pace. When her tray is empty I start to try and make her understand once more but she holds up her hand to stop me, and then a finger in the air by way of saying, I won't be a minute. I watch her stroll back to the bar of the beach shack restaurant and then out of sight through a beaded curtain to what I presume is the kitchen. After a while she re-emerges with a guy wearing a grubby apron that would suggest he's been doing the cooking. She points me out to him and they have a little conversation. Eventually he gestures me over. I perch on a bar stool and before I finish introducing myself I get that feeling again, like I'm preparing to be kicked in the teeth. I know she isn't here, long before I get to the end of my routine.

The Indian guy, who I assume to be Mr. Souza, I'm not sure because I can't be arsed to ask, tells me that Maggie helped him out for a couple of weeks, while his wife – assumptions being the slow-paced waitress – had been ill. With his missus back at work, and the season drawing to a close, he no longer needed her services. My enquiries as to where she might be now are met with the familiar non-committal roll of the head.

I trudge back across the sand with the mid-afternoon sun beating down on my back, starting to turn my under-wrapped, vitamin D deficient, sun-starved, translucent skin lobster red. I've done it again, dared to be optimistic when I should have known better.

I drive back down meandering coastal track, no I-pod this time, totally pissed at allowing myself to be suckered once more. Buoyed by memories of music and good times past I'd let hope into the equation, not only that, I'd allowed it to take over. I'd become almost euphoric with expectancy and I hate myself for it. There's no way back now. The void within me is slowly starting to fill with familiar hopeless cynicism. Negativity begins to course through my veins and the futility of this whole venture now appears as stark and as clear as the Goan day itself.

I make a decision to call the whole thing off and I use the putter-putter drone of the Bullet's engine to transport me back to the numb zone where all emotions are barred; it's one skill I've remained good at. But somewhere lurking at the back of this self-induced vacuum of solitude is a dull ache that has always been there – I think it's called loneliness.

The only other feeling I have now is a physical one, a throat that is as parched and as dry as Ghandi's flip-flop. I need a drink desperately and a little further down the road I see three hippy-looking dudes on Harleys turn down a track and disappear behind the red dust cloud that their bikes create. I slow to a halt in front of a faded wooden sign that says *Vagator Beach* and I follow them down the bumpy, dusty trail that soon opens out on a secluded little palm tree lined cove. Around a dozen or so assorted bikes and scooters are parked above the horseshoe shaped bay. I park my Royal Enfield with the others and follow the matted-haired hippies down a set of crude steps that have been hewn out of the cliff side. They head for one of three shacks on this little piece of tucked away paradise and I decide that Vishnu's looks as good a place as any, so I find myself a spot under the thatched palm tree roof of this watering hole, well out of the sun and order myself a large Kingfisher. This is definitely a stoner place. The three Harley dudes have joined a group of hippies around a large, low table where two ornate dope laden bongs are doing the rounds. Even the guy who brings me my beer looks nicely out of it. He slaps two laminated menus down in front of me; one has food on it the other is a selection of herb of the smoking variety. With a nod and a lazy smile, the dude leaves me to peruse; I think I like this place.

I slake my thirst and take in the sheer beauty of this small enclave: Soft, silver sands, and sea embraced by the circling arms of the rocky cove that make the water almost lagoon-like. This semi-remote place, shielded with a back drop of bent and leaning palms seems to have eluded the majority of the tourist trade, and that makes me like it even more. Amidst the strains of chill out music, gentle hippy chatter, and the tinkling of tin bells that adorn the necks of beach cattle, one or two beach sellers patrol the shoreline in laconic fashion, strolling along to the gentle rhythmic lapping sound of tidal water.

To one side of the haphazard rows of sun-beds are a make-shift volleyball net and a large trampoline. Three giggling kids, no more than toddlers, and as naked as the day they were born, are having bouncy fun. One of them, and probably the eldest, is a Caucasian boy, four at the most. A golden blonde mane of dreaded hair rises and falls against his bronzed back as he jumps, a hippy child, for sure. The second, and slightly younger looking, or maybe she's just smaller, is an Indian girl. She wears beads made from coconut husk around her tiny neck and nothing else. Her hair is jet black, and short, and from behind she could be mistaken for a boy. Her eyes are two deep pools. The third... the third is a little white girl, the youngest of the three, and she has me transfixed. She's the one giggling the loudest; she's the one bouncing the craziest; she's the one with sand-caked legs and the wild tangle of fine blonde hair like she's only recently emerged from the sea. I watch her and my heart knots itself. She is my Maggie, of that I have no doubt. Reason tells me it cannot be, impossible. But my heart tells it differently. The knot pulls tighter and I find my heart harder to ignore than mere rationale. I wipe my sweat-stung eyes and try to put it all down to dehydration or maybe the mind-set that hope just recently placed warped inside my already fucked up head. Nothing helps and I continue to stare. She's just as I remember her; same age, same height, same hair, same mad laugh. It's the manic little giggle that does for me; I remember it as if it were yesterday. But how can that be? Up to now I couldn't even form her features in my head, let alone her voice, and yet I am so certain.

I resist the urge to get up from my seat and walk over, and all of a sudden I become aware of how hard I'm staring. I must be displaying all the mannerisms of a predatory paedophile and my eyes avert shamefully back to the laminate in my hand, hoping no one was paying too much attention to my intense scrutiny.

'Food, smoke – or both?' says the bright female voice, making me jump out of my skin.

'Jesus...!' I blurt.

'No deities I'm afraid, despite the name out front – just food, drink and blow.' The waitress with the English accent,

116

razor sharp wit and pearly white teeth grins down at me in anticipation.

'I – I'm sorry...' I manage embarrassed, 'I was miles away.'

'Now why would you want to be miles away in a place like this?'

'Good point,' I say after a brief ponder, dropping my gaze to the menu to avoid further embarrassment. 'I think I'll have the roasties with melted cheese.'

'Anything else?' She nods to the Marijuana menu.

'Sure,' I say. 'I'll go with your recommendation.'

'Bong, spliff or takeaway?'

'I'll take an ounce of your finest.'

'Okay,' she says with a smile before whipping the menus away and heading back to the kitchen clearing tables with efficient speed as she goes. Not wanting to be observed as some gawping freak, I catch just enough of her features to leave me intrigued and I make small surreptitious glances at her back as she goes about her duties. She wears a sage green bikini with a matching patterned sarong that is tied around her slim waist and knotted to the side. Her shoulder length blond hair is kept in a simple ponytail by a colour co-ordinated bobble-band, exposing her slender neck and petite ears, around and on which hang simple jet necklace and earrings. Moderate exposure to sun shows her skin delicate, like fine beaten gold. A tiny tattooed butterfly adorns her left shoulder – Could it be? A voice inside my head tells me not to be so fucking stupid. Stop torturing myself. I've made my decision; this futile escapade, this mission impossible is aborted. End of. There are dozens, probably hundreds of English girls doing this, why should I expect this particular haystack needle to be my Maggie. My fucked up head is making her fit the bill, like the crazy notion of the kid on the trampoline. I laugh inwardly at my stupidity.

The voice tells me I need to start treating all this as a well-earned holiday and nothing else. My lonely, aching heart reluctantly agrees. I let out a long resigned sigh, take a pull on my Kingfisher and wait for my dinner and dope to arrive.

'Is it okay?' she indicates to the plate of potatoes smothered in melted cheese and the dark lump of resin sweating pungent in its cling-film wrap. My heart has overruled my head again and I find myself staring.

'What?

'Everything okay?' she smiles.

'Oh...yeah, great. Thanks – er, can I ask you a...'

'Putaly...!' The stoned waiter from behind the bar interrupts with a shout.

'Excuse me, I won't be a sec,' she says, and in the instant she answers his call, she also answers my question. Her name isn't Maggie, and once again I'm a dickhead for thinking it could have been. I put that familiar, endearing, cheeky, almost insolent Smith type smile of hers purely down to coincidence and try and put my head back in the driving seat once more.

'Sorry about that,' she says on her return. 'What were you saying?'

I start to ask her about her unusual name but then think better of it. The girl is obviously busy and I decide to spare her my pointless interrogation.

'Got any brown sauce?'

'I think we might have some in the back,' she grins Smith again, 'but I can't guarantee HP.' And she skips off with her ponytail bouncing off her shoulders, instantly reminding me of a younger Jeanie. She couldn't be more Smith if she tried, and if I ever find my Maggie I'd be happy to have her half the person this young woman appears to be.

I try detached. I try disinterested. I bury my head in my

118

meal. I gaze out to sea. It only works half the time. Every now and then I find myself tracking her movements as she goes about her chores. And then like a knob I pretend she's not there when she takes my plate away and asks me once again if everything's okay. But my brain records the smile. I burn it onto my retinas, and I'll keep it there as some fantasy image, like some sicko would. Who knows – maybe I'm already that person. I contemplate building a spliff and then decide against it, seeing as I have to steer the old Bullet back to Chakras and aren't too sure of the way.

I drink another Kingfisher then pay my bill as the sun drops towards the horizon. As I climb the steep cliff steps I look back to see my fantasy waitress daughter taking time out to play with the three naked kids who are now building castles in the sand.

Thirteen

I BUILD A second smoke under the gnarled and twisted branches of the Banyan tree and watch the last rays of the setting sun toast its ancient boughs red, like the dying embers of a fire. They match my eyes, old, lined and puff-red now that I've rediscovered the art of weeping. I'm sat here getting quietly mashed and my mind's gone walkabout. I think about rainy Marsden streets, the grey and the damp. A bunch of guys playing music no one wants to hear any more, the grey and the weathered. Crown Court proceedings, the grey and the grim. And yet I still ask myself the question – what am I doing here? It's not homesickness; this type of loneliness is ubiquitous. I'll carry this melancholy wherever I go, and this place is far enough. No more foolish optimism, no more dream chasing. Wallowing in a swamp of self-pity is what I do best and this batch of ganja is helping the process along nicely. I've learned that the optimistic route is fantasy driven, a sure-fire way of ending up back inside, courtesy of a section under the mental health act and I'm sure as hell not going down that road.

A shadow severs the sun's diminishing rays and I look up to see Kerin standing over me in silhouette.

'How did it go?'

I look up, take a toke and say nothing, let my stingy eyes tell their own story.

'No joy, eh?' she says, following the tracks of my tears.

I shake my head. 'Paper trails. False dawns. Red herrings.'

Kerin sits beside me taking up a lotus position like it was the most natural thing in the world. We sit in silence for a while. I pass the joint but she refuses, saying she rarely uses the stuff except on the odd social occasion.

'Using dope as a crutch won't help in the long run, you know.'

I scoff a laugh. 'Where I've been any comfort you can lay your hands on helps, crutch or not, believe me.'

'I understand,' she says sincerely, like she genuinely doesn't want to sound judgemental. 'What made you come and sit out here?'

'Dunno, seemed as good a place as any, I suppose.'

'Well, you certainly chose the right spot – or maybe it chose you.'

I look at her sideways through my stoner eyes and pray she isn't about to get trippy on me. 'What do you mean by that?'

'It's a magic tree.'

'It's a nice old tree, I'll give you that,' I concede looking up into its twisted gnarly depth.

'It has healing properties.'

Oh shit, she is getting trippy. 'How so?'

'Have you heard about auras?'

'Sort of, yeh.'

'Well, out here and especially where we are now, a person's aura becomes quite prominent and that makes them easier to read.'

'And I suppose you can do that, can you?'

'I like to think so, yes.'

'Go on then, do your stuff.'

She gives me a look that forgives my flippancy and takes a deep breath. 'When you arrived yesterday there was a swirling

mass of anger and sadness all around you, like a fog of bitterness. It was more a sense rather than an observation, because
your aura itself wasn't clear, it was shrouded in what I can
only describe as a sulphurous cloud. I could tell that you'd
been through some trauma that had been deep-seated and long
lasting and the legacy it had left was still eating away at you.
Now I can see your colours more clearly...'

She proceeds to give me a master class in the electromag-
netic field that surrounds the human body and the meanings
behind each colour and frequency. I do my best to feign interest, but I have to admit, she has me off to a tee, and by the end
of her analysis the sceptic in me has relaxed a little, or could it
be that by now I'm nicely out of it

'...There's a soft, bright band of turquoise around you that
represents healing. It's not part of your aura but it wants to be.'

'I'm not stopping it.'

'No, not entirely, that's why you unconsciously came and
sat here in the first place, but there's a part of you that *is* stopping it. In your aura it shows up as a band of dirty grey, it's an
energy blocker, it represents negativity and lack of harmony.'

'How do you know all this?'

'I suppose it's a bit like reading the growth circles in a tree
trunk. Scientist can tell how old it is, when there's been a bad
winter, a drought, that sort of thing. I can see times in you
when you've been so low that you've almost given up, abandoned all hope. It's left a band of cynicism that manifests as a
barrier, a wall you've built up around yourself to stop you
from getting hurt. Only sometimes you drop those defences
and allow a little bit of optimism in and, when that optimism
fails to deliver, you feel the hurt even more – that's what happened today, isn't it?'

To a fucking tee.

The sun drops pretty quickly round these parts, dusk to dark in an instant, Nature's evening scents come alive and insects begin their night time chorus. Soft veranda lights illuminate the old magical tree. I resist the urge to give it a hug and condescend to giving its ancient bark a friendly slap. Kerin unfolds herself and gets to her feet in one lithe movement, entirely without the use of her hands. 'Come on,' she says, taking hold of mine. 'I'll make us some dinner.'

'Isn't Ramon cooking tonight?' I enquire.

'I've sent him away for a few days,' she says with a smile.

What the hell is it with me? What was it I was born with that most other guys weren't? I mean, it's not as if I'm what you'd call good looking anymore, rugged, maybe, but mine's more of a homeless rugged, not the Hollywood meaning of the word. I could accept the phenomenon back in the days when the attention was welcome, but now it's all a bit disconcerting, I'm on the wrong side of fifty for Christ's sake. Don't get me wrong, I'm still a red-blooded male whenever the demons aren't messing with my head and causing shut down in the nether regions, but whatever it is I still have that women seem to want is a complete mystery to me.

I'm laid here with the skinniest of towels covering my lily-white arse having my lobster-red back smeared with cucumber and yoghurt. I stink like a Greek salad and to make matters worse, I've got a raging hard on. Talk about wrong time, wrong place. Kerin caught me stepping out the shower, and despite my protestations, insisted she tended my sunburnt body with her special treatments before it blistered. My reluctance stems from the fact that she won't go into detail as to why she's packed her fella off, or how long he'll be gone for, except to say that they both need their own space now and again. Fucking dilemma, oh, for a prison cup of tea right now. I try to turn my thoughts mundane in order to relieve the situation while she jabbers on about how desperately my knotted muscles are crying out for a bout of reiki, thermal stones, crystal therapy, and I think she just uttered the words: Hopi ear candles. My circumstance isn't being helped by the fact that she has the most amazing touch, like a thousand volts flash down my spine whenever her hands come near, and I sink my teeth into my knuckles trying to stifle groans of ecstasy.

'Okay,' she says eventually. 'Flip over; let's see how bad your front is.'

'Er – I don't think I'll be able to manage that just yet,' I say, having partially raised myself onto my knees in order to relieve the discomfort.

'Ah...' she says, observing my plight. '...Don't worry about it,' she continues, totally unembarrassed. 'It happens sometimes.'

Kerin informs me in a matter of fact manner that the body is littered with erogenous zones and that she must have inadvertently stimulated a few of them while in the process of applying her special batch of after-sun. She persuades me onto my back anyway and proceeds to smear my chest with her cooling lotion while I remain painfully conscious of my ridiculous situation – draw a couple of eyes on the towel and I'd have a cartoon ghost sat on my groin.

'At least we know that your Kundalini and Svadhistana are in good working order, which is a good sign.'

'Come again?'

'The Kundalini is the life giving energy that links the seven Chakras within you. The Svadhisthana is the second or sacral chakra that is located in the lower abdomen. It is likened to a lotus with six petals and is orange in colour. It deals with sexuality, libido, and emotions. The demon to this Chakra is guilt, and all these sensitivities seem to be alive and strong in you – particularly strong in some areas,' she adds with a cheeky glance to my nether regions.

'So, what alternative therapies can you recommend to reduce this particular problem?' I ask in all innocence.

'I know of only one solution to this eventuality,' she says in her husky tone and a glint in her eye. 'And it's more tantric than ayurvedic.'

Oh shit – I've said the wrong thing again, she's talking about sex, she probably thinks I'm dropping hints, but the way she's caressing my chest and that look in her eye suggest she wasn't waiting for a prompt. She comes in close. Underneath the flimsy cotton of her see-through sarong the dark, rock hard nipples of her relatively small breasts make contact with my torso. Casper the cartoon ghost does a quiver and I make a half-hearted attempt to protest.

'Oh, Christ – look, I'm sorry – I didn't mean to...' I feel a hand slip away from my chest and slide under the towel, gently taking hold of my manhood in a cool, slithery grip. I groan a mixture of ecstasy and despair. Kerin discards the towel. Casper disappears. I look down the length of my Neapolitan body to watch her stroke my avocado coloured erect todger. '...Kerin, please...' I groan. '...This isn't such a good idea...' *déjà vu* '... I've got issues – you wouldn't understand – I get visions, I – oh, Lord...'

'The only visions you'll have tonight will be pleasant ones,' she reassures. And with that, she crosses her arms, lifting her garment clear of her lithe coffee toned body in one swift movement. She unties whatever it is that keeps her hair in its pineapple-constructed style and her long sandy coloured tresses fall about her wiry shoulders. She transfers them to my loins and takes my penis in her mouth – cucumber and yoghurt? Totally organic I suppose she would reason.

Strategically placed burning candles, the pungent smouldering of incense sticks; ambient floaty music, Ramon packed off out of the way; it's hard not to perceive that this was all planned rather than spontaneous. She knew where to hit the spots, and some. The Smith lure strikes again.

This tantric sex malarkey is the business though. We've been at it for almost two hours now, and although the finish, for me at least, has been in sight a few times, she's pulled me back from the brink with expert dexterity. Her mastery and control of the cock is awesome. The positions and techniques she uses leave her in total charge. I can tell she enjoys the dominance and I'm quite happy to yield to it, sit back and think of England, good old England – Billy and Digweed shaking their heads in mock disgust, the disastrous encounter with Caroline – a quick glance at the shadows on the wall – no demons here, just the curling wisp of candle smoke. But I'm also thinking of poor old Ramon and the pangs of guilt the thoughts bring with them. Why did I never get this feeling all those years ago when I was being such a bastard to Liz? Maybe I have changed, maybe there's a moral conscience within me after all. Kerin turns with her buns towards me. She hovers and squats, holding onto my knees before impaling herself deep and wet onto my sword with a slow grinding, gyrating motion. I don't see myself throwing her off and jumping back into my strides anytime now so I quickly dismiss that notion.

From treatment room to bedroom, I fuck her, she fucks me; we fuck each other every which way, long through the night and into the early hours of the morning until exhaustion, at least on my part, finally takes over and she allows me to fall into a totally spent slumber. JD Smith thought he knew it all; he knew nothing – end of lesson.

Shafts of light stream through gaps in rattan shutters; dust specs dance along their length, disturbed by the beaten air of a ceiling fan. The sun is high in the sky, almost midday. I stretch out a contented yawn and take in the calm serenity of my surroundings: Kerin's bedroom, where the power of the spirit is so tangible you can almost touch it, and nature's elements seem drawn to its space to celebrate life itself. Sight, sound and smell. My senses come alive like they've been amplified by some dirty great big five hundred watt Marshall Stack. And for the first time I can remember I feel alive. I'm a man again, totally empowered. I recall the events of last evening with a smile on my face. I recreate the scenes from a few hours ago, like I'm viewing pornography and I find myself becoming erect once more - *chakra, chakra burning bright* - The remainder of the day beckons and I need to wash away the smell of sex and sour yoghurt. I spring out of bed and catch my reflection - *the guy who tries not to look in mirrors* - Still strawberry and vanilla, but I see the shape of a new man, not quite the young Stevie Marriott any more, God bless him, yet not so much bin-man rugged all of a sudden. I pat my gut and pretend not to hold it in; definitely not Brad Pitt status, nor will I ever be, but at least now I can shag for as long as that bass player from The Police. I grab a towel; wrap it round my battle-hardened loins and head for the shower. From the treatment room where the door is ajar I hear the mournful sound of whales having a chinwag and I see the Lincolnshire pig farmer's daughter swinging a crystal in circles above the prone torso of a female punter. From her whiny accent she sounds like a Kensington crusty, as Kerin calls them, one of the legions of privileged part time pseudo hippies who migrate here for six months of the year and effectively keep Kerin in business. Although they try to look the part, their threads are more haute couture than Oxfam. They don't live in thirty rupee a night beach shacks, but hire out villas at a grand a month with servants and all the trappings. They send their kids, Moon-beam, Inca and Rainbow to private, English speaking nurseries at less than a fraction of the cost of what it would take to hire a nanny in London. They try to rub shoulders with the working classes, go on protest marches against the poll tax but will never in their lives need to worry how to pay the rent; scream against police brutality, but wouldn't be without the state of the art alarm system in the Chelsea flat that is linked direct to the nearest cop shop. They ride around on the obligatory Royal Enfield albeit a brand new sparkling Thunderbird straight out of the factory in Mumbai carrying a hundred thousand rupee price tag.

'It's not the same as it used to be,' complains Kerin. 'Times have changed.' This place is no longer the hidden hippy jewel of the East it once was thanks to the cut price charter brigade, the kiddie fiddlers, the Kensington crusties and the Russian Mafia who seem to be muscling in everywhere. The idyll is fast slipping away, but, as she concedes, the presence of these undesirables does help pay the bills.

Feeling as brand new as the gleaming Bullet Thunderbird parked outside, I scour the kitchen in search of sustenance. Amongst the rabbit food selections in Tupperware tubs I pick out the least severe looking bran-based muesli-type mixture and try to cheer it up with some goat's milk. Out on the ve-randa I find a shady spot, stick on the I-pod and munch my way through what looks like, and what I imagine tastes like cat litter – *come back Ramon, all is forgiven.*

Despite my restoration as master libertine, I'm still pain-fully conscious that I'm still the same old love rat I ever was. Somewhere back in the ether, a voice trying its best at justification is churning out the old clichés: *a standing prick has no conscience – it takes two to tango – never look a gift horse in the mouth*, meanwhile the counterpoint lurches to the frontal lobes: *karma – cause and effect – do unto others...* My shitiness takes the gilt off my new man persona, so I banish all thoughts and concentrate on the music, swearing to myself with a ninety-nine percent conviction that what happened last night won't happen again. Thing is I'm not sure my conviction is any match for the will of this woman. Whatever it is she has, she has it in spades. When she casts a spell it stays cast. I don't like things messing with my head, but at least when she's inside it nice things happen.

I've got the I-pod set to shuffle, Terry Reid is wailing on about it being The Season of the Witch, and I laugh quietly to myself. I sing along when Jimi plays Dolly Dagger, smiling at the poignancy of the lyrics: *been riding broomsticks since she was fifteen, blowin' out all the other witches on the scene,* when lo and behold, and as if by magic, she appears right in front of me making me almost choke on my muesli.

'Morning,' I splutter, removing my earphones.

'Afternoon,' she corrects.

I give up my late breakfast as a bad job and abandon the remnants that are left in the bowl. 'Kerin...' I begin, as the contents in my mouth seem to get bigger.

'So, what are your plans for what's left of the day?' she asks, ignoring my aphasic attempts at speech.

'I don't have any.' I manage to utter, truthfully

'Good,' she says. 'I'll cancel my afternoon appointments in that case - don't worry,' she adds quickly at seeing the apprehensive cum horrific look on my face. 'I'm not planning on raping you again.'

'Oh, right, good – I mean...'

'Look, all I want to do is help. I don't want you going back to England in the state you came. I'm offering to help detox your mind, body and spirit. It'll be a bit of a crash course but if you're willing to give it a go I'm sure you'll appreciate the results.'

'Well, I do appreciate the offer, but I'm not so sure I'm the right candidate for this sort of thing.'

'Nonsense, I'll not be asking you to sit cross legged for hours on end chanting Ohm or anything like that. It'll require minimal effort on your part. All I insist is that you keep an open mind and banish any rubbish or negativity that may be floating around in your head – what do you say?' The look of apprehension that has remained on my face says it all. 'What have you got to lose Jack?'

I'm standing under the old tree learning how to breathe. First lesson. Now, you may think, as I used to, that this is the height of crackpot quackery, but within half an hour of practising this ancient technique taught to her by the Buddhist monks of the Himalayas I am coughing up the legacy of smoking prison snout for the past twenty-five years.

The healing and the purging go on for the rest of the day and into early evening. I have my Prakruti assessed. I am informed that according to Vedic philosophy I am half Rajasic, half Tamasic. The imbalances in my Doshas are identified; my Vata, Pitta and Kapha are all out of sync and are treated accordingly. Acupuncture: I resemble a human pincushion; Kerin consults charts. I fight off cynicism, she locates meridians; she unblocks them. I resist scepticism; she blends aromatic oils and potions. I feel nauseous; she swings crystals. I thank God I'm spared the hot rocks because of my sunburn, and as promised, she manages to stay clear of my erogenous zones.

'Who's Lauren?' Kerin asks out of the blue while we quietly sip our Honeybee and take in the warm night air. The question takes me aback. It's the first time she's broached anything that pertains to me or my troubles - and how the hell did she know about Lauren?

'How do you...'

'The other night, the night you arrived, I came into your room and watched you while you slept.'

'You did what?'

'You intrigued me,' she says shamelessly. 'This guy turns up at my door, a cloud hanging over him so large I thought the monsoon must have started, oozing negativity from every pore, spilling his kilesa all over the place, yet managing to cling to the tiniest scrap of hope, clutching a grubby piece of paper that stood apart because it had been compiled with optimism. This guy comes in search of his daughter, but he doesn't describe her, offers no background, has no inkling of her movements, past present or future, makes no mention of the other important people in her life...' With that she pauses and raises her eyebrows at me. '...It strikes me that this guy is looking for someone he knows nothing about, like he's searching for a total stranger – am I right?' I lower my head and nod slowly. 'And yet, despite this, you came with love, unconditional love. That much amongst all the fug was clear. I was intrigued. I wanted to get inside your head, so I came into your room and watched while you slept. You were restless, tormented. You ground your teeth and rolled your eyes, almost as if you were possessed. I knelt at your side and caressed your third eye, and before you drifted off into calmer waters you uttered that name.'

'Lauren,' I breathe. 'Lauren, oh Lauren...' I swirl the brandy around my glass and watch the flickering candlelights make patterns with the golden amber liquid before making it disappear down my throat. I take a deep breath, a real breath, a proper breath; one that opens every tissue of lung cavity, then I spend the rest of the warm, still evening telling her my story; the whole caboodle; from thread to needle.

An hour before sunrise Kerin kisses me on the forehead and we go to bed; she to hers and me to mine. Behind me I leave a burden that no longer has form of thought or a willing physical mass to cling to and it slowly dissolves and dissipates into what is left of this magical Goan night.

Fourteen

MORNING SEES ME in my favourite place. I've only had about three hours kip but the witch is still up before me. Sleep must be for mere mortals. I'm trying to master this breathing lark but I'm finding it difficult. Kerin says to empty my head of all thoughts and accompanying crap and the process becomes much easier – easier said than done. I keep getting visions of Billy and Digweed falling about, taking the piss at my New Age indulgences, but I feel I owe it to Kerin at least to be seen to be making the effort after all she's done for me. She's drawn so much shit out of me, both physically and mentally, that I feel like a different person; even my lobster skin is beginning to turn golden. I feel great and I want to be able to maintain the feeling – she says, all I need is some discipline – cue Digweed in my head singing Dinah Mo Hum from Overnight Sensation. I know I'm never going to attain Nirvana. You'll never catch me munching brown rice or wanting to hug every fucker I meet, but I'll try and heed her words, keep the cynicism at bay, try to be less sceptical.

Last night, after it all came out, I tried to ask about Maggie but she wouldn't tell me anything. "Her story is for her alone to tell, and any impressions you have of her should not be created second hand. These are things to learn after you find each other." I tell her I'd given up on that particular quest, and as for *her* knowing about or wanting to find me..."Earlier you told me you came here with only two goals left in life; one, to find your daughter, the other to clear your name. If you give up so easily on the first quest how do you expect to achieve the other? Things aren't necessarily going to happen how and when you want them to, it doesn't work like that for most people. You have to treat the disappointments as lessons in life and learn from them. It's simply karma playing itself out. Think of the parents who are presented with the burden of coping with a severely handicapped child, or the eight year old that has the daily job of caring for its Mum who is crippled with MS. They can't so readily walk away from their responsibilities. Their life lessons are forged by how they cope with what their own karma has thrown up. You have to realise that spirit doesn't recognise linear time. It's no use being impatient; things will happen as and when they're supposed to. Your job is to always stay positive, and if things are meant to be, eventually they will be. You may not think it, and despite occasionally walking up blind alleys and finding dead ends, no doubt your life is playing itself out the way it's intended. Believe it or not, the world is littered with souls whose stories are far more tragic than yours – turn the page Jack, it's a new chapter – Que sera sera."

And so here I am trying my best to apply the teachings and assimilate the wise words of the witch into a philosophy I can readily get my head around. Turning the page doesn't quite seem like an epiphany; I'm finding it hard to acknowledge there's anything more tragic than being wrongly accused of murder and having most of your life taken away from you as a result, but I'm trying.

* * *

'I've made a phone call, and I'm not entirely sure I should have,' says Kerin, pouring out two cups of green tea with a concerned look on her face.

'Oh,' I say and wait for her to continue.

'There's something I haven't told you, and there's a very good reason for not doing so, but now I've made the call, I suppose I'd better fill you in.' She finishes playing mother, sits down opposite, takes a sip of tea and pulls a face. 'Maggie has a partner, an ex-partner I should say; they're estranged, and he lives here in Arpora.'

'Oh,' I say again, trying not to sound surprised.

'The split wasn't amicable, and – well, I'm not prepared to go into the reasons, because it's none of my business. I know that Jordi, that's the guy's name, is desperate for reconciliation, but whenever Maggie is in town she does her best to avoid him and refuses to have any contact, despite his efforts. A few weeks ago, at Venta, they bumped into each other. Words were spoken and it all got a bit heated. There's a lot of bitterness, especially on Maggie's part. That's why I was reluctant to make the call, but I thought either he or Edgar, his business partner, might know of her whereabouts. Anyway, they've both agreed to come over as soon as they finish work. I've not gone into any detail; they know nothing about you. I'll make the introductions and leave you to it. Remember, there'll be no guarantees. Are you okay with that?'

'Er, yeah, I guess so,' I say, a little bewildered at the revelation.

When afternoon tea is over Kerin goes back to her clients and I go back to the sanctuary of my tree to wait the arrival of some bloke who seemingly had it all then blew it. It all sounds strangely familiar. I practise my breathing some more but my concentration levels aren't right. Little scenario bubbles keep floating in my head then popping out again. I consider building a smoke until a bubble with the witch's wise words inside appears and kills that notion, so I stick on the old I-pod to while away the next couple of hours and I'm joined by a butterfly displaying vivid mauve, violet and blue colours. It does a dance before my eyes before daring to settle on my hand. I think it's come to join its mates that are jiggling around in my stomach.

Jordi and Edgar are two young, soft-spoken, bearded, hippy Dutch guys who build and then export their own acoustic guitars out of a little workshop in Mapusa. They both look like any other new-ager you can see around these parts: lean, laid back, laconic. Edgar is the slightly taller of the two, fair in hair and complexion, Jordi the exact opposite. They both resemble Corsairs, like they've just returned from a bout of buccaneering off the Spanish Main, but their manner couldn't be far more removed. As far as the good-looking stakes are concerned, at least, Maggie hadn't made a bad choice.

The guys don't have the information Kerin thought they might and Jordi looks sad in that knowledge, but they're both keen to hear my story. I give them a shortened version as to what brought me here, as I am also eager to learn about what went on between Jordi and my girl.

'I never knew she had a dad. I don't ever recall her mentioning you. For some reason I had assumed that you were dead.'

'My ex-wife, her mum, might have told it that way,' I concede.

'So, you're Titily's old man,' says Edgar.

'What did you just say?

'I said you're her dad.'

'No, that name – what was that name you used?'

'Oh, you mean Titily – it's just a nickname we use for her. It's Hindu for butterfly.'

'Or Putaly,' says Jordi. 'It means the same thing in Nepalese. She prefers Putaly.'

I freeze rigid. The old girl down on the beach at Souzas, she used the word Titily – she meant Maggie. The stoned guy at the nice beach; he called her over. Putaly – that's what he called her – the tiny tattoo on her shoulder, of course – I'm a dickhead, an Idiot – she *was* my girl.

'Putaly!' I blurt. 'Maggie! – My Maggie, I know where she is. I know where she works; I've seen her. She's the waitress on that beach – that beach...' I snap my fingers impatiently. I can't remember the fucking name. '...V – begins with a V...'

'Vagator?' says Jordi.

'That's it, Vagator,' I exclaim.

Jordi and Edgar look at each other. 'Vishnu!' the word comes out as one.

I race to my bike as fast as my flip-flops will let me.

'Wait!' shouts Jordi in pursuit. 'I'll take us; I'll get us there quicker.'

'Jordi, that's not such a good idea, man,' Edgar bellows after us. 'Let me take him. You should stay here.'

Jordi kicks his bike into life; I jump on the back.

'Not a good idea, man,' repeats Edgar, catching up and holding on to the ape hangers.

'I need to see her, too,' states Jordi in determined fashion. 'Out my way, brother.' He revs the engine and we take off in a mad wheel spin and a cloud of red dust. Through the rear view mirror I see the faint images of Edgar and Kerin, standing open-mouthed, fade into the distance.

If I had the time or inclination to think about it this would be weird; two complete strangers pursuing the same woman in single-minded, determined fashion for two completely different reasons; two guys who've barely spoken a dozen words between them racing along Goan track with the wind in their hair, both on a mission bent on reconciliation, both seemingly driven by blind love.

The crimson orb that is the sun is beginning to dip itself into the sea by the time we arrive at Vagator. Jordi hastily rocks the bike back on its stand and without a word sets off down the cliff side, negotiating the haphazard steps like a young mountain goat. Half way down he casts a quick backward glance to make sure I'm following before his impatience at my lack of agility gets the better of him and he's off again. I have no idea what estranged my girl from this guy, but whatever it was he seems hell bent on rectifying it. By the time I'm two-thirds down the cliff side, he's pounding over the sands towards Vishnu.

I arrive at the beach bar breathless and totally knackered, the benefits of Kerin's breathing technique having yet to manifest. The place is empty save for three dreaded stone-heads tucked away in a corner. One of them is sprawled comatose across some beanbags, the other two stare blankly at a board full of chess pieces. Jordi is having a conversation with the stoner waiter guy. I keep a respectful distance; I wouldn't understand the discourse anyway. I get that feeling again, like a balloon farting its way to deflation. Despite trying to hang on to Kerin's philosophies these things hit you like a punch to the solar plexus.

Before I get chance to catch second wind, we're off again. 'Come on, we need to go,' says Jordi racing past me.

I catch the Flying Dutchman by the arm and yank him back. 'Slow down, fella.'

'She's not here,' he says exasperated.

'I gathered that – explain.'

'There's no time; she's leaving for Mumbai tonight.'

'So, where to now?'

'Engle's bazaar.'

I look at him, none the wiser.

'I'll explain on the way. We must go now.' He looks down at his restrained arm and pulls himself free of my grasp. 'Please,' he says with a desperation I know only too well. 'I need to speak to her as much as you do.'

By the time we re-scale the obstacle course that is the cliff ascent all light is lost and I stumble across loose stone and rough sand, occasionally losing a flip-flop and stubbing my toes on tree root. Jordi revs the Bullet's engine impatiently as I stagger and stumble my way towards his headlight.

Before the muscles of my beleaguered backside have chance to hit the saddle we're away again, racing off into the hot, ink-black night where the once still air, now disturbed by our desperate mission, turns my sweat to a cooler, sticky state and the journey of unsuspecting nocturnal flying creatures is halted by my face or arrested by my hair.

'Where d'you say we're going?' I lean forward and shout above the growl of the bike.

'Engle's Bazaar,' he yells back. 'It's a giant night time market.'

I groan inwardly. Not another fucking market.

In over-the-shoulder shouts Jordi explains that Putaly – Maggie, was doing the rounds, collecting wages owed to her from the various stop-gap jobs she'd been doing before heading to Panjim this evening to catch the midnight bus to Mumbai; this would be our last chance to find her. As with Anjuna, the nearer we get to this place, the slower the progress as bikes, taxis and tuk-tuks fill the roads. I'm not feeling confident.

Engle's is every bit as big as the Wednesday market, and at night, even more spectacular. We park the bike amongst a sea of two wheeled vehicles and venture into a cauldron of noise, light and colour.

'Keep close,' advises Jordi. 'You don't want to get lost in this place.'

We weave our way snake-like through the heaving throng and my girl's thwarted paramour swats away any hawkers or peddlers that slow our progress with a Konkani put-down or an irritated sweep of the hand. We pass minstrels, jugglers, fakirs and fire-eaters in a kaleidoscopic blur. I see all manner of animal on open roast spits, beside which bizarrely stand vegan stalls selling every type of pulse, bean, nut, grain and dried fruit known to man. From saffron to sandalwood, my senses are assaulted from all directions. Here, it seems all that can be wrought from the Earth has been natured, nurtured, grown, beaten, woven or shaped into a saleable, consumable commodity.

At the far side of the market is a spion kop of stalls sitting on terraces that have been hewn out of a hillside. This is the hippy sector, and some. Here trade characters that make you double-take. This is the domain of proper hard-core trogs and swampies. As we climb the terraces I take a trip back through myth and legend. Scenes from the Arabian Nights unfold before me; Sinbads' abound. From Aztecs to Indians, artisans from all continents trade amongst half-Goth, half-pirate, and tribes a bit closer to home that can't quite decide which part of history they want to belong to yet. I'm visiting another dimension; the last remnants of an enclave that just about still affords a hedonistic, drug fuelled fantasy escape from the real world.

High up the terrace we find our mark. *Dharma – Leather*

says the crude sign above the stall. Simple but straight to the point, the place is full of the stuff; woven, beaten, buckled. The emporium of dead animal hide smells great, and sitting cross-legged in the middle of it all, working on an intricate bracelet is a wiry little dude wearing three-quarter cut stripy pirate pants and, over a skinny bare torso that is as tanned as his merchandise, a well-worn leather waistcoat trimmed with woven leather lace. A battered roll up hangs from the corner of his mouth as he concentrates on his work.

'Jacques...'

'Hey, Jordi, my friend,' says Jacques looking up from his endeavours. 'Long time; how are you man?' Jacques offers his hand without getting up.

'Good, man – listen, have you seen Putaly at all?'

'You just missed her; she was here five minutes ago.'

Here we go again. At least this time I can understand what is being said.

'Did she say where she was going?'

'Panjim. Mumbai. – Hey when are you cats gonna get back together...?'

Not hanging around to reply, Jordi is already on his way. I leave Jacques holding his bodkin in the air with a bemused look on his face and tear after the Dutchman before he's out of sight.

I bump, jostle and shove back through the crowds trying to pick out any trace of blonde hair in an ocean of bobbing heads. I'm getting fed up of this. For some reason my heart isn't in it any more. Taking on the mantle of desperation, Jordi is forging ahead, shouting out her name at intervals. Somehow I just know it's going to be a waste of time.

Back at the entrance we peer helplessly into the night that is weakly illuminated by the odd bike park floodlight. Could she already be on her way to Panjim? Or is she still in there, collecting debts or buying last minute provisions for the journey north? I glance back into the maelstrom of noise and colour and personally decide against continuing this hopeless search – and then he sees her.

'Look,' he says pointing across the bike park into the gloom.

'Is that her?' I ask doubtfully, catching just a glimpse of what could be a blond ponytail about two hundred yards away.

'It is her,' Jordi says with conviction in his voice.

'Maggie...!' I shout into the night.

'Putaly...!' he supplements.

Amidst the background noise of surpeti drone boxes, the mournful wail of pungi and ottu horns and the general hubbub of the market I hear a scooter engine fire into life.

'Putaly...!' Jordi shouts.

This time the blond responds. She turns and stares hard in the direction of the calls.

'Putaly...!' He waves his arms in the air then sets off through the maze of bikes towards her.

In what I take to be a moment of recognition, I see her shake her head, ponytail swinging from side to side. I hear the scooter rev, I hear Jordi call her name, I see her hurriedly rock the bike from its stand, I see Jordi stumble and fall into the first bike, I see the bike crash into a second, then a third, then a fourth, all in slow motion, domino effect until at least a dozen bikes and one desperate man lie prone on their sides. I see my daughter give a final backward glance, before roaring away into the night. I watch the scene unfold with the words of the witch in my head: *Things will happen as and when they're supposed to...*

142

Fifteen

IT TURNS OUT I'm a granddad. That little girl on the beach, the one on the trampoline, that's my granddaughter. Nina's her name. She'll be three years old in a couple of months. She's the same age as my Maggie was when I last saw her, as a toddler that is.

Jordi hasn't seen *his* little girl in almost a year, and now I understood his frantic determination. A year, twenty-five years, what does it matter? The separation still hurts and I understood that too. He'd wanted to follow her down to Panjim once he'd untangled himself from the mangled mess of motorbikes. He had questions; he wanted answers. He'd have chased her all the way to Mumbai, I'm sure of that. I told him I'd done chasing, if he wanted to pursue her some more that was up to him but I'd had enough. Thankfully, and I suppose the thanks are entirely due to Kerin, I felt no sense of defeat in that decision any more. I'd walked up a blind alley; a dead end, and I would simply turn around and tread a new path until I found the road I was looking for. With that, the poor lad had fallen into my arms and wept openly. I'd felt awkward, not just because the guy was bigger than me, or that I barely knew him, but maybe because I'd only just become accustomed to dealing with my own set of tangled emotions let alone someone else's. But I suppose ours was a shared type of grief in a way, so I did my best at comfort, which consisted of some tenuous hugging and a few consoling slaps on the back, before suggesting we make our way back to Chakras and a dose of Kerin's home spun healing philosophies, lest we got confronted by the irate owners of a few scratched and battered bikes.

Edgar wasn't so understanding. He argued that if Jordy had let him go in his stead, she might have waited, she might have listened, and most importantly she might have been re-united with me, her father. For that Jordi apologised. Because of his obstinate single-mindedness he's realised he's possibly screwed it up for me, but I tell him not to beat himself up about it, I understand his blind doggedness only too well, and after hearing his story, his hopes, his dreams, his fallibility, and above all his strength of love and regret, I feel there is nothing for him to feel sorry for and nothing for me to forgive. I content myself with the fact that at least I've seen my daughter. After all these years I now know what she looks like, how she talks, how she walks; even that to me at this stage is priceless. I'll keep that day on the beach in my head for as long as I live, no matter what the future holds. Of course she's still blissfully unaware that I exist, and how she'd react to the knowledge that the old English geezer with sunburn and the vacant stare, who liked his roasties smothered in HP sauce was her old man is still a bit scary for me to contemplate.

Granddad. I say the word over and over to myself in my head. It tingles.

As with my Maggie, Little Nina wasn't planned, she just happened, but her creation managed to start the rift. He'd wanted Maggie to settle down here with him in Goa just so he could provide a bit of stability for her and their daughter. She was a free spirit and wasn't having any of it. She was a true traveller with gypsy blood and the built-in wanderlust. He argued that Nina, his little Nina was too young to travel the more remote and inhospitable regions of the world, but from what I briefly saw of the tiny spraffer, bouncing, healthy, carefree, her brief, nomadic existence hasn't done her any harm at all.

Jordi came to resent their absence. He begged her to leave the kid with him if she insisted on pursuing her transient career, but she remained steadfast and there was nothing he could do about it. He had no legal recourse; they weren't married, so wherever she went, her child would go with her. And it was during one of her recent absences that the resentment twisted his reasoning. He cheated on the woman he loved and she found out.

'Was it just the once?' I venture.

He nods his head then lowers it in shame while my own catalogue of misdemeanours flashes behind my eyes.

'That ain't so bad,' I inadvertently reflect out loud, for which I'm briefly confronted by a battery of raised eyebrows, plus a knowing look from Kerin.

Jordi couldn't get his head round her intransigence; her refusal to let him have contact with his little girl. That's all he was asking for, time with Nina whenever they were in Goa; surely she could accede to that. But she wouldn't even discuss it. He'd hurt her beyond redemption; he realised that and he regretted it so much, but using the little one as a weapon of revenge against him wasn't right and what was doing his crust in all the more was that he was being denied the opportunity to reason with her. I felt sorry for Jordi in his misery and frustration, while at the same time having an insight as to why Maggie was being so hard. It had to be her mother. I can only guess what Liz had told our girl about me, and possibly men in general. My ex-partner had every right to be bitter, and if she'd managed to instil only a small percentage of that bitterness into Maggie, then I could well understand her uncompromising stance.

We talk long into the night. The story of the butterfly; cathartic for me as I find out all about my girl and paint pictures in my head, painful for her fella as he imparts bitter-sweet memories at my behest. Finally, fatigue takes hold of me. The last two nights catch up. Spiky eyes and heavy lids demand rest. I draw a close to another eventful day; wearily get to my feet and say my goodnights. Before I shuffle away to my beckoning bed Jordi and Edgar invite me over for a tour of their workshop in Mapusa. I graciously accept the offer.

I sleep peacefully, long and hard as is evident by the slaver on my pillow on emerging from slumber. I rise and am happy to note that the new man feeling is still with me despite the events of last evening that now seemed like a far off dream. I feel I've turned an all-important corner in my life and I feel impelled to seek out the woman responsible and tell her so.

I find Kerin in her treatment room blending aromatic oils.

'Morning,' I say cheerily.

'You seem to use that greeting no matter what time of day it is,' she turns to me glancing at her watch and smiling. 'So, how are you today?' she asks turning back to her potions.

'Actually, Kerin, I feel great, and it's all down to you. I just wanted to take this opportunity to thank you for all you've done for me.'

Just a few weeks ago I wouldn't have been able to utter those words; I'd have choked on them, now they flow out of me, easy and heartfelt.

'Not so much the cynic anymore, eh?' She turns to me again, her eyes flitting across my features in close scrutiny. I no longer flinch under her gaze but give her a cheeky Stevie Marriott type smile.

'I'm trying,' I admit.

She nods, seemingly satisfied with her handiwork. 'Not bad, not bad. Tan's coming along nicely, too.' She brushes a hand across my chest as if it was her God given right and I get a whiff of Ylang Ylang and Black Pepper.

'How's the old aura looking then?'

She looks at me through narrow eyes as if trying to detect any remnants of flippancy.

'Better, better,' she says cautiously. 'How are you feeling about Maggie?'

'Que sera,' I shrug using her phrase. 'Not so sure about poor old Jordi.'

'It's going to be hard for him; another year without seeing them both, especially the little one.'

'Isn't there anything you can do for him?'

'I talked to him at length last night after you crashed, but there's little you can do about cause and effect; only time and tide can swing the balance and make things as they should be. Remember, things happen for a reason. You were sent to me for a reason. Things didn't happen turn out like you might have expected them to, but that tiny speck of faith you kept in and amongst all the shit helped turn the tide for you a bit, didn't it?'

'I guess so.'

'Things will change for Jordi and Maggie and little Nina in time, but none of us can say when that will be. All we can do is stay supportive, be positive and try and be there for him when he needs us.'

'I go home on Tuesday; I may never see him again.'

'You won't if you think like that. We have things called computers and e-mail these days. Just because you're remote or far away doesn't stop you from being a friend. You both have a common goal; staying united halves the task, shares the pain. You must stay in touch. Nothing is greater than the power of love. You both have so much to give. Combined you can work miracles, never forget that.'

'I won't, I promise.'

We hug and I feel the power of the witch surge through me like I'm connected to the national grid.

'Good, now bugger off. I've got a Kensington crusty to see in five minutes.'

* * *

The guitar-building process on visiting the workshop in Mapusa had fascinated me. It was a small but intimate place and on entering I immediately got that kid at Christmas feeling, the one I used to get whenever I visited Celia's basement all those years ago. The smell of Indian Rosewood, mahogany, ebony, shellac and varnish; my heart sang with joy as the scents flooded my receptors; stock wood and shavings, clamps and glue, chisels and band-saws. I was in the company of craftsmen and felt privileged and envious. Here my spirit soared. Here, I felt at home. Jordi and Edgar very kindly gave me a master class, from design to finished instrument that hung in elegant rows across one wall; identical steel strung acoustic guitars displaying intricate abalone rosette inlays, mother of pearl fret markers and tortoise shell scratch-plates, all screaming out to be played.

'What's the V on the guitar head stand for?'

Edgar smiled. 'In our first year we only sold twenty guitars; Vis is the number twenty in Konkani. At that time we didn't have a name for the company, so now that's who we are, Vis Guitars, hence the V.'

'I see, so how's business these days?'

'Well, we were doing great until our export manager left us,' he said while firing an accusing glance at his partner. 'Now we have to do all the selling ourselves and neither of us is very good at it.'

Before the split Maggie had set up deals wherever she went. She was selling guitars as fast as they could make them. Vis had begun to build a reputation internationally and they had received one or two lucrative commissions from renowned artists. But this pair of luthiers weren't au fait with the logistics of the export game. They were craftsmen first and foremost and didn't possess the business acumen that Maggie had, and since the estrangement had found it difficult to keep that side of things running smoothly.

Jordi took a finished article off the wall and handed it to me. I admired the quality from close quarters.

'Play it,' he invited.

I shook my head and handed it back as if I was holding nitro-glycerine. 'I can't,' I said. 'I'm cack-handed; I never learned to play the right way.'

'We'll build you a lefty, won't we man?'

'Sure,' said Edgar.

'Maybe one day,' I said trying not to sound too ungracious.

* * *

...I can't seem to get my ass in gear – too much dope and too much beer... goes the chorus of the much celebrated hippy anthem that is sung with such raucous gusto down here at Venta by the side of the Mayonna creek every Sunday night. From all over Arpora and surrounding districts bohemian xenophiles come together for a gathering of the tribes to jam, sing and basically do what it says in the song. The place is

heaving. Everyone seems happy and high. Tourists attracted by the noise and the light wander in and out, not certain what to make of the Circean atmosphere. I'm sitting with Kerin, Jordi, Edgar and Ramon, ensconced round a table drinking beer and feni chasers; a local brew that is distilled from cashew nuts. It's an acquired taste but quickly gets you in the mood, although a certain night on the red wine not that long ago reminds me to take stock of how many I sink.

Ramon, the not-so-happy wanderer re-appeared as mysteriously as he had disappeared. I try and engage him, being as bonhomie as I dare without sounding like a hypocrite, telling him how much he'd been missed, especially his cooking, but it is hard going; a conversationalist he certainly isn't. I never do get to find out where he'd been or what he'd been up to.

Halfway through the evening Edgar gets up on stage with his custom-built guitar to do his spot. He plays a thoroughly acceptable version of John Martin's May You Never and one of his own compositions that leaves everyone impressed. The acoustic sounds wonderful and he receives a good ovation for his efforts.

On returning from the stage Edgar immediately strikes up a hushed, conspiratorial conversation with his mate in his own tongue; double-dutch you might say, like they're planning something covert.

'So, what sort of stuff did you used to play in your band then, Jack?' asks Jordi, out of the blue, having to raise his voice above the next troubadour who has taken to the microphone, with what sounds like some old Bert Jansch tune.

'Oh, old rhythm and blues standards; Willie Dixon numbers, y'know, Walking the Dog; stuff like that.'

They both nod eagerly at the response and I sense something is in the air. They're both looking at me oddly, expectantly.

'When's it your turn then, Jordi?' I ask nodding at the gig bag propped against his chair, just for something to say.

'What, this?' He points to the bag then proceeds to unzip it. 'No man, I can't play this.'

'Why not?' I ask as he reveals its contents.

'Because it's a lefty, man...' he says holding the guitar triumphantly aloft.

It takes a few seconds, but when the penny drops, so do my guts, bowel contents take a decided shift. The pair of assumptive Dutch cunts expects me to perform. 'No, no, guys; you don't understand, I haven't played in public for over twenty-five years, and how the hell have you managed to build a left-pegger so quick?'

'We just switched the saddle and the nut and re-strung it; still sounds great – try it,' says Edgar enthusiastically.

'Look, I'm a bass player; I stay in the background. I don't do this solo shit. Believe me, I don't sing too good. I stay clear of microphones.'

'Who cares? This is amateur night. Everyone gets up and has a little jam. You saying you can't live with this guy...?'

Bert is wailing his way up the mountainside picking wild mountain thyme with his lassie.

'... Go on, no one gives a shit here, honestly; it's just a bit of fun.'

I look at Kerin who's sat there with a seductive smile on her face. 'Such a lovely looking guitar...' she says wistfully in that husky tone of hers.

'Christen it for us,' says Edgar. 'We'd be honoured.'

'No, I couldn't do it; it's been too long,' I convince myself unconvincingly, while unconsciously conjuring images of young Ben shaking his head at my lack of spine along with

Billy and Digweed strutting and scratching about, flapping their arms making clucking noises.

'I thought you were a musician,' says Kerin.

'I *was*,' I counter, rather pathetically

'What do you mean *was*? There is no *was*. You either are or you aren't – which is it?' she challenges.

Pressure, pressure – fucking pressure. No hiding place, no cocoon. Stand up and be counted you spineless twat.

'Fuck it!' If Bert deserved the ovation he was getting, what had I to lose? I down a shot of feni and stuff the glass in my pocket. 'Is this bloody thing tuned?' I demand snatching the guitar.

'Ready to soar, man,' says Jordi.

'Don't forget, it's an electro acoustic, you can plug it in,' shouts Edgar as I head for the stage.

'Remember to breathe,' adds Kerin helpfully.

I wrack my brain for a tune I can remember the chords and words to, and something I can play in the right key for my dodgy voice. I pluck something from my I-pod; an old obscure little blues ditty that hopefully no one will have heard of and can tell if I'm doing right. The place is buzzing, and thankfully not many people pay attention as I set up, nervously check the tuning, bugger about with the strings, the volume, and the tone and try to figure in my head how the damn thing goes. I shuffle my arse comfy on the stool, stick my feni glass on my third finger, tentatively tap the mike and courageously, or stupidly mutter into it: 'Er – this is an old Blodwyn Pig, Mick Abrahams number, and it's called Truck Driving Man...'

I deliberately slow the tempo of the song down to a pace my fingers can cope with the opening arpeggios, praying I manage to bring the slide and vocal in at the right place. The action of the guitar is unbelievable, and the sound I manage to get from it takes me by surprise. My playing doesn't sound as rusty as I expected it to, but my singing reveals no surprises as the old vocal chords wobble and waiver trying to hit the right pitch. Then, in the bridge when glass hits brand new steel and screeches the length of the neck, I'm born again. Angels herald the return of the prodigal son, and the ghost of Robert Johnson welcomes me home. I stop fighting my voice and let its untrained rawness ride with the slide. I'm in the zone, where the odd bum note or fluffed lyric don't matter, 'cos this is the blues, and I can still do it, and come the second bridge, I've picked up the pace, added a flurry, bent an extra semi-tone, giving the Vis the ride of its life on its maiden voyage, and it loves it, the fucking thing's masochistic, inviting all I can throw at it, begging me to hurt it some more. And then I wind it down; slide, bend, vibrato, quiver.

The applause snaps me out of the zone and I become aware of the audience again; clapping, whistling; cheering. I glance over to my table, just to make sure the appreciation is for me. They're all on their feet, Jordi and Edgar giving me the thumbs up and Kerin with her crinkled smile putting her hands together and nodding with pride like I was her prodigy or something. This isn't so bad; in fact this is a bit of all right. I pat the guitar by way of thanks. This thing could play itself, I'm sure of it.

I hear a few shouts of *more* ringing out from the gathered and I look to my table to make sure it's okay. Everyone nods vigorously.

'Thank you, thanks very much...' I mouth into the microphone feeling a little pop star pretentious, but fuck it; I am actually beginning to enjoy this. '... This next one is... er... this is an old Leadbelly tune,' I small talk while dropping the tuning down to D modal. 'It's called Out on the Western Plain, and

I'm gonna attempt it in the style of the late, great Mr. Rory Gallagher – thank you...'

Back in the frozen wastes of Marsden guitar virtuoso Billy Marshall tears down the *bass player wanted* poster and rips it into tiny pieces while Digweed the drummer looks on in approval. Close by a young dude called Ben dusts down an old Fender case and lovingly polishes its contents with a smile on his face.

...come a cow-cow yicky, come a cow-cow yicky, yicky yea...

Sixteen

IT'S FUNNY HOW smells define a place, a feeling, or a mood. Entering a place of foreboding the smell is usually the first thing you'll sense. In a place of habit and routine, smell will have set up home there and will be forever associated with the vibe of that environment, be it a sad, happy, stressed or evil place. Smells can be broad and expansive; ambiguous. Smells can be specific and refined, like diesel fumes in the rain, box files and manila envelopes, dust on venetian blinds, stale coffee grounds and late nights at the office, the stuff the cleaner squirts into the ear and mouthpiece of a telephone. These are the smells of the real world we're talking about here; depressingly reassuring, grindingly familiar and a million miles away from a place where even the sun and the sky have their own smell, encapsulating bougainvillea, patchouli, feni and leather. Of course it's all smell by association, tricks of experience that the senses lock into memory for later recall of good, bad or indifferent.

Like days spent wasted gazing out of a classroom window, I didn't really want to be here. Like the resistant force of two polar opposed magnets, a whole bunch of real world smells are fighting those that near memory have turned almost to fantasy, where yearning has skewed reality into something it probably wasn't in the first place. I brought home a bottle of Honeybee brandy, quid a bottle, Asda price; but it doesn't taste the same.

In the background a phone rings. 'Good morning, Knapton and Dupree solicitors, Elaine speaking, how may I help?' sings Elaine – the real world stinks.

Caroline has my file, my case notes spread across her desk. Their age comes with them like some ancient sarcophagus rediscovered; their contents waiting to be re-examined, the curse ready to be unleashed. Inside these piles of foisty paper and cardboard are thousands of words constructed by wise men and women along with the not so clever; fact, circumstance and lies all fashioned towards a conclusion of convenience, moulded to a cold clay finger of accusation and guilt that pointed and will always point to me. And somewhere deep inside of me still lingers a small enclave of doubt that dreams and nightmares tried to twist real; a gut-wrenching fear manifested by irrational guilt, where the voices say it must be right because the Crown and the State deemed it so.

Caroline has five red manila files spread fan like in front of her. For her, here in her real world domain, this is simply dealing with business. She sits Queen like on her soft leather throne while the buzz of her day-to-day court goes on around us. As her station demands she cuts an imposing figure in her sharp charcoal suit, crisp white blouse, and the severe, nononsense tie-up of her ebony hair that manages to accentuate those cheekbones and understated jewellery. She exudes a powerful air of professional detachment that gives me great comfort as I embark on another journey into the unknown – and she still looks gorgeous.

'Bernard Williams,' she states lifting a folder and throwing it to one side. 'Died nineteen ninety-six – emphysema.' She lifts another file and repeats the performance. 'John Gill: died in two thousand – lung cancer.' She holds up a third but doesn't slam it down with the other two. 'Now this one, this one leaves me intrigued, she says waving it in the air. 'Albert Novac; remember him?'

'Vaguely – young Polish-Lithuanian kid; about my age – not very bright as I recall.

'Committed suicide in nineteen eighty-nine,' she says as a matter of fact. 'But there's something about his statement taken on that day in the scrapyard that just doesn't read right.'

'How do you mean?'

'Well, for one it's contradictory. It reads very nervy, like he's trying to hide something. But what could he possibly have to hide?

'You don't think he...'

'...No, the notion's absurd. All the other statements made by the pickers are almost identical; they just catalogue the events of that afternoon as they happened. The line of questioning by the police at that point was simply fact gathering, yet this kid acts defensively throughout. Now, I understand he wasn't the sharpest knife in the drawer, but why act like that?'

'How did he – you know...?'

'He didn't work much after you got sent down. He ended up on the sick, long term, allegedly suffering from trauma and depression. He parted company with Sutherlands in nineteen eighty-three. The young Mr. Novac was also a petty criminal; shoplifting, picking pockets, nothing too serious but habitual; a handful of cautions, a suspended; couldn't leave it alone; did three months in Armley in eighty-six; ended up in PC after being badly beaten up for thieving from other inmates. He lived with his mum still; she came home from the shops one day to find him hanging from the banister.' Caroline puts the statement to one side away from the others and pats it like she hasn't finished with Albert Novac yet. 'George Mcintyre: went back to Scotland; retired, living in Fife. That just leaves one

157

Ronald Hodgson: last known address Laisterdyke, Bradford; not a million miles away from where this Novac character lived.'

Three out of the five original pickers are dead. Of the two still alive, one of them is over two hundred miles away; the other still lives locally. I wasn't sure how all this was meant to help me.

'Let's go back to the donkey jacket,' says Caroline leaving the red folders in their respective piles. 'You never took it home, it never left the yard?'

'Never.'

'So, scenario number one as reasoned by the boys in blue...' Caroline re-familiarises herself, wading through reams of paper, forcing me to relive the genesis of my nightmare...

* * *

"...You raped her, you took her life, you drove her body to the yard, you unlocked the gates with your key, and then you dumped her in the boot of a car, knowing full well that when it went through that fragmentizer there would be little or nothing left to piece together. But before you did that, you couldn't resist a little trophy could you, Jack? You tried to pull the engagement ring off her dead finger; the same ring your mate Nick Fadgely had presented her with as a token of their love only a fortnight previous. You couldn't stand the thought of them being happy together could you? Your own relationship was on the rocks. You still held a candle for Lauren Feeney, but when you tried it on that Saturday night, smashed and off your face, like you've admitted you were, she rejected you. Didn't like that did you Jack? Got a bit of a reputation as a ladies man, haven't you. Hurt your pride a bit, that; dented your ego, so you flew into a rage and did her in. If you can't have her, nobody else can, eh, Jack? But, try as you might, the ring wouldn't budge, would it? So, in your rage, you hacked off her finger with the ring still attached. In a blind panic, you dropped them into your pocket, covered your tracks, adrenalin still pumping; the booze and the drugs, swishing about inside you, and then, after the comedown, in the cold sobering light of day, you forgot all about it..."

I wearily looked up at my accuser through tortured eyes. "I've told you, I never even spoke to Lauren that night, I was with someone else."

"Oh yeah, the elusive blonde, the bird with no name; piss poor description, no fixed abode; can't even remember if she was a good shag can you, Jack? That's because she doesn't even exist. You've made her up; she's just a figment of your imagination."

"I've got a dose o' crabs says otherwise," I muttered futilely.

The Inspector ground his fag butt into an ashtray on the desk and leant back in his chair, forming a pyramid with his fingers. He looked at me with eyes that had hate in them. He detested longhaired types like me, especially socially immoral longhaired types. I stared blankly into his hateful features wondering, how the hell did I end up in this shit, what the fuck was I doing there? How did a mess of body parts and a ring that mysteriously ends up in my donkey jacket pocket get me to this? It was all a mistake, some big misunderstanding. I refused to believe those bashed-up bits of flesh and bone belonged to Fadge's flirty fiancé, my ex-girlfriend. She'd simply done a runner, I told them; she was always doing it, and I prayed silently for the stupid little bitch to stop fucking about and put in an appearance, give us all a break. But that morning

I'd been informed that Fadge had positively identified the ring to be hers, as were the shattered fragments of bone, enamel and calcium that had been matched to dental records. My world was already spinning on a different axis – it was about to turn upside down...

* * *

'Could anyone else have had a key to your locker?' asks Caroline as she continues to speed read through piles of paper.

'I didn't have a key, no one did, they didn't lock; they were battered old things that came out of a demolished mill. The lads just used them to store their jackets, overalls, mucky boots and mucky mags. Nobody kept valuables in them.'

'So they were accessible to anyone?'

'I suppose so, yeah.'

'Did you wear the jacket at all that day?'

'No, I was operating my shear. I had a little heater up there, nice and cosy. I only wore it when we were all called to give statements and were told to hang about in the non-ferrous shed.'

'Did you have any enemies at work, Jack?'

'No, well, not amongst the guys I rubbed shoulders with; didn't have much to do with the pickers.'

The frown on Caroline Dupree's forehead grows deeper and she blows air from her cheeks. I can see that she's struggling with this. Whichever way you look at it, the thing still points to me; there's never been anything to say otherwise. No wonder it made her old man ill.

She deliberates the other scenarios, and I let her get on with it, knowing, having deliberated them a thousand times myself, she will reach the same implausible conclusions.

Only five people held keys to the yard, me included. I never mixed with the other four socially and none of them knew Lauren Feeney. There had been no sign of a break-in over that weekend.

Monday: eight am to two pm: a regular flow of punters, from tatters to car dismantlers. I was a shear operator; I had little or no contact with these people, not my department. Scenario: punter, having weighed in car and dead body, accesses changing rooms, clairvoyantly identifies my locker, deposits ring in jacket pocket – unlikely.

Nick Fadgley? No one would have blamed him for dumping her, but not in that way. He was as soft as shit. There was no way he'd have lifted a finger to her, let alone do her in, despite her tiresome efforts at making him jealous. That's why he rang me on the Sunday night, close to tears. She hadn't come home; had I seen her? I must admit I hadn't been too sympathetic. I'd been trying to sleep off the acid comedown and was feeling a bit spiky myself. Should he call the police? "Nah, she's playing you for a mug, mate. She'll turn up when she's good and ready. Best thing you can do is ignore her, play it cool; act as if nothing happened. She'll come crawling back once she realises she's not the centre of attention. Now fuck off, Fadge, I've got my own domestics, let me back under the covers..."

Caroline comes to the end of her re-scrutiny and I can tell she's found nothing new; not one chink in the prosecution armour.

'So, what do I do now?'

She thinks long and hard before answering. If she feels as defeated as I do she doesn't show it. 'You find out why Albert Novac topped himself.'

'That's going to be hard, he's dead.'

'Most suicides leave a note.' She gathers the folders and files together into one big pile, and I can't help noticing the top most. It bears an embossed coat of arms and a Home Office stamp. Below it is another stamp in red and a date. The stamp reads *DENIED* in bold, and the date: twentieth of April nineteen ninety-one is one that will be forever etched on my memory. It is the day of the refusal of my last right of appeal and the day before Steve Marriott, my childhood hero, dies in a house fire...

* * *

It was Sunday evening and I was lying on my back staring blankly at the diamond-shaped metal springs of the top bunk. There was a lot of screw activity around my cell that night; I was on suicide watch. I'd had visitors the previous evening. The heavy metal demons came to mock while the banshees serenaded me with their tortured wails. Afterwards I went to see Gertrude. I asked him for some pills. He said he knew what my little game was and gave me a slap, not because he was looking out for me, but because he didn't want to lose his guitar tutor – selfish twat. We compromised, did a deal. I promised him an extra lesson in return for some blow. Got blocked and went back to my cell to hide in the numb zone. Spent all day there, didn't eat. Johnny paid a call; said Gertrude wanted his extra lesson now. I told him to tell him I wasn't up to it just yet. Wrong answer. Johnny said he'd give me an hour to get my ass in gear. He didn't need to tell me the consequences. No sympathy from *that* fat, ugly, cross-dressing cunt, then. You never knew where you were with the schizophrenic psycho. Catch him in one of his Dusty Springfield Empire creations and he'd be all sweetness and pie, then at other times he'd be threatening to rip your arsehole inside out, turn it into a hand-bag and use your guts as a strap. I'm sure the foul fucker actu-ally had periods.

I spent the hour thinking about Stevie and his last moments on Earth and wished myself with him wherever he is. He was only forty-four, what a fucking waste. At least the original mod had been allowed to live the life he'd been given to the full, and some: umpteen top ten singles with The Small Faces be-fore he was even twenty. Endless sell out tours of America with Humble Pie. The sweetest rhythm and blues voice this country has ever produced. The guy was a fucking legend. But it seems all the greats die young: Buddy, Janis, Jim, Jimi, to name but a few. Strange; it's as if their fates had been foretold and so they crammed all this creative genius into a few short years, living life as it's meant to be lived – chance would be a fine thing. I'd be fifty before, or if, I ever got out of that place. What a fucking waste.

'Where d'you think you're off to, Smiffy?' asked the land-ing lurk-about screw with menaces.

'Gertrude's,' I muttered. 'I've been summoned.'

'Off you go, then,' the shiverer responded, changing his tune as soon as Gertrude's name was mentioned. 'Make sure you're back by eight thirty,' he added trying to throw a bit of authority back into his voice. Even the screws were scared of Gertrude.

Gerald Sankey was an Essex boy. He was also, among other things, a homophobic cross-dressing schizophrenic psy-chopath, a walking, talking fucked up contradiction of living matter – oh, and a serial killer. He had a penchant for rent boys, for murdering them that is. He was serving three life sen-tences, and there were at least double that waiting to be pinned on him if he ever fessed up to them. He'd already done a stint in Broadmoor but he didn't like being locked up with the basket cases. Most nutters plead diminished responsibility for their actions, but not Gertrude. He maintained there was nothing wrong with his head, he knew only too well the magnitude of his actions and demanded to be treat like any normal villain, whatever one of those was. Besides, being classified as an out-and-out head-the-ball sullied his reputation. You see, for Gertrude, slaying young men was merely a sideline, a hobby if you like. Murdering notoriety aside, he was also a big figure in the criminal underworld. Extortion, blackmail, narcotics, armed robbery, you name it, he'd done it; a gangster of renown and he still ran his empire from his cell in Parkhurst as was evident by the blatant turning of blind eyes from certain quarters as well as the privileges, perks and favours afforded him. He was a bit like the Grouty character from Porridge, only a thousand times as nasty and not half as funny. The official line relating to his transfer from Broadmoor was the divided expert opinion amongst the trick cyclists as to the genuine extent of his schizoid behaviour. The unofficial word was Gertrude knew people; people of influence who knew how to petition in the right places on his behalf – and I couldn't even get right to appeal, let alone the chance to win one.

Big Mick and Shergar, two of Gertrude's goons were stood flanking the cell door. They nodded me through like bouncers at the VIP entrance of a top nightclub. Inside, Gertrude was sat perusing a French lingerie catalogue full of black lacy numbers. Johnny, his number one minder and gopher stood idly watching over him. At least the big ugly pig was in his sweats and not squashed into some gold lame creation with sequins, which was a relief. He didn't lift his head to acknowledge my presence and I stood there feeling like a prick, a depressed, suicidal prick who didn't want to be there.

'Gert,' I began to plead. 'I really don't...'

Without lifting his head, he raised a fat finger that silenced me immediately. At the end of it was a long, grotesque false nail painted black, evidence of his last dressing-up session. With the same stumpy digit he pointed to an empty chair that I went and occupied without another word. I sat quietly and watched him flick pages with his Cruella Deville nails. I'd been his musical mentor for ten years by then. You got to know when to speak and when to be quiet. And yet there were still things I didn't know, like how he came by his name for instance. Everyone called him Gertrude or Gert, and he was happy to respond to that. He was also known as Sugar, as befitted his surname, I suppose, but no one ever called him that within earshot, unless they had a death wish that is.

Gertrude dictated his lingerie order to Johnny and I made my gaze flit across the luxury appointed cell, trying to seem as disinterested as possible.

'...Did you want two or three of the vixen camisoles, boss?'

'Three – better make it a couple of bustiers as well, F cup don't forget...'

Johnny finished taking down the details and as he looked up our eyes met and locked. He scoured my face for the slightest reaction. My teeth ground together, my jaw as rigid as a nonce's pecker at shower time. We stayed like that for what seems like an eternity, and for the first time all weekend I silently thanked God for my depressed state. Johnny finally unlocked his stare and left the cell. Guts uncoiled; tendons relaxed.

'Cheer up you miserable fucker, what's wrong wiv ya?'

I dropped my head and shook it slowly, *like you'd care or understand.* 'You could've given me the night off, Gert.'

'What for, so you could toss it off up there on your own,

feeling sorry for yourself? – Nah, you're better off dahn 'ere wiv your auntie Gert – ferget abaht your worries and your strife, as the cartoon bear said.' He took a thin rolled snout from a silver cigarette case and lit it, blowing smoke in my direction trying to engage me. I stayed shtum and stuck to miserable. 'It's abaht time you shaped up and faced the facts, my son. You are going nowhere for a very long time yet. My advice to you would be: change your plea, settle dahn, do the stir and be aht of 'ere at least five early.' *Stick the knife in and twist.* I fired him my bitterest look. He held up his bingo arms in mock defence and looked to the ceiling. 'Okay, okay; I know, you didn't do it. I believe ya, but you ain't doin' such a good job to convince them ahtside what matters are ya? You carry on like this my son and you'll end up a ding in no time; padded walls wiv the fruits indefinitely, like in that place what I checked aht of, you mark my words. Change your plea, Jackie-boy, and you're already halfway there.'

I quickly did the maths in my head; plead guilty, earn maybe a five-year reduction, that'd make me forty-four. I'd be starting a new life the same age as Stevie ended his.

Sick irony and despair collided and shattered somewhere inside what had been my skunk-addled numb zone and the shards of bitterness flew out in all directions. 'But I'm fucking innoceeennnttt!' I jumped to my feet and screamed at the four walls. Padded fucking cell? – Bring it on.

I didn't see or care about the macabre looking hand that batted me across the side of the head even though the force of it put me back in my seat with a thump.

'Behave, you fucking little cunt,' said the ugly frowning mush hovering menacingly above me.

'You alright, boss?' asked a worried looking Shergar peering around the door with his monkey mate.

166

'Yeah, yeah,' the gaffer waved them away with his manicured hand. 'The boy's had a bit of bad news is all; he's a bit upset. He'll be all right, won't you my son? – Close the door boys.'

Gertrude waited till his henchmen had gone before tearing into me. 'Now you listen here, you little prick. I'm sorry you've been knocked back again, genuinely I am, but don't you ever, ever come beefing on my manor like that; you understand?' He stared at me hard, taking a pull on his roll-up. 'You're an ungrateful shit, d'you know that, Jack? There's not one lag on this landing hasn't got a grievance abaht sommink. If I had a pony for every poor geezer what maintained his innocence in this shit 'ole I'd be a fucking millionaire. You got a short memory you have, Jack; too much wacky baccy, that's your trouble. Remember when you was a fish and all the beasts and nonces was licking their lips, lining you up to turn you aht? If it weren't for me you'd have a keister as slack as your defence and as wide as the Dartford tunnel by now.' He growled up a lurgi from the back of his throat and fleggged it into his slop bucket. 'Where's the gratitude, Jack? Fuck's sake, I'm a lifer too you know, you don't have to tell me how fuckin' hard it is.'

I gingerly rubbed the side of my stinging head, slowly lifted my eyes and took in the relative opulence of his cell. There weren't many penthouse suites as cosy. Hard came in different leagues for me and Gert.

As for being ungrateful, well I didn't mean to be, and of course he was right; without his timely interjection I'd have been skin beef long ago, but the Prison Baron's philanthropy came at a price, and it was all down to the man in black...

Seventeen

I'D BEEN IN Parkhurst for less than two weeks and was trying to fathom out who or what I'd become. JD Smith the young, good looking, arrogant, cocksure philanderer was dead and had been replaced by a scared, bewildered, naive and vulnerable wreck of a human being. Word had started to get around about the nature of my crime, and I wasn't too sure if certain lags had dumped me in the same league as the child killers. I'd already had whispered threats and promises that chilled my blood. I'd been stared out, leered at, had gestures sent my way that I would soon learn the meaning of. I was a fish primed to be skinned and de-boned – terrified.

I had my head down, concentrating on, but not taking too much notice of the contents of my food tray that I was nervously pushing around with my fork. It was the ciggie breath I noticed first, then the realisation that the lag I'd been sat next to had disappeared, tray and all, to be replaced by the impassive, expressionless features of the bloke I would come to know simply as Johnny.

'You the fish what's been sent dahn for the full jolt?'

I stared at him. Fear poured out of me. I didn't have a clue what he'd just said.

'You play guitar?' The guy waited patiently for his answer.

I nodded, weakly.

'Be at Gertrude's six o'clock sharp.' He got up to leave.

'But...but I don't know...'

At last his face broke into a smile cum sneer. 'Ask anybody; they'll tell you – six o'clock, don't forget.'

When he'd gone I looked cautiously around to see I'd become the centre of attention for what seems like the whole canteen. I buried my head back in my tray and decided I wasn't hungry.

Unless you're a kiddie fiddler some lags liked to wear their misdemeanours as badges of honour, it added to the status and notoriety. My cell mate Jimmy - found out his wife was being unfaithful and stabbed her twenty seven times -was filling me in about the prison Baron and top psycho Gertrude and what atrocities he inflicted on his rent boy victims, and couldn't understand why I'd gone such a funny colour and was swallowing hard trying not to retch, especially after hearing what I'd been sent down for. In between gips I told him I didn't do it. He gave me one of those looks; one of those patronising looks of mollification that I would have to get used to over the coming years whenever I protested my innocence.

At five minutes to six I walked the landing, fear and trepidation mounting with every step and with every echoing taunt and cat call that accompanied my journey. Halfway along the lower landing Johnny was waiting for me. He was stood outside the cell idly chatting to a screw. They looked me up and down contemptuously as I shivered towards them.

'You look like shit,' remarked Johnny distastefully.

I looked up at the screw, my eyes pleading for deliverance. He just smirked, turned and walked away.

Johnny checked inside the cell to see if my summoner was ready for me, and then beckoned me forward with a jerk of the head.

Jimmy had warned me, but I still wasn't prepared for what

now appeared before me. It stood about six foot tall. It had hairy arms and a five o'clock shadow. It was a bloke, there was no mistaking that, but it was wearing an off the shoulder, multi sequined, black split knee length dress, black fishnet stockings, ruby red high heels with matching pashmina shawl, all accessorised with white pearl necklace and earrings. On its head it wore a bouffant blonde wig with Marylyn Monroe kiss curl – and it was smoking a roll-up.

'In you come, my son,' it said. 'Pull up a chair, close your mouth.' It spoke in the most friendly, cheeky-chappy cockney accent, no affectation at all. I blindly obeyed.

'I hear you play the guitar.'

'Er, yeah, a little,' I whimpered cautiously.

'What do you think of this?' he produced an acoustic from somewhere behind him and passed it over.

I took it and looked at it aimlessly; it was an old Eko. 'Very nice,' I offered.

'Nah, I mean is it any good; can you play it?

I dragged my fingers across the strings. 'Needs tuning, but yeah, it's okay.'

'Good, go on then.'

'What?'

'Let's hear what you both sound like.'

'What, here – now?'

'Nah, next bleedin' Tuesday you muppet – o' course now.'

I quickly brought the thing into tune and looked at him-her expectantly. 'Er, what shall I play?'

'Know any Johnny Cash?'

I shook my head.

'Anyfing then, I don't bleedin' know; just play it,' he commanded.

I couldn't think of a single tune. My head was in a spin and my hands were shaking. Eventually I started to strum a crude approximation of Steve Marriott's Sad Bag of Shaky Jake, which turned out to be unintentionally appropriate. Without the singing it sounded crap so I inserted a few twiddley arpeggios. It still sounded crap, but Gertrude seemed happy and showed his appreciation with a cry of, *"go on, my son."*

'Well done, that man,' he said when I'd finished. 'You'll do for me; you're hired.'

'What...?' I managed to croak.

Gerald Sankey – *you can call me Gertrude, my son* – had recently watched a screening of the Johnny Cash film, the one where he plays San Quentin prison in California. He'd become obsessed with the man in black and wanted to emulate him. He made a vow to learn guitar and play and sing just like his new found hero, and, as luck would have it, he'd just got wind of a young fish that had recently landed on his wing, who murdered women and played the guitar – me.

He wanted me to give him lessons and in return he'd give me protection from some of the nasties who were already jerking themselves off in anticipation of breaking in the new pretty boy.

'Okay,' I agree. 'But it'll probably only be short term.'

'Why's that?' asked Gertrude crossing his fishnet legs and modestly pulling skirt over the revealing split.

'Because I'm appealing.'

'Well you're certainly appealing to most of the beasts and nonces on C wing so I'm told...'

* * *

I could still hear the laughter resounding harsh and hollow around the cell walls as Gertrude and Johnny split their sides at my innocent naivety. Ten years later, sat in the same cell, the desperate hope and faint optimism that had ridden on the back of my innocence and naivety finally gave up the ghost as the door to appeal was closed forever.

The deal we made still stood. The cost: three lessons a week for the past ten years. One thousand four hundred and forty lessons and the big useless bastard still hadn't mastered the basic open chords. The gain: an undefiled sphincter I could call my own and thankfully only used to shit through.

'No, no, Gert, it's a B seven after the E.' He looked at me blank. 'B seven: forefinger D string, first fret. You're never going to do it with those fucking nails on,' I sighed frustrated.

'All right, all right,' he snapped, ripping at the black talons. 'Took me bleedin' ages to put these on,' he grumbled.

'I hear the train a rollin', it's comin' round the bend...' he crooned, not even managing to get the lyrics right, while his pudgy chipolata fingers, now minus the nails tried to cope with E to A to E to B seven.

'It still don't sound like the CD,' he moaned struggling to the end of Folsom Prison Blues.

'Course it doesn't. You're just playing chords; he picks at notes. You're not ready for flat- picking yet. Plus he's got his band behind him don't forget.'

'You don't think it's the guitar? We've had it ten years. I might put in for another.'

'There's nothing wrong with the guitar. Let's try Wanted Man; D, E minor, A – ready...?'

We both struggled through the unscheduled lesson, finishing off as always with House of The Rising Sun; not Johnny Cash, I know but it was the first tune I ever taught him and the only one he'd just about mastered after all that time. Maybe Gert wasn't cut out for the guitar, or perhaps I was a bad teacher; whichever, he showed no sign of giving up. Maybe I should've taken a leaf out of his book.

Lesson over, I wearily took my leave. Outside the cell, faithful lap-dogs Big Mick and Shergar, standing duty until lights out, took the piss at my earlier outburst.

'Ooh, I'm innocent I am; it wasn't me what did it, officer,' mocked Shergar, the big fucking goon.

'Fuck off, hoss-head.'

Once more I trudged the landing back to mine with mocking laughter ringing in my ears.

Eighteen

MY RENEWED SEARCH for answers finds me in the old district of Thornbury, amongst rows of stone built terraces, where time has stood still, where the modern medium of tar macadam has yet to spread its black reach and most of the litter-strewn streets are still cobbled. Regiments of satellite dishes and the exodus of indigenous mill workers, who have been largely replaced by an Asian community, seem to be the only noticeable sign of change around here, probably since the industrial revolution.

I've been knocking on the front door of number twenty-seven Gladstone Terrace for the past five minutes now and I fail to spot any movement behind the dense, dingy yellow net curtains that adorn the window, so I walk to the end of the block and make my way round the back, gingerly stepping past supermarket trolleys, old tyres, soggy mattresses and exploded black bin liners and try at the rear of this Ritz for rats. Three little Pakistani kids sit on the large stone roof of the old midden next door and curiously watch my every move like I'm from another planet. I take out my new contact list just to check I'm at the right location once more and I get the sense that there's some skewed parallelism going on here; something to do with children playing and scraps of paper with names written on them. I rap hard on the door, silently hoping that any symbolic allegory with what went on in India stays at that.

There's a smell of Garam Masala in the air and the tea-pot-lids continue to stare. I decide to give myself a slow, silent count of fifty before abandoning this latest bout of straw clutching. I get to twenty-five and knock hard for the last time. On the count of sixty-eight I hear the sound of a bolt being slid back. The Karen Bickerstaff applied science of positive thinking pays dividends and I feel chuffed with myself for not walking away at fifty.

The door opens the few inches that the security chain allows and a frightened looking, little old lady peers up at me.

'Hello, love,' I say in my cheeriest voice. 'Are you Mrs. Novac?

She warily eyes me up and down, doesn't respond.

'Mrs. Novac?'

'Yes,' she says cautiously. 'Who are you; what do you want?' she demands in a thick Polish accent.

'My name's Jack Smith, I'm an old friend of your son,' I lie. 'I used to work with him at Sutherlands.'

I don't ever recall even talking to the guy except maybe to take the piss for lunchtime entertainment in the canteen.

'My Albert is dead.' Her words are sad and tainted with bitterness. 'Please go away.'

I stick my foot between jamb and door before she has chance to shut it in my face.

'Mrs. Novac, I need to talk to you about Albert – it's very important.'

'My boy has been gone a long time, what can be so important now?'

'It's important because it concerns me. Please, just give me ten minutes of your time; that's all I ask.'

'What did you say your name was?'

'Jack – Jack Smith.'

'I don't recall my Albert ever talking about any Jack. Ronnie was his friend, his only friend. He talked about Ronnie a lot.

'Ronnie Hodgson?'

'Yes – you knew Ronnie too?'

'Yes.' I put syrup in my voice. 'I've travelled a long way to get here today,' I lie again. 'Will you let me in for just ten minutes – please?' I remove my foot and cross my fingers. After cautious contemplation the old girl finally relents, undoes the security chain and lets me in. Once she's half certain I'm no predatory con man, she relaxes a little and even offers me a cup of tea.

The inside of the house is a museum to post war austerity. It reminds me of visits to my gran's when I was a nipper. A three bar electric fire stands instead of the old Yorkshire range that originally came with these dwellings, and on the mantelpiece sits a walnut carriage clock, loudly ticking away the passage of time while all around it stands still.

I look around for a photograph so I can put a face to the late Albert Novac, but all I can see is an old, faded black and white framed portrait of a dashing looking chap in air force uniform, sporting slicked-back Brylcreemed hair and David Niven tash.

Mrs. Novac delivers tea on a tray with a saucer full of ginger biscuits. I look up at her to smile and say thanks but she stares back cold, her face set rigid – she's just twigged who I am.

I do my best to allay her fears and try and convince her she hasn't just served tea to a murderer. I try and explain to her as best I can my confusing and unconvincing story and end up doing both, confusing and unconvincing her, that is. In an ancient looking armchair with a grubby crocheted antimacassar she sits with her baggy woollen cardigan wrapped around her and shakily sips at her tea. I can see she's struggling to get her head around anything I'm telling her.

'I'm seventy-nine years old now,' she says setting down her cup and saucer with an unsteady rattle as if to emphasise the fact. 'My memory isn't what it was, but I do remember the shocking business with that poor young girl.' She falls silent for a moment, the clock ticks and I crunch a ginger nut while she formulates her thoughts. 'Forgive me, Mr. Smith, I'm a little slow, and perhaps I've missed something in what you've told me, but I'm still not sure why you're here and what any of this has to do with my Albert.'

'To be perfectly honest with you Mrs. Novac, neither do I, but now I'm out I owe it to myself to go back into the past and look for any new information, anything that may have got missed first time round. I have to clear my name.'

'Are you suggesting that he had anything to do with the girl's murder?'

'No, not for one minute, but he may have known or seen something that he was too scared to tell the police at the time.'

'Like what?'

'This is what I'm here to find out. Who's the handsome looking fellow in the photograph?'

'That is my father. He flew Spitfires during the war. He got shot down over the channel in nineteen forty-one. They never found his body.'

'I'm sorry, I don't mean to pry, but I can't help noticing you don't appear to have any photos of Albert anywhere.'

She sighs. Her hand goes to a gold locket around her neck. 'He's here,' she says with her voice breaking. She opens it and invites me to see the tiny portrait of a child. 'He is four years old. This is how he was just before his father deserted us. Just upped and left, went back to Poland without a word. After that it was hard bringing him up on my own. You see Albert was a problem child. He wasn't like the others at school. He had learning difficulties. They used to tease and bully him. Can you imagine what that's like, Mr. Smith?'

'No, no I can't,' I say hiding my shame and guilt.

'As he got older I found it harder to control him. I did my best. I tried to bring him up a good Catholic boy, but he rebelled. He became a sinful child; deceitful. He stole and lied, broke my heart. I wanted to believe it was all part of his illness rather than the work of the devil, but how could I be sure?'

My eyes go to the picture of the Pope above the fireplace, the Virgin Mary next to the ticking clock; one, two, three, four crucifixes strategically placed around the room – no place for an image of a sinner boy here.

'I prefer to remember him as the sweet, innocent child he once was and not what he became,' she says, crossing herself and clicking shut the locket.

'Have you any idea why he might have wanted to take his own life, Mrs. Novac?'

'I blame it on his time in that place...' Her hands turn in little circles trying to remember the name. '...What was it? - Armley. They did unspeakable things to him in there. It was like he was back at school again; only what they did to him was a million times worse. By the time they put him in protective custody it was too late, the damage had already been done. He'd been disturbed long before that, though. After he lost his job at scrapyard his stealing had begun to get out of control. Every week the police picked him up. Eventually they had to take him in. It's as if he wanted to get caught; a cry for help. But look what they did to him, look what they made him do. Nobody helped him; no one.'

'Didn't he leave a note or anything?'

'Oh, yes he left a note, but a lot of what he wrote didn't make much sense to me. It just shows what a confused state his mind must have been in.'

'Do you still have it?'

'The note? – Yes, of course I do.'

'May I see it?'

Mrs. Novac hesitates, not because she's reluctant to show a stranger something as personal as a farewell letter from her son, but because the old girl is really slow on her feet, and it takes an almighty effort to trudge up and down the steep and narrow stairs of these old terraces.

She hauls herself out of the chair with a grunt. 'I may be gone some time,' she says wearily. 'Help yourself to more tea and biscuits.'

'Thank you, Mrs. Novac,' I say, feeling guilty for putting her to so much trouble. 'I really do appreciate it.'

She mutters something under her breath in Polish and shuffles out of the room.

I still can't picture this guy, don't seem to remember him at all so I put myself in his shoes and think there but for the grace of God, well, a cross-dressing psychopath actually, go I. It's only now I truly start to appreciate what old Gert saved me from, and I suddenly realise what a small price years and years of fruitless guitar lessons was to pay. Albert Novac got no protection because he had nothing to offer in return; nothing to barter with. He was always going to be a victim, and his compulsion to thieve and pilfer, along with an inability to carefully discriminate who you pilfer from, only made him more of a victim.

The clock on the mantelpiece ticks away to itself, I crunch another ginger nut.

Breathless with the effort of granting my request, Mrs.

Novac hands me the suicide note. 'Here you are,' she says. 'But I don't know what good reading this will do you – have you finished with your tea?'

She gathers up the tray and shuffles into the kitchen. I unfold and start to read the child like scrawl.

Kochana Mamo,

The time has come now I must leave you. I'm sorry I never became the son you hoped I would be, but I couldn't have been that in a million years. I don't know how or why I became a bad person; I never meant to harm anyone, especially you, Mamo.

I know what I'm about to do is wrong and my soul will go to a dark place, but my life is already a living hell, so whatever it is awaits me on the other side, I'll be ready for it. Please don't think me evil, most of the things I've done were stupid, not bad. I've only ever done one thing in my life that was both and everynight I close my eyes the nightmares force me to re-live it, Pierścionek tamta ręka, ciągle mnie prześladują, may God forgive me.

I've paid for most of the wrong I've ever done, but one thing will always remain beyond redemption and for that I can no longer live with myself.

Tell Ronnie I'm sorry I wasn't able to get the latest batch of stuff he asked for; I didn't mean to break up our little partnership like this. I hope he understands.

Muszę już iść, Mamo. Nie bądź na mniezła, przepraszam. Kocham Cię - Caluje.

Albert.

'Some of this is written in Polish; I don't understand it.' I say offering back the letter when she re-enters the room.

She lifts her reading glasses off the mantelpiece and holds the letter close to her face. 'He's just saying goodbye,' she says, her voice cracking up. 'Just saying he's sorry and that he loves me.'

'What about this sentence here.' I point to the middle of the note.

'*Pierścionek i tamta ręka, ciągle mnie prześladuja,*' she reads aloud. 'It says *the ring and that hand still...* how you say... scare him, to haunt, yes *...haunts me.*'

I take the letter back and re-read. '*...Every night I close my eyes the nightmares force me to relive it – the ring and that hand still haunts me – may God forgive me...*'

'Have you any idea what he meant by that?'

She removes her glasses and wipes away a tear. 'No, like I said, his mind was confused at the time; there were lots of things going on inside his head. He should have been in hospital; he should have had treatment. No one would listen.'

'What was this partnership with Ronnie that he mentions?'

'It was some little business they ran together. I don't know exactly what it was they did. Albert always insisted he was a partner, but I'm not sure if that was the case. He always seemed to be running errands for Ronnie, or missions, as he liked to call them. It didn't sound too much of a partnership to me, but Ronnie seemed a nice man. Albert liked him; wouldn't have a word said against him. He was a good friend – his only friend really. I never saw him after Albert died. He never came to the funeral, I don't know why. There are still things in his room that Ronnie never collected.'

'You mean stuff from his missions?'

'Yes, that's right. I kept them thinking he would call round for them, but he never did.'

'Do you mind if I take a look?'

'Well, I suppose not,' she says hesitatingly, thinking more about the trek back upstairs rather than anything else.

We make the painfully slow ascent up the dark and dingy steps, past the wooden banister from where I assume Albert did the grisly deed.

'I don't go in here much,' says Mrs. Novac reaching for the door handle. 'It's just as he left it. I've not moved a thing.'

She opens the door to a cold, damp, Spartan room. The carpet is threadbare. The candlewick counterpane that sits on the metal- framed single bed looks moth-eaten. In the corners of the grime-covered windows, green mould grows in between rotting frames and condensing glass. Layers of dust coat the old walnut wardrobe and dresser. Depressing.

The dresser drawers, unaccustomed to being opened for such a long time, jerk and stick, resisting old Mrs. Novac's attempts to reveal their secrets. I come to her aid and the drawer finally explodes open, spilling its contents; a treasure trove. Gold and silver in the shape of watches, bracelets, necklaces, brooches, tie-pins, cuff-links and rings; a proper magpie's haul.

'Is this the stuff Ronnie should have collected?' I ask dropping to my knees, picking up each item of jewellery and placing them back in the drawer.

'I think so, yes.'

'You do know why Albert was sent to Armley, don't you, Mrs. Novac?'

'Yes,' she says, bowing her head in shame.

Nineteen

I WALK THE streets to my next point of contact, thinking about Hodgson-Novac Enterprises; Albert playing Dodger to Ronnie's Fagin; thief and fence, try to make sense of what it was I'd just uncovered; one naive old lady and a curious phrase from her disturbed son, a loser, tired of life. I wonder what Caroline would make of it all.

The districts of Thornbury and Laisterdyke sit next to each other. Names apart, there's nothing much else to discriminate with; same time warped, neglected back streets, same air of decay and desolation.

The address I have for Ronnie Hodgson is a little over a mile away.

Next door to number six Fenton Street, two women, arms folded stand idly gossiping.

''Scuse me love, does Ronnie Hodgson live here?' I enquire.

Gossiping stops. 'Yes, love.' Gossiping resumes.

I knock on the door and wait. I knock three more times – and wait. He's either as deaf as old Mrs. Novac or he's not in.

'Is it Ronnie you're after?' One of the women breaks off.

I nod thinking I'd already established that much.

'He won't be in at this time o' day, love; he'll be down at t'club.'

I ponder the universe and put the last wasted five minutes

in their rightful place. Is it me? 'Which club?' I dare to venture.

'Labour club.'

'Right. Thanks.' I walk away marvelling at their uncanny ability to resume the conversation mid flow, to pick it up without pause for reflection as if nothing had happened. What a skill.

I find the club without too much trouble and wander in. It's quiet, not a lot of activity in a place like this at one o'clock on a Tuesday afternoon.

'Ronnie Hodgson?' I enquire at the bar. The steward points to a bloke sat nursing what looks like an oxygen tank and mask. It has to be him there's no one else in the room.

'What does he drink?'

'Bitter.'

I order two pints and stroll over. On the table in front of him a newspaper is spread open at the racing section. He is an old man and he looks to be on his last legs. Fucked. I would never have recognised him as the forty-odd year old we used to take the piss out of as he bit into his bacon and egg sarnie all those years ago. His watery eyes are glued to the telly on the wall, studying the field as they circle the paddock. He doesn't notice me approach.

'Hey up, Ronnie – remember me?' I say, setting down the pints.

'Aye, course I do,' he wheezes, barely glancing away from the telly.

'Here, I've brought you a pint.'

'I can't buy you one back you know, I'm a pensioner.'

'That's all right, here, gerrit down your neck.'

He finishes the dregs of his gill then growls his way into the top of his fresh pint.

'You don't remember me, do you?'

'Here, shhh – you see these?' he rasps in what's supposed to be a whisper, while totally ignoring my question. He produces a Golden Virginia tin from under the table and looks around conspiratorially. His bony hands shake and struggle with the lid. 'I'm not supposed to have these.' He reveals three skinny roll-ups, takes one out and puts it to his lips. 'It's me lungs you see – knackered.' He lights it with total disregard for the recent smoking ban and laughs, but the laugh quickly turns into a coughing fit. 'Fuck 'em, eh? – What do you say kid? – Want one?'

I refuse, and take the top off my pint wondering how I'm going to get any sense out of the old boy with what looks like the onset of Alzheimer's taking hold. 'Ronnie, it's Jack - Jack Smith; I used to operate the big shear at Sutherlands, remember?'

He looks at me and frowns. 'Aye, you're not him; he were a young lad, long, fair hair. He got sent down you know, murdered a young lass, sent her through the fragmentizer. Cocky little twat; never liked him. – Nah then, here we go. Total Recall, likes the going; top weight, but Mcoy's on him, not a bad price, might be worth a punt.' He circles his selection, chest heaving; cig smoke curling into his eyes.

'What about Albert, Ronnie, remember him?'

'Aye; topped hi'self; found him strung up over t'bannister.' He says it like he knows people who regularly do that sort of thing, an everyday occurrence.

'Best mates, weren't you?'

'Nah, not really.'

'Business partners?'

He chuckles hoarsely. 'He used to nick stuff; I'd flog it for him.'

'Why do you think he hung himself?'

'Well, he wasn't all there, was he? – 'Ere, you're not a copper are you? All that was a long time ago.'

'No, I'm not a copper,' I reassure. 'What was it tipped him over the edge then?'

'Who?'

'Albert. Was it his time in Armley?'

'Well, it can't have helped.'

'Why?'

'Let's put it this way, somebody should've told him to keep his soap on a rope around his neck, know what I mean...?' He laughs himself into a coughing fit again, and this time has to take a blast on the nebuliser. '...Nah, it was the nightmares what sent him doolally.'

'Nightmares; did he tell you about them?'

'Aye, he used to go on about devils and demons, wailing witches and body parts that would come alive and go for him. He used to be scared to go to sleep. That's when he started robbing at night, tried to stay awake as long as he could. Trouble was he kept on getting caught. He was a crap burglar. He got so bad I had to go sign on.'

'These body parts he used to dream of, were they anything to do with the girl that got murdered?'

'Definitely; they were recurring; always took place in the picking shed. That's where we used to work you know, terrible place. He'd jabber on about the screams, the blood and guts; severed heads that talked to him and the hand with the ring that would go for his throat. I didn't like him talking about it, it gave me the willies; I mean we'd all gone through it for real, it affected us all for a long time, only more so for him because of the business with the hand and the ring I suppose.'

'What do you mean, Ronnie, what about the hand and the

ring?'

He suddenly stops. 'Nah,' he says looking around furtively. 'He swore me to secrecy on that one.'

'What did you swear secrecy to? It was a dream, a nightmare.'

'Not that bit; that bit was real.'

'What was? – Ronnie, you've got to tell me. Albert's dead now; it doesn't matter.'

'Rogue Fantasy; good form, won by three lengths last time out...' Hssssff, goes the nebuliser. '...Be odds on, that bugger.'

'Ronnie, – what bit was real?'

He takes a coffin nail pull on his roll-up, a good measure of his ale and growls satisfied. 'We worked at the scrapyard me and Albert – Sutherlands. We used to stand in this tin hut called a picking shed, sorting bits o' non-ferrous metals amongst a load o' shite that used to come down this moving belt; ally in one bin, copper in another; filthy fucking job, you'd have to be mad to do it...'

I decide it's futile to try to explain who I am again in case he loses his train of thought. I keep quiet and let him get on with it.

'...I didn't mind the shite so much, I could put up with all that. It was the noise that did me. It made you shudder; rattled your brain; never got used to it. Beast of a machine was that fucking fragger. It could chew up a whole car in seconds and spit it out in bits – clever, no doubt about it, but what a fucking monster...'

'Ronnie...'

'Eh...?

'Tell us about that lass; the one that went through the fragmentizer.'

I don't really need to hear all the gory details. I've lived

187

through them so many times, but I need him to tell me what he knows about the finger and the ring, and I can see that I need to steer him gently around the holes and spaces of his occasional dementia.

'Aye, I'll never forget that day as long as I live. We all thought it was a dog at first. You sometimes got some sick bastard who'd put a dog in the boot of a car; used to make a right mess. This one was different; no fur on this poor fucker. Mac saw it first. He just screamed and ran. Ripped his mask and ear defenders off and legged it. Bernard fainted, cracked his head open as he fell. I saw all this... this stuff. I didn't know what it was at first. It was... bits of skull with hair on; all matted... brains, guts... I saw, I saw... dear God...'

Ronnie takes a drag. His trembling hand reaches for his pint. Gurgled slurps calm him down; while his watery eyes stare into space as long term memory springs to the fore as sharp as a pin, clear as day.

'... I – oh, Lord,' he wheezes and rasps. 'There was bits of bone, all shiny and all this stuff, all this mess, all...oh, all slow, slow motion. I remember, I remember hitting the red button and the claxon sounded – then I threw up...'

He turns to face me but stares right through me. His eye sockets are brimming with moisture.

'Ronnie... Ronnie, what about Albert, what was Albert doing?'

He slowly shakes his head. 'I, I don't know...' he mutters vaguely.

'But what about the ring, the hand and the ring?'

'Oh, he never told me about that till years later,'

I sigh, then turn it into a Kerin style deep breath – *keep calm, persevere*. 'What did he tell you Ronnie, what did he say?'

His features register back to the now, and he gives me a look like I've just landed. 'You're not a copper are you?'

Short term – fucked.

'No, Ronnie, I'm not a copper. You said Albert had these dreams, these nightmares, and some aspects were real. What did he tell you about the ring?'

'What do you want to know about him for? He's dead; hung hi'self from t'bannister...'

'Ronnie – the girl; the ring.'

'Aye, he told me a tale about that...'

Any time now, please God.' What did he tell you?'

'He came to see me one night; dropped in some watches and other bits o' stuff. He looked terrible, fucking shocking, said he hadn't slept for days; too scared to close his eyes. Said he needed to get something off his chest – well, I couldn't be arsed listening to that crack-pot prattle on; as long as he didn't fall asleep on the job and get caught again, that's all I was bothered about. So, he grabs me arm and says he had to tell somebody. Jesus, I thought he was going to start frothing at the mouth. He demands I listen to him, so I thought best to humour him in case he throws a proper wobbler. So he sits me down and starts going on about the day that lass came through the fragmentizer. I says woah, enough o' that Albert, lad, let it go; all that happened a long time ago. He grabs me and sits me back down all determined like, his eyes blazin'. He says he done a bad thing, a stupid thing. So I says, it wasn't him what done her in and put her in that car was it? – Joking, like, but he wasn't in no mood for jokes that night, I can tell you. He says when all them bits o' body parts come rattling by he didn't know what to do, said he was transfixed, just stood and stared horrified but fascinated. What he sees next is this hand coming towards him, but it's got a finger missing. Then he sees the finger amongst all the other shit, and on this finger is a bloody diamond ring, so what does he do? He only reaches in amongst the blood and slime, lifts it off the belt and stuffs the fucking thing in his pocket. Couldn't resist owt shiny; proper little fucking magpie was our Albert.'

'What and none of you saw him do this?'

'Well, I never saw him, I was too busy revisiting me dinner. Mac and Gilly had legged it and poor old Bernard was out flat cold. After that it went mental, everybody running around like headless chickens. It was total fucking chaos, as I remember...'

Ronnie starts to drift away again, wheezing vacantly.

'What did he do then?'

'Who?'

'Albert; what did he do with the ring?'

'Oh, aye, well, after all the panda cars start appearing at the top of the yard, he says he starts to panic a bit. Then, when we're all told we'd have to give statements; he says he proper starts to brick it. Somebody tells us to go wash off, get presentable. So we all go get a shower except Bernard who's in first aid getting patched up. So Albert hangs about, waits 'till it gets all steamy and nobody's looking, doffs off, takes the finger and the ring, opens a locker and drops it into some other fucker's pocket. – Hey, and get this, it only turns out he's dropped it into the pocket of him what did it; what was his name...?'

'Jack Smith.'

'... Aye, that's him Smithy, cocky little twat, never liked him. – Hey did you know him?'

'I used to... a long time ago.'

'Well, I mean, how fucking weird was that. So I says to Albert, what's your problem? Okay it might have been a bit naughty swiping a ring of a dead un like that, especially just a

190

fucking finger - grisly cunt; but think about it, I says, in the long run you've saved the boys in blue a lot o' spade work. You helped bang him up; you did 'em a favour. Why are you getting so cut up about it after all this time? I told him to go home and get a good night's kip. He gets up and mumbles something about when he finally gets to sleep it'll be for an eternity. He thanks me for listening, drops the bag of goodies on the sideboard and leaves.'

'When did he tell you all this?'

'About a fortnight before he topped hi'self. That evening was the last time I saw him alive, but even then he looked half dead. Poor fucker must've had some proper demons in his head.'

I nod in solemn agreement because I know all about Albert Novac's demons; they come from the same hell that I visited on many occasions. Our nightmares must have run parallel, our torment concomitant.

Hate and pity hit me in alternate waves as I think of the late Polish petty thief and what he inadvertently did to me. I slowly get to my wobbly feet and start to walk away on jelly legs. Inside my head ironies and circumstance collide and collude to brew a hysteria that, if I let it, would manifest in howls of laughter or wails of exasperated indignation. I favour neither and breathe hard, breathe deep, but all it does this time is make me feel dizzy.

'Hey,' rasps old Ronnie at my back. 'Don't I know you?'

'You never knew me, Ronnie,' I say without turning round. 'You just think you did.'

I find myself out on the street. A meteor shower of implications born out of what I've just learned is hurtling around my cosmos of emotions. I try and catch them, thread them onto a bead of cohesion, but I fail to tie them off and they fly away

191

into an irregular, haphazard orbit about my head. I need to speak to Caroline – must speak to Caroline.

Across the road is a bookies. I wander over; check out the field for the two-ten at Kempton. I stick a fiver to win on Total Recall. I stroll back across the road, fold the betting slip, hand it to the steward; tell him it's for Ronnie. Ronnie sits in his corner, head buried in the paper. Nebuliser goes hsssff-hsssff. He doesn't look up.

I aimlessly wander the terraced streets in a daze; emotions wrung out like some damp, overworked dishcloth. Time does its suspended thing. Don't know how long I've been walking, but I'm lost. I look around the grey surroundings and am pretty certain I haven't a clue as to where the hell I am; yet it all appears vaguely familiar, like some déjà vu vibe. I turn the corner at the end of a terrace and then I see it. Big, bulbous, grey and rust rotten monster; the imperious edifice of numb steel that is the old gasometer that loomed daily, sun blotting, shadow casting over Sutherlands scrapyard, and in that instant I know exactly where I am.

I cross the road, drawn by a morbid curiosity and am immediately dwarfed by the giant Yorkshire stone wall that runs the entire length of one side of Gasworks Lane. Cut into the wall, halfway down the road are two large stone pillars that once held mammoth iron gates that formed the entrance to the scouring mill. I wander through the old Victorian portal, where I'm confronted by signs that invite me to visit Ali's Trade and Discount Carpet and Flooring, Factory Direct Bathrooms and Kitchens and Budget Busters Lighting Emporium. I stroll through the mill yard until I can get a better view of the old building, carved up, dissected for use as modern industrial units now. Further down the yard and over to the left is a low wall. Over the wall is an embankment. At the bottom of the embankment is a railway line. Across the line at the other embankment is a siding. Twenty-five years ago the siding would have been full of wagons waiting to be loaded with fragmentised scrap that came off a moving belt from the scrapyard. The laden wagons would make their daily runs down to British Steel Cooperation furnaces in Sheffield and Rotherham; loud, noisy, smelly industrious times. My eyes follow the line, up the embankment, over the way to where my life ended. The theatre to where the overture of lost liberty was played. I can't curse it now because it's not there; gone like it never even existed; gone as fast as the wounded and ailing British manufacturing base was asset stripped and put out of its misery. Decommissioned and taken apart, the scrap maker that was scrapped, the behemoth that ate itself. Foreign containers in neat, stacked rows now stand on the site in uniform silence. The building that housed the sub-station that powered the awesome machine that was the fragmentizer now looks to be a transport office for lorry drivers. The spot where my Henschell used to sit obscured by a metal box endorsing Fyffe's bananas. I turn away and look back to the old mill. I recall the earth shattering, bowel loosening explosions created by un-slashed, un-drained petrol tanks of scrap vehicles as they went through the fragmentiser and the old building in front of me losing half the glass in its windows as a result. I still hear the noises, I still sense the smells; I took them with me into my nightmares. Now, I'm back; I'm actually here – no noise, no smells; no history, no evidence. Only a surreal notion of the ultimate mind fuck, bookended by the old Mill and the gasometer, witnesses to the truth but unable to tell their secrets. I guess this is how an Auschwitz victim must feel being confronted by a holocaust denier. My insides feel like they've been scoured hollow and the oft beleaguered and tortured part of my brain, the part that tries to deal with reason and rationale has gone scurrying away and locked itself shut in the back of my head.

I try Caroline's mobile for the third time, it goes straight to voice mail; she must be in court.

The journey home is public transport slow. Apart from that I don't recall any part of it, and I spend the time in a vacuum. Back at Jeanie's the house is empty and quiet. I kick off my shoes, slouch on the couch and tune in to teletext. In the two-ten at Kempton, Total Recall romped home at fourteen-to-one. I can't stop thinking about Albert Novac. What were the odds? I try and remember how many lockers there were in the changing rooms at Sutherlands scrapyard – probably fourteen.

Twenty

THE MAITRE D' looks down at me like I'm some piece of shit Caroline has dragged in on her shoe. He gives her a polite smile that he manages to tinge with patronisation as he catches her coat that elegantly, effortlessly slips from her shoulders. He makes a point of giving me a wide berth as he heads for wherever it is they put them. I'm glad I didn't bring a coat; the sour faced fucker would probably have taken it in the back and trampled on it. All this was my idea and now I'm beginning to regret it. Only my second date with Caroline and already it looks like turning into another bloody disaster. I insisted she choose the restaurant, and of course with Caroline being who and what she is, we end up at some place whose name I can't even pronounce.

I'm warm, overheating, and I tug at my shirt collar as we're led to our table where I'm convinced all eyes are on me and the hushed chatter pertains to my presence. I'm certain my perspiration stinks of prison. I don't want to be here; I don't fit in a place like this. Despite my Indian sojourn that managed to dispel a million inhibitions, I painfully remain socially inept in such an alien environment.

As soon as we're seated a waiter produces a wine list and I'm instantly petrified.

'Are you alright?' asks Caroline at seeing the look of abject terror on my face.

'No,' I whisper.

'What on earth is the matter?'

'I don't know – I don't feel right.'

'Why, what is it?'

'I don't know – Everything; this place, this suit. I don't suit suits; they make me irritable, uncomfortable.'

'Nonsense, you're not used to wearing one, that's all. You look great. Relax, you'll be fine.'

Caroline buries her head in the wine list while I look around nervously. Two waiters stand at the other end of the restaurant; they're looking over here, looking at me, whispering, sniggering, and all the while Digweed's whistle is rejecting me and me it. I thank God I ignored Jeanie's suggestion that I bought my own suit instead of borrowing Digweed's threads whenever I went on a date, and vow never to wear one ever again after tonight.

'Anything on there you fancy?' she asks breezily.

'Caroline, I can't even read it; it's all in bleedin' French.'

'That could have something to do with the fact that you're reading the French selection. How about the St. Estephe?'

I slam the menu shut. 'Whatever you say.' I try and act nonchalant but fail, having already scanned the prices.

The St. Estephe duly arrives; the waiter dribbles a mouthful into my glass.

'Go on then pal, don't be shy; top her up.'

'Perhaps sir would like to *taste* the wine first?'

'What for; It's got to be right at these prices, hasn't it?'

He gives me a look of contempt and snakes over to Caroline.

'Would Madam care to taste?'

He coats the bottom of her glass, straightens up and studies me with disdain while she sips and approves. *Philistine* – I catch the gist of his telepathic accusation. *Wanker* – I send back at him through the ether. *Wanker – wanker – wanker* – I continue to fire at his back as he creeps away from the table.

'Lighten up,' she demands in a loud whisper. 'I know the prices can be a bit scary in this place, but we can go Dutch, it's not a problem, really.'

'It's not the prices,' I lie through my teeth.

I know it's a long time ago but my last ever weekly wage wouldn't even have covered the cost of the Bordeaux.

'What is it then?' she asks, downing a few quid's worth in one sip.

What can I tell her? Can't she see the divide, the social chasm? I can't believe I had the bottle to ask her out again, and I can't believe she accepted, especially after last time. But she said yes without hesitation. She seemed genuinely thrilled that I'd asked, as thrilled as when I presented her with the cheap jet necklace that I purchased from Anjuna market, that she wears around her neck this evening, that she somehow manages to make appear expensive. In reality we're leagues away from each other; different worlds, and yet there's something that draws me to this woman despite the obvious incompatibility. The more I see of her the more I'm attracted, and I sense, I hope, that the feeling is mutual.

I shake my head. 'Nothing.' I gaze into her face and raise my glass to hers. 'You look lovely tonight – as always.'

'Thank you.' Her eyes sparkle at the compliment and our glasses chink.

Out of the corner of my eye and clutching two food menus I see the stern-faced maitre d' approach from a distance. He presents one to Caroline with unnecessary ceremony and hands me mine with what I detect to be a slight smirk.

I put on a brave face, stare at lines of foreign words while

Caroline makes her selection. I knew that hors-d'oeuvres was a kind of starter, and paté de foie gras involved some sort of cruelty to geese, but after that I was totally lost.

'What's this?' I ask cautiously, pointing to something on the menu as discreetly as possible.

'Ris de veau? – Sweetbreads.'

'Sweetbreads – aren't they pigs knackers?'

'No,' she laughs mockingly at my ignorance. 'They're not knackers, as you call them, and they don't come from a pig. It's a special gland taken from a cow or a calf. They're very nice.'

I curl my lip, decide to keep quiet and keep my head down. She casts an occasional glance from over the top of her menu and can see in my misery I'm struggling. Eventually she puts it down, sighs and tilts her head to one side; the ultimate show of pity.

'Look, do you want to get out of here?'

'What? – No, I'll be fine, honestly...'

'Waiter...' Her command attracts instant attention. '...Could you put the cork back in this wine to take away with us? We're not staying to eat, I'm afraid. I'm not feeling too well.'

Smooth. I watch the head dude make guppy shapes with his mouth. He takes a while to compose himself.

'As madam wishes,' he finally manages with a huffing restraint as Caroline grins broadly at me over the table. God I'm beginning to love this woman.

I sit in the back of the taxi and study my contrary date as she opens her compact and applies fresh lippy in the shadowy sub-light. She purses and pouts, and I watch in silent fascination as the flash of passing street lights catches the shiny gloss of her ebony hair. She drops her stuff into her bag, closes the catch with a snap and turns to me, pulls that face, the face that melts... 'Jack, you'll have to forgive me again; I didn't think – as usual.'

'I don't know what you mean.'

'That's the trouble with being a lawyer, you see, we tend to be thinking all the time and then at times we forget to think at all.'

'I still don't know what you mean.'

'Dragging you along to that place, trying to seduce you on our first date; it's all very selfish of me and I'm terribly sorry. You must think I'm an awful person.'

'I was just a bit out of my comfort zone, that's all...' I fight with the cork on the St. Estephe. '...And actually, I think you're a wonderful person.' The cork relents with a dull thoop. I put bottle to mouth and take a long swig. I offer her a go; she smiles; I smile. She takes the bottle and tilts back her head revealing her neck that tempts me, Christopher Lee style. I watch her knock it back like some seasoned old wino. She'll do for me. 'Fancy a curry...?'

'...An ambiguous extract from a suicide note and a statement from a dying man in the early stages of dementia isn't enough to go to the police with. You must realise that Jack, even though it all makes plausible sense, explains everything perfectly to you and me, and is the absolute truth.'

The lawyer tells it how it is. I tear a strip off my roti and dip it, frustrated, into my bhuna.

'But it's the ring and finger that got me sent down; it's what they used against me and it was all bollocks.'

'What we've discovered explains an odd, unfortunate and circumstantial anomaly that The Crown conveniently used to secure a conviction. The information we now have remains useless until we gather firm evidence as to who actually carried out the murder. As your file officially remains closed, to go to the police at this stage would certainly get us both into trouble.'

'So, where do we go from here?'

'We've already established that the killer, or an accomplice, if there was more than one person involved, entered the yard in that five hour period up to the discovery. It had to be a regular; someone who had knowledge of the scrapyard and the effects a machine like a fragmentizer would have on any evidence...' She puts her napkin to her perfect mouth to brush away something imaginary. Perfect, precise, and then she adds a frown. '...What I can't understand is how you fit into all this. What we now know about the ringed finger means that no one was trying to fit you up, but you knew Lauren Feeney intimately and she ends up dead at your place of work...'

I chew on my bhuna and shrug my shoulders. 'Coincidence?'

'Bizarrely, it's beginning to look that way. You definitely had no acquaintances in the scrap game in or out of work?'

'No, and neither did Lauren to my knowledge. Ronkers, tatters and merchants weren't our kind of people. I came to work, did my job and went home again.'

'Even if it was someone either of you knew, why would they risk the chance of bumping into you on the day, knowing where you worked? It doesn't make sense; it simply has to be coincidence. I'm not entirely ruling out whoever did this didn't know you, but they more than certainly didn't know you worked at Sutherlands.'

'So, how do we go about finding the punters who weighed in that morning?'

Caroline blankets a piece of chicken in her naan and hesitates. 'This is where we hit a brick wall,' she says despairingly. She puts down her food and looks across the table at me. For the first time I see defeat in her eyes. 'The finger and ring conveniently wrapped things up for the police. They never checked or recorded the weighbridge dockets from that day. Sutherlands went out of business in two-thousand. No records were kept. There's no way of tracing who came into the yard and weighed in that morning.'

I wrack my memory; back to a period I'd spent desperately trying not to remember. From the ashes of time, hazy recollections marinated and hampered with a drug and booze soaked aftermath of weekend excess; fuzzy fractured images of a scrapyard bustling busy with noise and industry; merchants, dismantlers, Dennis the foreman locked in square-up confrontation with wide boy pikeys and ronkers. Two-hundred customers a day back then, and out of half of those, at least one who was responsible for me spending half of my life behind bars, secretly harbouring that knowledge, quietly blessing a quirk of luck and circumstance; one in an anonymous legion who's certain, now, after all this time that the secret will go with them to their grave.

'I don't know where we go from here Jack, I really don't.' Caroline stares at her plate, suddenly losing interest in her meal. 'I know this is scant consolation, but DNA testing would probably have absolved you if it had been around at the time. Similarly, if whoever did it had any previous, the databases we have now may have picked them up.' She looks up at me through long, dark lashes; a look of sympathy, but tinged with guilt. I know she's explored every avenue, left no stone unturned. She thinks she's failed me and now all she can come up with is *if onlys*. I send her the same look back. She's got nothing to feel guilty about. I know I'll never find the words to express how grateful I am for all she's done; all the unpaid hours of ploughing through my old file trying to find a scrap of something. Deep down, I suppose I already knew I'd be looking for a minor miracle. Like the bad luck and circumstance that got me sent down, I'd need circumstance and good luck to clear my name.

I don't know what makes me think of Kerin at that precise moment, but a clear image of the smiling, sari swathed siren pops into my head and a floaty, mantra type version of the old chestnut phrase *patience is a virtue* plays around my consciousness. I dismiss them gently, and at the same time, probably for the first time ever, the untamed, unsaddled colt that is my frustration gives up the fight, ceases to buck, slows from a canter to a trot, to a controlled walk, and I lead it in total submission around the corral inside my head. I take a good swallow of my Kingfisher; it doesn't taste the same as Goan Kingfisher.

'Why are you smiling?' she asks, curiously confused.

I could tell her it's because I'm slowly exorcising demons, dealing with my lot; starting at last to live one day at a time, getting on with the rest of my life. Or I could tell her about something that hasn't really happened to me before, least not like this. Something that since my return from India has grown and started to open out like the lotus flower Kerin spoke about. I could tell her that I thought I was falling in love – but I don't.

'No reason,' I continue to beam.

Twenty One

I NEVER THOUGHT anything would occupy my thoughts more than the quest to clear my name, but lately something has. I can't deny feeling a little guilty about it, but at the same time the distraction it has managed to create, despite playing with my fragile and oft frayed emotions, comes as a welcome relief.

I can't get Caroline out of my head. I never thought as much or felt about anyone like this when I was younger, Lauren Feeney or Liz included. It's a scary feeling, one that knots you up inside, and right now I haven't got a clue what to do about it.

In my mind I relive our last date, and, as in the bedroom scene a few months back, I continually change the end of the evening, hit the auto reverse button and play it all out like it should have been.

When the taxi pulled up outside her apartment I was dying for her to ask me in for a coffee or a night cap or something, just so I could show her how my Indian sojourn had left me better equipped to cope with intimate social situations and mind fucks – but she didn't. I wanted her to lean over and plant me a kiss with those meltdown lips so I could respond in a way that showed her how I was beginning to really feel about her – but she didn't. All I got was a quick peck on the cheek, the incendiary smile and a *'thanks for an interesting evening,'* to send me home walled up and hollowed out with. It's my entire fault. I haven't learned how to process thoughts that have feeling attached into words yet. And, now that I don't want her to, Caroline, with tons of misplaced guilt, has brought professional detachment into the relationship.

Out of all the human emotions I've experienced in my life, and I've hit the extremes of most, jealousy has never been one of them. I suppose the absence of any green-eyed monster in my psyche frustrated no one more than Lauren, who, in her most flirtatious mode would try and use the thing to tame or destroy the men in her life. The fact that her little mind games had no effect on me when we were together probably meant that our eighteen month relationship petered out with little more than a whimper rather than the heart wrenching drama she favoured. But over these past few weeks I'm pretty sure I've begun to get a taste of the phenomenon, as at this very moment, the absence of contact with Caroline since our ill-fated date in the restaurant is beginning to gnaw away at me. I haven't heard from her for nearly three weeks now and I'm beginning to think that she's come to her senses. Having a relationship with someone like me, business or otherwise was always going to be a non-starter. She tried to play out her schoolgirl fantasy and it failed; didn't live up to expectations. A silver haired, uneducated ex-con and a high- flying sophisticated lawyer were never going to hit it off in the compatibility stakes, who were we both kidding? I let myself get carried away with her easy and eager seduction, her insistence and reassurance that I was worthy of her attentions. It was always doomed to failure, and deep down I must have realised that, but the old ego being what it was, and I suppose still is, allowed itself to be stroked, and, like the old fool that I've become, I have let it all grow into an infatuation that has somehow nurtured this fucking jealousy thing. I've called her at work without ever thinking what I'm actually ringing for but she's always been out of the office or in court. I've tried to get her on her mobile but it diverts to voice mail. I don't leave messages, I don't want to sound desperate although desperate is how I feel and I hate myself for it. I've even begun to picture scenarios where some handsome, Armani suited professional colleague is wining and dining her in the restaurant whose name I can't pronounce, swapping choices in fluent French, flexing their combined knowledge over the wine list, making all the right choices. I imagine them in the bedroom, Mr. Adonis undressing to display a body sun kissed from a winter Caribbean break, honed to perfection under the guidance of a personal trainer; confident, cocksure – fucking cocksure? How the hell is it possible to hate a figment of your imagination so much? *Ah,* responds Mr. Amateur trick cyclist inside my head, *the person you actually hate is you.* Okay, I think I've already sussed that, I find my subconscious self-responding sarcastically. Tell me this then, smart arse, why am I beginning to hate a guy I only met half an hour ago and who has nothing to do with the woman who now occupies my thoughts daily? The Jung-Freud part of me disappears with a pop and I stare hard at the guy in question, not sure what particular shade of green I'm displaying at the moment.

Fergus plays a left-handed translucent gold Ernie Ball Music Man Stingray with a matt black scratch plate, and he plays it in that cool, detached, disinterested, laid-back manner that is unique to all self-respecting bass players. In fact he looks so detached, bored even, as to make me think his mind is somewhere else, probably on the upcoming European tour with Tony T.S. McPhee. Nevertheless, the guys sound awesome, incredibly tight, and their version of T. Bone Walker's Mean Old World is having that goose-bump tingly, hair prickling effect on me. Jed the vocalist cum harp player strikes an imposing figure, reminding me of a greying version of the late, great Bob 'The Bear' Hite from Canned Heat. And the boys were right, his voice is rangy, raw and powerful and his harp playing soul-twistingly divine. He fits the band perfectly, and in the years I've been away; looks to have made Blizzard his own. Billy is Billy. William Marshall, the devil's messenger; in the background stooped over his Les Paul wrenching all manner of manna from his old Gibson; physically unrecognisable from the guy I knew but musically the guitar God I've always known. I love the gnarly old fucker. Digweed: Mr. Reliable, deceptively holding it all together in that animated, pretend sloppy way of his, pulling faces at me as I sit and toe-tap, knowing, having laid the bait, I'd take it up like some dumb animal to become a prisoner of the blues once again. Then there's the new boy. Fergus is a stone-faced picture of proficiency. He plays the bass like it's a job, which to him, is probably all it is. He plays it left-handed, like me, and there any similarity between us ends. He's a journeyman, a wandering minstrel of a mercenary, playing for the highest bidder or some tread-water convenience residency until the next attractive gig comes along. It's patently obvious he doesn't fit into this line up. Like a vegan at a butchers' convention, he doesn't belong. And he's only thirty-two, *nowt but a bairn,* as they would say around these parts. I didn't come down here with the intention of being disingenuous, I really didn't, I mean sure the guy can play, and I suppose he's doing all that's been asked of him, but play like you mean it boy else get off the goddam' stage.

No one can remember exactly how many bass players they've had over the years; at least six or seven Digweed speculates vaguely. Billy concurs with a disinterested shrug, like they've had some sticking plaster over the slot all this time, just waiting for the time when I would come and reclaim my rightful place, slightly forward of the riser, stage right – always. Well, thanks to two Dutch men, a Lincolnshire pig farmer's daughter and an unscheduled, improvised semi-acoustic spot at Venta's, Shaky Jake Smith is back to do just that. And right on cue, as if to emphasize the fact, Billy segues into Leaving this Town, and Jed lurches into the mike to growl out the words.

'Feel free,' Fergus casually nods over in the direction of his smart looking axe, with a smile, as he disappears outside for a fag break, and I immediately feel a proper dick for my irrational show of jealousy.

'Yeah, cheers,' I respond with lazy laconism, while inside I react with a surging mix of nerves, excitement and fear that want to scramble around in my gut. Desperate to stay cool I nonchalantly glance at the rest of the band waiting for the official nod, but they're having a breather. Jed is tapping spit out of his harps. Billy is knelt over his pedals, making adjustments, and Digweed has his bumpers and socks off and is sat at his stool busy picking at his stinky feet. Come on you bastards; put me out of my misery.

After I got back from India, and when the house was quiet, I brought the old Fender out of hibernation and secretly started to practise scales. I even bought her a new set of strings, D'addario flat wound chromes. I didn't bring it with me tonight; didn't want to appear too keen or pushy; told Digweed I'd be content to just sit in and listen for now. With a touch of irritability in his voice he warned me I couldn't just keep thinking about it for much longer. They were playing the Colne Rhythm & Blues festival in a few months and needed to get up to scratch. They were even including some of the old favourites in the set list just to make it feel like old times, and if I didn't pull my finger out sharpish and make a commitment they would have to think about auditioning.

Young Ben was right, you're never too old for the blues; shame on me for thinking such a thing. And let's face it, apart from a woman who's becoming unattainable, I've nothing else in my life, and unless you count my estranged, elusive daughter, never have had, never will have. Even some of the best old delta based black boys came back to their muse after a long enforced sabbatical in the state penitentiary. Why should I be any different? Plus I need to start paying my way in all fairness to Jeanie, and by all accounts the money the guys earn from gigging these days isn't too bad. Digweed offered me a job driving a forklift at his place. Says that's how he started out and now he's a shipping manager. I passed on that one; any kind of work sounds like too hard work to me. I don't need no flash German motor. If bass and benefits get me by I'll be happy with that.

Billy has a nice little set up here, three sizeable rehearsal rooms all his own that he rents out to bands, all the gear they need in-house; a far cry from the old chapel cum scout hut. He even has plans for a full-blown studio with recording facilities. I'm not too sure what Jed does for a living, but the guy certainly isn't starving.

All in all, I like what I see; I love what I hear. It's like I've come out of a coma and the hazy mist is slowly lifting to reveal what I've been missing. I've come back to where I belong. The prodigal son returns and is itching to go.

I'm not sure if the bastards have been tormenting me on purpose but after what seems like an eternity of them fucking about I finally get the nod. I get up as nonchalantly as I can manage and strap on the Stingray with my heart thumping

208

against my chest.

'Dust My Broom – in D,' adds Digweed with a nod and a wink in my direction just in case I've forgotten. 'One, two, – one, two, three, four...'

Once again, Jed growls into the mike. I fall into the rhythm as easy as I'd never been away. Three Cheshire cats grin in my direction, and I feel taproots emerge from my heels and plant out – JD Smith has come home.

Twenty Two

PATTERSON, MY ANDROGYNOUS looking spachelor probation officer seems pretty pleased with herself today, probably spent last evening stroking her pussy. She's ticking boxes for fun, her pen skipping across the pages with gay abandon. I can't be bothered being arsey with her right now, so I allow myself to cooperate, feed her compliant answers to inane questions, ease her workload, give her a steady day – gets her out of the house quicker. I guess she's unusually giddy because the shrink assigned by NACRO to assess my resettlement progress signed me off the other day. I made it easy for him to tick the boxes as well; can't have hindered I don't suppose. It'll be nice to be shut of them all one day, but at least still having the state under my skin helps jolt my resolve, especially since the trail went cold.

'Doctor Lomas seemed very pleased with your progress,' says Patterson as she ticks away.

'Yeah, he did, didn't he?'

He'd asked me if I still had the nightmares. I told him that I didn't. "Good to see the Diazepam and Imipramine doing their job," he'd said smugly, peering over his bifocals. I'd smiled and given him the thumbs up, not having the heart to tell him that all the Benzos had got flushed down the lav. When his pager buzzed and he excused himself from our session for a few moments, I wandered round the other side of the desk and decided to have a nosey. I flicked open the manila file and there, right in front of me, was my release report. I daren't risk reading the whole thing; my eyes flicked across the summary.

...As often in crimes of passion, or cases where the murder is the result of the perpetrator flying into a jealous rage having been humiliated or belittled by the victim, the resulting shock and instant remorse is sometimes masked by total denial, especially where the subject is normally placid and non-violent in nature. Coming to terms with their actions can be a long, drawn out process, where, often during therapy, answers to certain questions or phrases used reveal a hidden desire to release the burden without actually admitting guilt.

Certain subjects remain IDOM for the duration of sentence and beyond. Such case studies show a tendency towards, nightmares, depression, schizophrenia and attempted suicide.

Although these conditions have manifested in varying degrees at some time or other during his time in Parkhurst and Wakefield he has responded well to all treatments and prescribed medication (listed on page 3) Subject reports no instances of night sweats/bad dreams in over two months.

In conclusion, whilst remaining IDOM, I can detect no sign of duality in persona. During counselling the subject has demonstrated satisfactorily that he is of no danger to himself or the wider general public and I hereby sign him off this current programme.

Dr. J.S. Lomas MD, MB, MRCPsych.

Of all the shrinks I've seen over the years, and there have been a few, I don't think there has been one who, deep down, didn't harbour some seed of doubt over my guilt, and this Lomas guy has been no exception. You can see it in their faces. Usually after about two weeks of so-called therapy it starts. They begin to avert their attentions when confronted with a stare of bitterness and injustice but where battered and bruised integrity still manages to show through. Heads down, not as much eye contact, the scribbling becomes more intense, questions from the script less measured. Ninety minute sessions become fifteen if you're lucky. But questioning the judgement of twelve men and women good and true isn't their brief. Their task is to get people like me, In Denial of Murder, to fess up and clear the system quicker, save the taxpayer a few bob. The state hates people like me.

Lomas returned to his desk, spoke about nothing for five minutes, or if it was something, I wasn't listening, shuffled some papers, stood up and shook my hand in a limp and clammy manner. Inside, I shivered while he smiled his insincere smile and wished me luck, no doubt pleased at having another statistic off his books and some more brownie points from the Home Office.

Patterson looks as if she's about to make a statement, an announcement, a revelation. Maybe she's coming out or something, I don't know. She flicks pages back and forth, clears her throat a couple of times like she's ready to cough up a fur ball, then she hits me with it.

'Jack, with regard to your continuing stance on the IDOM issue...' *here we go* '...Considering you've made such good progress...' *what did I tell you?* '...Well, I mean, it seems such a pity that after all you've been through, you're going to have this life licence around your neck for some time to come, probably for the rest of your days, all for the sake of a signature on your behalf. You have the opportunity to wipe the slate clean; start afresh, forget the past...' *they never give up; bless 'em.* I smile at her; a smile with all the bitterness and frustration removed. Inside, I'm chuffed to bits that I've mastered it at last, after all this time – my smile gets wider.

'Shame on you Ms. Patterson,' I remonstrate, trying to keep the mocking tone to a minimum. I can't believe she still doesn't get it. She raises her eyebrows and shakes her head – she never will.

'Well, Jack,' she says, gathering up my weighty file, 'I think you'd better start calling me Bryony from now on, seeing as our little soirées are set to become regular for the foreseeable future...' *fucking Bryony? Fuck me, well I never.* '...Thanks for your time,' she says with a frustrated sigh.

Like the perfect gentleman, I get up and show her the door. 'Don't mention it; I'm used to it – giving up my time, that is.' I continue to smile.

'See you next month,' she says with assured resignation, and walks off down the path.

'Don't bank on it, Bri.'

She half turns and gives me an odd kind of look. My smile remains fixed.

'Oh – do you know something I don't?' she asks curiously.

'Watch this space,' I reply with a wink, and close the door.

Readjustments are hard, of course they are; didn't expect otherwise, but I was never going to take a lead from some over qualified shrink with less than a perfect grip on the real world, following the dictum of the state, ready to dispel chemical suppressant with a cavalier stroke of a pen, or be dictated to like some remedial class infant by a glorified social worker who's unsure of their own sexuality.

The sanctuary of solitude: that fine line between sheltered haven and loneliness, where thoughts, memories, feelings and emotions are harboured, cherished, embellished; kept to dwell on because there are no outlets for them to grow or dissipate, form into importance or fade into trivia. Where the warping of time conspires to keep things that normally would be forgotten fresh. Incarceration contradicts theory and senses become heightened, not dulled; a smell for a time and place of instant recall; a piece of music to invoke the moment long ago like it happened yesterday. To the normal mind, a hazy whiff of retrospect; a half curious, disinterested archaizing nod to the past. For me, not just a wistful memory of an earlier time, not even some sentimental yearning. Yesterday is still my today, time compressed - it's all I have.

Twenty Three

WE'RE TRAVELLING THROUGH Bronte country, rolling over the hills from Yorkshire into Lancashire in a laden Iveco that doesn't sound too healthy. Billy's at the wheel with a frown on his face, Digweed's leant on my shoulder snoring away to himself. Jed's sprawled out in the back giving us a rendition of John Lee Hooker's Groundhog Blues on his harp. And I'm trying hard not to think of three things. One is Caroline; two is a trail that has gone cold, and the other is our pending gig at The Colne Rhythm & Blues fest.

It's not such a smooth start to my comeback weekend. We limp into Colne on a wing and a prayer with one very sick motor. After we land, Billy sticks his head under the bonnet. The layman diagnosis is knackered petrol pump. He makes a phone call, and then announces that part and mechanic can't be with us till tomorrow, which isn't such a great problem as we're here for two nights anyway.

Blizzard has played The Great British R&B festival in Colne twice before but only in the roadhouse venues, which to you and me are the town's pubs. This time the guys have been invited to play The British stage, certainly a step up.

We unload our gear to a designated area backstage, and then wander off to the international stage to sample a few pints and some of the acts that include Albert Lee, Maggie Bell, Zoot Money, Steve Cropper, Nine Below Zero and Walter

Trout.

Jed downs pints like there's no tomorrow. 'Just lubricating the old voice box,' he grins with the residue clinging to his beard, then raises a hairy eyebrow when I go onto shandies after a couple of rounds after mistaking my pre-concert jitters for diligence and professionalism.

Because the schedules are so tight, we don't get to do a sound check. It's a case of go on, do your stuff and get off again, and anyway on the subject of sound checks: *"You're better off reading a book or having a shit,"* according to the late, great Lee Brilleaux. Our allocated slot is nine till ten, and that's to include a couple of encores if requested. As the time nears I make a few unscheduled visits to the bog, and then find a quiet corner in which to do some serious breathing. Jed is stood in the wings with a bottle in his hand, his giant frame pumped up with adrenalin and alcohol, head shaking and feet tapping to the band that precedes us; no fear at all. Digweed sits idly twiddling his sticks between his fingers, nonchalantly chewing gum, stretching and snapping it occasionally, while Billy calmly chats away to a bunch of musicians who played an earlier set. My own seasoned air of detachment went west when I lost my liberty, now I feel an absolute beginner, like I have to start and learn my craft all over again. I know that a few months ago I could never have dreamt of being where I am now, but nerves aren't allowing me to dwell on that sort of progress. Funny really, along with the jealousy thing, stage fright was never a phenomenon I used to suffer from, but like all departments of my new life, I'm having to look at things from a different perspective. Lomas said there was no evidence of dual personality; I'm sure he's right about the schizophrenic slant, but there certainly is, or has been, two Jack Smiths. One has slowly morphed into the other and it's only recently I've started to become aware of the bloke I now am. Whenever I used to play the bass in public I was only ever doing it for myself, that and the love of the music, when did I ever become aware of an audience? When was I ever concerned about how we were received or if I was playing all the right notes in the correct order?

The band onstage finishes their set and the in-house roadies go into action. Like techies the world over, this small army of hairy dudes race back and forth, going about their business with chaotic efficiency. The sudden flurry of activity puts me on cue for another visit to the bog that, thankfully, a few concentrated deep breaths manages to quell. And I silently pray for re-election to the detachment club; that exclusive establishment where the aloof and the cool come together, the place I used to frequent without even knowing it.

Twenty minutes goes fuck-knows-where and I hear the MC garble into the microphone. It's just a blur of words until: '...*ladies and gentlemen – for the first time on the British stage – please give a warm welcome to – BLIZZARD...!*'

Jed fires me a manic, almost demonic grin, his spittle-flecked ivories, gritted, determined, flashing beyond the tangled forest of his beard; eyes blazing wild. My heart responds machine gun fashion up against my ribcage, screaming to be let out.

Taking up the rear, I follow the guys out into no-man's-land. I don't really hear the polite welcome from the five-hundred plus crowd as Digweed turns to me, placing his hand and his sticks on my frozen shoulder.

'Just like old times eh?' he winks and cracks his gum before bounding away up the riser. *Boom-boom!* He tests his pedals against the bass drum, paradiddles the snare and rakes a flurry across the tom-toms like he means business. It serves as a wake-up call. I try and work some saliva around my Gobi desert gob while I plug in and watch Billy make final adjustments to his pedals and switches. Jed, absolutely full of it and raring to go, adjusts his mike and casts glances around his band, making sure everyone's set.

'Alrate?' he greets the audience. 'We're from Marsden, just over yon' hill...' He jerks his thumb in the general direction. '...And we're gonna play you some rockin' blues – two, three, four...'

I never analysed my playing, my style or my prowess with my chosen instrument. In the seven years Digweed, Billy and I were together the sound we created formed and developed all on its own, naturally. The sum of the three parts came together as a whole organically, and apart from informing each other of what key we were in we never discussed how each of us should be playing a particular piece. And although we were a rhythm and blues outfit, we belted out the standards in what we liked to think was our own brand of the tried, tested, and safe old formula. If you had to pin a badge on us, just for comparison, I suppose the early Magic Band style was the closest to our take on the genre, even more so now that we have Jed at the helm with his contradictory, soulful, gravel-filled vocals.

My own mentor wasn't really a blues man. James Jamerson belonged to Motown; one of the founder members of the legendary Funk Brothers who played on all of the early Motor City hits. But if I ever thought of emulating anybody it would be him and his smooth rolling, understated finger style that held the rhythm section together like super glue.

I survive the first twelve bars of our opener and as the butterflies flutter away and my guts stop squirming, I realise it's just like riding a bike; you never really forget. Why I ever thought the real thing should be any different from rehearsals,

I'll never know, even though it is, it has to be. I'm playing in front of a live audience who have paid money to come and see me perform and only now do I really start to appreciate how much that means.

Jed, pulses his giant frame with surprising agility to the beat as we belt out a pacey, rambling version of Look on Yonder's Wall. Semi-improvised harmonica and guitar solos stretch the overture to over ten minutes long, way too long for a blues standard, but as we finally wind it up we're met with a roar and thunderous applause. The reaction makes us all smile broadly; even Billy lets his face slip. Jed shakes beads of sweat from his already matted brow and under his face-fuzz crinkles a look of encouragement in my direction – welcome back Jack.

Our set comprises four blues standards and four of Jed's own penned compositions that go down well with the crowd. We leave the stage with unified stamping of feet, cheers and triumphant whistles ringing in our ears.

I stand in the wings, wipe myself down with a towel and savour the moment like I've never done before. I am getting to like adulation. All of a sudden I get a shove from behind; Digweed ushering me back out.

'You've got five minutes,' some guy from promotions shouts a warning in the background.

'Yeah, sure,' laughs Jed bounding to the front of the stage and throwing his sweaty towel into the pumped up crowd.

We play Willie Dixon's I'm Ready, and then we segue into our old jam rehearsal favourite, Rattlesnake Shake. This is Billy's party piece and when Jed ad-libs, '*I know this guy, his name is Billy, and he don't care when he ain't got no filly – he does the shake – yeah the rattlesnake shake – yeah Bill he does the shake- you watch him jerk away all his blues...*' for the next eight minutes Billy performs musical masturbation on his old

Les Paul. The audience are in raptures, they want him to come on their collective faces and he obliges with an ejaculatory crescendo of guitar work the great maestro Pete Green himself would have been proud of.

We overshoot our set by a good ten minutes, much to the chagrin of the promoter and the final band of the evening who give us the evil eye as we saunter off backstage with an air of a job well done.

'Follow that,' says Jed immodestly to anyone within earshot. 'Where's the bar?'

In the morning I feel absolutely drained and a little hung over. In addition to the ale, years ago I'd also have a regular cocktail of pharmaceuticals swilling around inside me almost on a nightly basis - days of immortality. Christ knows how I used to do it.

The evening had gone by in a blur, that in itself was nothing new, but this time the blur was created by nothing more sinister than nerves, adrenalin and the taste of a past life revisited. And I guess we'd been good judging by the after-show plaudits, backslaps and free drinks that came our way.

'Of course we were good,' says Jed in that immodest manner of his, 'and that lot that followed us knew we were good, too,' he wheezes with a chesty chuckle. Big in stature, big in ego, this huge bear of a man is the perfect antidote to our laid back almost horizontal approach to things, because apart from the ravages of time, Billy and Digweed don't seem to have changed all that much; still taking life as it comes, everything in a slow-paced stride, playing for the love of it without any interest in glory or recognition. Perhaps if Jed had been around in the early days things might have been different, dragging the rest of them towards fame and fortune in his self-assured *we are the dog's bollocks* wake. I watch him neck a bottle of Heineken with his bacon and eggs and quickly dismiss that notion. Down that particular route the name Blizzard would have undoubtedly entered the rock and roll hall of infamy and its members been added to the scroll of casualties for sure.

We breakfast at lunchtime then head out to re-load the van ready for our matinee slot at The Admiral Lord Rodney, a local pub renowned for good live music, lively atmosphere and much more in keeping as the type of venue we were used to.

Apparently the guy fixing the van used to do a spot of roadying for the band, and as I hump the last of our gear on board and my head continues to pound I reflect that his services wouldn't have gone amiss this weekend. I wander round the front to see how the repair is going.

'Is it the petrol pump then?' I enquire.

'I've told you before,' says Billy emerging from under the bonnet, 'I may not always be right, but I'm never wrong – course it's the petrol pump.'

'So how much is that going to cost us; did we play for nowt last night?'

'Ere, our mate Wiggy always does us a good deal, don't you pal?' he says slapping the crouched-over grease monkey on the back. 'You remember Wiggy, don't you Jack? Purveyor of cheap transport and part time roadie?'

The oily mechanic looks up from the bowels of the stricken Iveco and performs a double take before jumping up and smacking his head on the underside of the raised bonnet, like he'd just gotten a jolt off the battery or something. He steps back in apparent shock, nervously wiping his hands on an old rag.

'No...' I say slowly, '...Can't say we've met.'

'You alright mate?' laughs Billy, 'You look like you've just seen a ghost.'

The guy stares at me wide eyed like I'm the devil incarnate. 'What...? No, no...' he stutters, '...Definitely not had the pleasure.'

'Ah, you must have come on the scene after Jack went on his holidays.'

'Yeah, yeh – definitely... Any road, that's it,' he says backing away. 'You're up and running again.'

'Great stuff,' says Billy. 'How much do we owe you, Wiggy?'

'Oh, no worries,' he dismisses with a wave of the hand. 'I'll sort it out with you later.'

'Please yourself. Are you staying for this afternoon's gig? You could help us shift the gear, you know, keep your hand in like the old days.'

'Nah, sorry mate, got to pick a couple of scrappers up this aft'.'

He continues to back away as if Billy and me are a couple of puff adders waiting to strike.

'Okay, whatever, dude,' says Billy, breaking the awkward silence and looking slightly nonplussed. 'See you later.'

The guy combines a quick nod of the head with a final furtive glance around him before diving into his vehicle and driving off. We both stand and watch him leave. I take in the words WIGGY'S AUTO RECOVERY written in big bold, blue letters. I get one of those déjà vu moments, ever so briefly followed by a cold shiver, like someone had just walked over my grave.

'Strange fella,' I comment.

'Yeah,' says Billy. 'He's not usually like that.'

'Bloody hell, he didn't hang about, did he?' remarks Digweed, appearing between us. 'Has he fixed it?

'Yeah.'

'How much?'

'He didn't say; said he'd sort it out later.'

'That's not like that tight bugger.'

'I thought he'd have stayed and given us a hand – miserable sod,' adds Jed.

The shy mechanic-ex-roadie has me intrigued. The guy most definitely had the jitters and I'm certain it was my presence that freaked him out so. I'm pretty sure I'd never laid eyes on the geezer before now, but I wasn't convinced of his insistence likewise.

I'm nattered to hell by the time we get to The Admiral Lord Rodney, so I decide to be a pest and quiz Digweed further as he builds his kit on the tiny but intimate stage.

'So, how long have you known this Wiggy character then?' I ask cautiously while he spins a wing nut over his hi-hat.

'Ages,' he replies casually. 'Why?'

'Something about him back there,' I say shaking my head unsure.

'What?' he asks looking up.

'Dunno, can't put my finger on it.'

He shrugs at my failure to expound and gets on with his setting up.

'Don't you remember him, then?' he asks while pushing me out of the way to drag a tom-tom into position.

'No – no, I don't, and he says he doesn't remember me either, but I'm not so sure. He was definitely acting a bit odd.'

Digweed shrugs again. 'You don't come face to face with a lifer every day of the week. He probably felt a bit uncomfortable in your presence; not sure how to react.'

'But he insisted he didn't know me.'

'Oh, he knows you all right, or at least of you. Your name must have cropped up quite a bit, especially in the early days.

Anyway, I could have sworn you were still around when he started roadying for us.'

I shake my head. 'I don't ever remember us having a roadie.'

'Can't have been long after you got sent down, then. Do you remember us having that VW Transporter?'

'No, the old Trani was the only wreck I ever recall.'

'Well, if memory serves me well, the VW was the first vehicle we bought from him. He's supplied us with transport and maintenance ever since.'

'So, you've never thought him strange, then?'

'To be honest I've never really thought him anything.' Digweed positions the rest of his kit with experienced proficiency; double quick time, before sounding it out. He sees the puzzling and the pondering going on inside my head and props his sticks vertically on the snare to lean on like he always did. 'He used to be a regular in the Melbourne, started to follow us around when we did local gigs, helped us out with the gear once or twice and we ended up buying his beer for the night in return for a shift. Apart from a period when he disappeared off the scene he's been around here and there pretty much ever since, doesn't move gear for us any more though...' He performs a club-land roll and cymbal crash. '...Can't tell you any more than that.'

'Cheers.' I nod, and head off towards the bar before it gets heaving.

'Here, you're not thinking...' I hear Digweed shout after me, but I pretend not to as I mingle with the ever increasing throng. I imagine him lifting his sticks and doing his shrug.

Although last night on The British Stage was a gas and we went down a storm, this is the type of gig we prefer and are used to; packed, noisy and intimate, with all the punters so close you can smell the ale and sweat, if not the dope and fags these days. We're an English pub band playing down home, dirty R & B, and this is all we ever want or are likely to be.

We kick off with Roxette, the old Dr. Feelgood tune; a sure-fire way of setting the mood and breaking the ice, not that anyone needs thawing out here. We soon have the whole boozer rocking its collective socks off, especially when Jed performs his Lee Brilleaux harmonica break.

This place reminds me so much of the heady, post-punk Melbourne days of old, so much so I can actually taste the bittersweet past as if it were yesterday. I allow it to take hold, and because of my heightened awareness of all things preterit, it gushes at me, overwhelming like I'm about to drown.

I'll never be certain if it's the memory of those times that triggers what happens next, unconnected as they are – Or are they?

Twenty Four

"I KNEW WE should've auditioned," I just about remember hearing Billy say in the hazy background.

"Don't be so hard, you twat," said a sympathetic Jed. "We all fuck up occasionally."

"What, second number in? –It's twelve bar blues, hardly rocket science for a fucking bass player is it?"

I'd screwed up big style, just stopped playing a few bars into BB King's Rock Me Baby, not because, as Billy thinks, I'd forgotten the number; like he said, it's not rocket science. It was what became unlocked from the memory vault in that very instant: all revealing, Earth shattering. A moment words couldn't describe. It stopped me dead in my tracks. I froze solid. Like a gorgon's victim, I turned to fucking stone.

Elaine glowers at me from behind her desk, not such the normally chirpy, syrupy voiced receptionist this morning, and it's entirely due to my almost aggressive insistence on seeing Caroline. I'm not taking no for an answer and threaten to stay outside on the doorstep until she buzzes me in or until my solicitor leaves the building. I'm determined to see her one way or another, despite her full diary.

I sit and wait, putting on a poor show of trying to appear patient. In my head I relive the recent events that had my guts churning like ice cubes in a blender...

* * *

"You think it's *him*, don't you?" Digweed had calmly approached and asked after the messy gig, while in the background Billy the perfectionist took the gear out to the van, chuntering to himself.

I'd managed to struggle through the rest of the set but my mind hadn't been on the job, and my erratic playing had somewhat soured a performance that had started out so well. My head had spun and my legs jellied. I let Billy have his grump and gripe, I didn't give a stuff about the gig, my head was on an altogether different plane. I'd had a breakthrough and I'd scared myself giddy and sick at the development,

"It *is* him," I'd hissed back in a half whisper. "I'm sure of it."

"How can you be so certain?"

"Wiggy's Autos," I'd said. "Wiggy's Autos," I repeated just for the effect the words had on me: Frighteningly ominous and jigsaw snap-in clear. There, on the stage, it came out of nowhere and knocked me for six; that afternoon in the scrap-yard all those years ago, through the painful mist of time, the haze of incomprehensible confusion, that one pivotal part of my life came sharply into focus – a Lazarus moment.

In amongst the chemical comedown a few grey cells had thankfully survived the self-abuse and had managed to store away the scene until now: The crash and thunder of the fragmentizer in full flow, the clung-snap precision of a shear blade, the rattle and hum of Hi-macs and Poclains unloading and sorting scrap iron, Dennis the foreman locked in battle with a bunch of dead-eyed pikeys, and Wiggy - Wiggy's Autos sounding his horn, waiting impatiently in line to deposit his macabre payload; three semi-crushed cars held down with a Hi-hab, one of which no doubt contained the still as yet intact corpse of my former girlfriend.

"It's fucking him," I'd hissed, letting Digweed know in no uncertain terms.

* * *

Elaine looks at me from behind her desk with disdain. I glance down to see my left leg pumping up and down involuntary. I stop. I breathe. I crack my fingers. I crack my neck. The leg starts again. I must appear like a smack-head craving the next fix, but it's not heroin coursing through my veins; it's resolve, pure and simple. Twenty-six years and seven months ago I had my former life taken from me. In that time I've gone from a naive, optimistically misguided young dude who thought everything, every wrong would eventually be put right, to a cynical, emotionally raped, wrung out old man, and right now even the calm teachings of Kerin the wise witch can do nothing to temper the dogged compulsion within. Elaine can pull as many disapproving faces as she wants. Kiss my arse suck my socks. Right now this guy doesn't give a fuck.

Patience is a virtue – patience is a virtue... the old adage goes round and round my head mantra fashion until, at last, after a torturous wait, a buzzer sounds on the receptionist's desk.

'Miss Dupree will see you now,' she says with barely concealed venom in her voice. 'You've got five minutes,' she states, sounding like that miserable chuff of a promoter from Colne. I don't even give her the satisfaction of a response. I'm at the office door in a flash.

I relate my discovery at a hundred miles an hour, like an over-exited schoolboy, and when I don't get the reaction I expect I repeat it with even more overblown emphasis. Caroline retains her annoyingly calm, measured, professional detachment throughout while taking down shorthand notes. After five minutes I'm literally jumping out of my chair. I want reaction. I want action, any kind of action and I want it now. Caroline keeps casting surreptitious glances at her desktop clock as I continue to fail to stir any tangible replication to my revelations.

'Okay, Jack,' she says eventually. 'I think I've got enough there to make some enquiries with. I'll do some investigating into this Wiggy character and let you know what I come up with.'

I deflate like a farting balloon.

'What – is that it?' I sound off bitterly.

She cocks her head to one side and looks at me in the way that I used to find sexy and endearing; now it's just fucking annoying.

'Just what do you expect me to do, Jack, go charging around like a bull in a china shop making unfounded accusations? You of all people ought to know by now that things simply don't work like that.'

'But Caroline, it's *him*; this is our man.'

She sighs. 'We've had all this out before. Evidence, Jack, evidence. We will need to gather it in the proper manner and present it in the proper way. That may take time.'

I jump up from my seat, banging my fist on the desk in total frustration.

'He knows I'm out, Caroline. You should have seen the look on his face; the way he reacted when he realised it was me. If there's anything left after all this time that we could nail him with, don't you think he'd be getting shut of it like, right now? Time is something we don't have. We have to act now.'

She remains unfazed, gazing up at me impassively with those fucking eyes.

'If you still want me to represent you on this Jack, you've got to trust me. I appreciate that this is the best lead we've had and it all sounds promising, but to rush at it headlong may jeopardise the only chance we have at overturning your conviction.'

'I want to trust you Caroline, I really do, but look what happened the last time I put my trust in your family.'

I strike a blow to her heart. I regret it as soon as the words leave my frustrated lips, but it's too late. The look on her face leaves me feeling like shit. I feebly try and recover the situation.

'Look... I'm sorry... I...'

She starts shovelling papers hurriedly into her briefcase.

'I should have been somewhere else ten minutes ago,' she says. 'I'll be in touch as soon as I learn anything of relevance.'

I nod my head and silently, shamefully turn on my heels leaving behind a soup of emotions; some hers, but mostly mine.

I ride the bus back to Marsden. On the way I make a decision. I didn't mean to cast a slight on the Dupree family, that wasn't my intention at all. It's the system I can no longer trust, the procedures, the maxims, the rubrication, the whole stinking bureaucratic legal process that does fuck all to serve the truly innocent. I can't let this window of opportunity slip away. I'd top myself if I allowed that to happen. I simply can't afford to place my faith in others anymore. If JD Smith is to ever find justice, he will have to serve it himself.

Twenty Five

THE GRIMY BACK streets of Blackmoor appear sinister and foreboding at night; an area during the working day frequented by scrap men; shady dealers and tatters; black market economists of the type that used to frequent Sutherlands; scheming schemes, operating scams and executing dodgy deals; a spit in the palm and a cast iron calloused handshake. It's a place littered with storage units and lock-ups; dungeon-like half derelict constructions where you'd imagine local gangsters take their hapless victims to torture and extort or do away with. Lawless. No-go; where a sense of evil and the smell of back axles happily co-exist.

I make three passes of Ludlam Street, slow and measured; second gear in Jeanie's little Micra, killing the headlights and bringing it to a halt where the road is unlit and opposite the place I'm looking for. I turn off the engine and sit quietly for a while, checking out the scene. I squeeze a button on my Casio and the time illuminates green: one twenty-five am. I let another couple of minutes tick by, and then I step out of the car and scan both ends of the street; dark, quiet and empty. I close the door with the softest of clicks and venture across the road gripping my unlit torch. The place is half old mill, half reclaimed wasteland; a mixture of blackened Yorkshire stone and barbed wire topped metal fence. The large iron gates are heavy duty chained and double padlocked with a deterring, curling pattern of razor wire as their crowning glory. Without the aid of the torch I can just about make out the sign: WIGGY'S AUTOS-CAR DISMANTLERS -- AUTO SALVAGE & RECOVERY – TOP PRICES PAID FOR SCRAP VEHICLES – EST. 1967

I step back into the road and size up the task: difficult, but not impossible. The wire would be the challenge, but nothing a few double draped industrial standard tarpaulin sheets couldn't help render less lethal. I walk to the end of the stone wall where the perimeter becomes wire mesh. Through the fence half flattened scrap cars are piled vertically in haphazard rows. Parked outside a dark building and what I guess is an office cum garage are a recovery vehicle, the one I saw in Colne, and a flatbed wagon equipped with Hi-hab, no doubt an updated version of the one that carried the body of Lauren Feeney all those years ago. Both vehicles are sign-written in the now familiar bold blue lettering that sends me cold.

I take a quick glance around, still quiet, street still empty. I flick on the torch and send the beam towards the vehicles and the building. I suddenly freeze as the light captures two pair of fixed, luminous yellow eyes. Their owners, a couple of large, hairy German Shepherds' begin a slow, menacing snarl of intent before springing into action. Heavy metal chains scrape at speed along concrete and two sets of snapping jaws strain towards the light's source until the restraining links reach their limit, yanking them to a vicious halt. An incessant volley of canine displeasure pierces the quiescent night air. I quickly kill the light and sprint back across the road to the car, fumble the keys into the ignition and drive swiftly away in total darkness, switching on the lights only when I turn the corner and the insufferable audible threat of Wiggy's guard dogs fades into the ink black night.

* * *

A week or so after our unscheduled, somewhat tempestuous meeting I get a call from Caroline. Her tone is friendly but business like. She invites me over to hers on Saturday night, no offer of a meal or a veiled hint of sex. We have a gig that night and I refuse. I suggest the Sunday evening but she has a date. A wave of that new phenomenon green washes over me and drenches me into silence at the end of the line. She can cancel, she assures me after the tumbleweed rolls by. I tell her not to bother on my account, but she insists it's not a problem. We fix a time and I put down the phone, angry with myself for feeling the pangs of an infatuation I'd convinced myself had passed.

I make no effort. I turn up ultra-casual, just the right side of scruffy in jeans and open necked shirt and with a decent amount of salt and pepper growth on my face. But at least now I feel comfortable within my skin, no longer feeling the need to impress. Gigging again has helped me become a gnarly, veteran version of my old don't-give-a-shit self. And tonight I'll go in with an open ear but not necessarily an open mind. I'll listen to what she has to say, see what she's come up with, but any stalling tactics of the legal sort that might allow this cunt off the hook will only serve to strengthen my determination to do things my way.

A laptop peaks like a summit amidst a mountain of paperwork on her dining room table. Caroline sits behind it all. She's also casual, dressed in jeans and a gossamer light blouse, but her casual is chic and fresh. The musky scent of her perfume wafts over to me across the table, and she's still annoyingly gorgeous. Even more potentially distracting to the job in hand is the recently opened, strategically placed obligatory bottle of wine. She offers me a glass and I refuse, being determined that tonight, or any part of it, wasn't going to resemble a date.

Wiggy's Autos: Founded by Walter Wiggington in nineteen sixty-seven. Two sons: Robert and Brian. Walter divorces in nineteen seventy-two. Eldest son emigrates to Australia in seventy-seven. Walter dies of a heart attack in seventy-nine; remaining son, Brian inherits the family business aged twenty-six - never marries. Charged with two separate accounts of assault in nineteen seventy-eight, attempted rape in nineteen eighty-three. None of the cases gets anywhere near court. Nineteen eighty-nine: serves six months of an eighteen-month sentence in Armley for ringing and illegally exporting vehicles.

As always I'm mightily impressed by her thoroughness, but when I make enquiries about her investigative methods she simply states she has her sources and would never be at liberty to divulge those sources to anyone, not even me, which is fair enough when you consider the risks she must be taking with such matters. She gives me the complete low-down on Brian Wiggington, and I can tell she doesn't hold anything back despite knowing that the likelihood of imparting all this stuff is bound to set me off again. She remains the consummate professional; calm, measured, reading out the facts with all emotional judgement removed. She looks into my face with every new piece of information revealed. Caroline trusts me, and in each and every look she's asking for the trust to be reciprocated, but I still have questions.

'I don't get it,' I say, failing to hide my obvious frustration. 'I just don't get it. They had him three times for assault and attempted rape and yet they never even went to court?'

'It happens a lot. The system isn't too sympathetic towards the victim in these cases. They often back out at the last minute for fear of giving evidence, re-living the ordeal. In alleged rape cases the defence can be intimidating and often brutal. The procedures *are* beginning to change at last, but not quick enough and far too late for thousands of women.'

'I'd hate to have your job.'

She shrugs like it's a given.

'There's more,' she sighs. 'Between May nineteen seventy-seven and January nineteen eighty-three there were no less than thirty-four separate reported instances of sexual assault with varying degrees of seriousness in or around HD3, none of which ever made it to court through either lack of evidence, dropped charges because of fear and intimidation, or simply CPS refusal to proceed.

'I don't understand the significance.'

'The Melbourne? – The pub where your band once held residency? – Slap bang in the middle of HD3....'

Another ticked box, one more dropped penny. Caroline's expression indicates she hasn't finished yet.

'...Out of those thirty-odd instances we know that Brian Wiggington was positively identified at least four times.'

She waits for me to digest it, giving me a half sheepish, half sympathetic look through the protective veil of those long, dark lashes. The implications of this scale of incompetence drops through my stomach like a millstone.

'This is all on top of the times when charges were brought then dropped?'

She confirms with a nod.

I shake my head in disbelief. 'They actually knew this guy. They had him in; had him on record and never pinned one fucking thing on him?' The calmness in my voice rises towards the inevitable bitterness I feel creeping up my craw.

'Same thing happened with The Ripper,' she says trying to convey the fact that my circumstances aren't unique. 'He continued to butcher all those poor women despite having been questioned, despite the police having built a profile on him.'

I look at her and say nothing as the resolve inside me tightens up another notch. Caroline waits for me to ask what happens next, but I don't. I'm certain I'll get an answer that for me, at this stage, isn't good enough. She clears her throat and outlines her strategy anyway.

'Okay, I'm confident we have enough here to go forward with. Our next move is to petition the Home Office to re-open and review your case.'

The cynic in me re-emerges. 'It's never going to happen, is it?'

'Hear me out, Jack,' she warns away my negativity. I hold up my hands and put a pause on the pessimism. 'We can now safely de-bunk the prosecution's evidence regarding the ring.'

'How?'

'I followed up your lead and obtained a signed affidavit from our friend Ronnie Hodgson. I also went to see Aniela Novac and secured her son's suicide note.'

My eyes widen in astonishment. Caroline observes my reaction with mild amusement on her face.

'You didn't think I was sat idle for all these weeks did you?'

I shuffle in my seat. 'Well, I didn't... I...'

'Once we get the case re-opened and we supply sufficient grounds to bring Brian Wiggington in for questioning, that's when the real work begins.'

I squirm away from the unwelcome stab of guilt over my irrational jealousy and feelings of abandonment that have followed me around for a month or more. This woman is a star, God bless her, and I feel a complete twat for ever doubting her commitment.

'But how ever did you prise a coherent statement out of old Ronnie?'

'It's amazing how a few pints of bitter and a cash incentive sharpens the memory.'

My eyes widen once again. 'Aren't those particular methods a little bit unethical?'

'We can close the file now if you're going to get all moral with me. Don't worry, I'll claim the cash back out of your compensation.'

'Okay,' I say with a newfound cautious optimism. 'We can explain what really happened with the finger and the ring, but like you've already said, even though we know what we do and everything points to this bastard, we haven't got the evidence we need in order for it to stand up in court.'

'At that stage we apply for exhumation.'

This time the eyes pop out of my head. 'You mean dig her up? Was there anything left to bury?'

'There must have been something; she was put to rest in her home town of Monaghan.'

'And what will that achieve?'

'DNA; it's the vital link in today's forensics, especially when dealing with events long past.'

'How is it likely to link him with the murder?'

'I'm not saying it will, but in the absence of a complete confession it's our only hope. And, if this guy is or was a serial offender, which I'm inclined to believe is the case, he may well have gathered trophies as well.'

'How do you mean?

'In some of those reported attacks certain items of clothing went missing, never recovered.'

'You mean like panties and stuff?'

Caroline nods solemnly. 'Our man may well be a collector, and if he is the DNA link could prove vital.'

'What are the odds?'

'Hard to say at this point, but you'd be amazed at what this new testing can detect and throw up still, even after the longest periods. The beauty of it is it can prove guilt or innocence beyond any reasonable doubt as has proven to be the case so many times in recent years. It has got to be the ace up our sleeves.'

It all sounded so promising, but I was never into games of chance, and when she tells me a decision from the Home Office could take weeks, maybe months I'm soon back to my cynical self. I really don't want all of Caroline's extraordinary efforts to be in vain, but I get a gut feeling that in the long run the whole meandering process could prove futile. The last thing I want to do having already slandered the name Dupree is to appear ungrateful, so I put away the cynic once again and do something I should have done straight away but probably didn't have the bottle to do. I go for the double; a show of appreciation and grovelling apology all in one.

'It's okay, I'm used to it, I'm a lawyer don't forget,' she dismisses my stumbling, bumbling attempts to say sorry and thank you.

'But I didn't really mean to insult your family like that...I...'

'I know,' she says holding up her hands and cutting me short. 'It's okay, really – want to know what else I found out?' she changes the subject, no doubt in order to save us both further embarrassment.

I nod my head.

'While you were in Wakefield you were on an IRA hit list,' she says in a most matter of fact manner.

'Come again?'

'It turns out Lauren Feeney came from a big family of provos; people with huge influence within the Republican movement. You were definitely a marked man while inside.'

'How the hell do you know all this?'

'I've told you, I have my sources.'

She picks up and begins to read a couple of sapling sheets from the ex-rainforest on her desk.

'She had three brothers, all pro-active. One died of leukaemia in nineteen ninety-seven. One blew himself up in a botched bombing of an army base in County Armagh back in eighty-six. The other served time in the Maze; released under the Good Friday agreement in two thousand; last known living in County Fermanagh.'

'Christ, how come no one ever told me this?'

'It was classified.'

'Shit.'

'Don't worry, you were protected.'

'Protected – how?

'Does the name Gerald Sankey mean anything to you?'

'Gertrude? – Don't tell me he was mixed up in all this.'

'Why do you think he was moved up from Parkhurst three weeks after your transfer to Wakefield?'

'I don't know. He always had friends in high places. He told me he'd wangled it so he could carry on with his guitar lessons.'

Caroline laughs and shakes her head at me like I was an eleven year old who still believed in Father Christmas.

'Gerald Sankey was an inside informer, a canary. He turned Queen's evidence on quite a few occasions. Why do you think he was afforded all those perks? Apparently he worked covertly for a number of government organisations. He was a man revered and reviled in equal measure. The powers that be decided it was time for him to move to pastures new, and knowing of your little musical arrangement, as well as the threat on your life, thought they could kill two birds with one stone. He and his cronies were sent north to mind you...'

My mind starts to flake, as is its wont. Layers of memory peel aside. My back pages flicker like celluloid in its infancy. The accumulative library of lapse inside my head searches for reference. And as always it's there in almost an instant, and, as usual, attached to it is a date – the seventh of April nineteen ninety four...

Twenty Six

I CAUGHT THE news on the radio, in the back of the Mariah, half way up the motorway. Lee Brilleaux, lead singer, harp player and founder member of the great rhythm and blues band Dr. Feelgood had died of lymphoma. As with Stevie a few years earlier, I couldn't believe the news and it sent me into a fit of depression already exacerbated by the long, lonely journey into the unknown. I'd been taken out of a comfort zone of sorts and wasn't really looking forward to a new life in Wakefield maximum security prison aka *the mulberry bush – mad mansions.* Terrorists, mass murderers; women and child killers, some choice names of notoriety, nearly all category A. I'd be in good company.

I spent my first solitary hours getting familiar with the new four walls. Most of the gaffs there were single cell occupancy, and I found it hard getting to know the ropes in those initial weeks when there was no one around to bounce off.

I sat quiet and fashioned a black armband out of the top of an old black sock that I intended to wear as a tribute to Lee for the first few days, while trying not to think too much about the more chilling tales surrounding *psychoville* that some of the lads at Parkhurst had happily sent me on my way with, making an almighty effort to stay buoyed by the fact that now I was close to home I could at least look forward to more regular visits from Jeanie and Digweed.

My first assigned detail was spud bashing in the kitchens. Amidst the echoing din thrown up by a stainless steel and steam environment a screw told me to report to my supervisor and pointed to a kid in a corner of the kitchen throwing vegetables about like he was a confirmed carnivore.

'Are you Dean?' I shouted above the metallic clatter and general industry. The kid looked up with a menacing stare. In his right hand is a knife with an incredibly sharp blade, judging by the chopping board full of massacred leeks and artichokes laid out before him. The guy just had to be category B, they wouldn't have allowed him loose in there with such a weapon otherwise – I hoped. He didn't answer straight away but clocked the symbol of mourning I was wearing on my sleeve. I was too preoccupied with the knife at first to notice that on the same arm of the hand that he was brandishing the potential weapon, he too wore a black band.

He used the blade as a pointer and spoke. 'What's with the armband?'

For some reason, like I'd forgotten it was there or something, I looked down at my home made gesture and fingered it before looking up to see the point of his implement still aimed at me. 'Someone I admired has just died – and you?' I nodded beyond his outstretched hand that I hoped he'd lower sometime soon.

'Same as,' he said guardedly, finally bringing the knife crashing down on a defenceless carrot and severing it in two. 'Friend or family?'

'Musician.'

Dean looked up at me all of a sudden with a renewed interest, like he'd just come face to face with a kindred spirit. He laid his knife on the chopping board, abandoned his vegetables, wiped his palms on his apron and, with all menace removed, came over and offered me a hand. I took it and allowed him to pump mine up and down while remaining slightly bemused.

'I couldn't believe it when I heard the news. He was a legend wasn't he?'

'Er... well... yeah, yeah, I suppose he was in a way.'

'I was up all last night thinking about him, hardly slept a wink...' Dean shook his head in sad reflection. '...Such a tortured genius.'

Jesus, steady on mate. I mean Lee was a lovely geezer by all accounts, and a brilliant front man, but tortured genius?

'I blame that screwed up bitch of a wife of his; I bet she drove him to it.'

Screwed up bitch of a wife? Drove him to what? I began to get the feeling we were not grieving about the same person.

'It won't be the same without him; there'll never be another band like Nirvana.'

Nirvana? The only Nirvana I'd ever heard of were a second rate psychedelic outfit from the late sixties. 'Er, who exactly are we talking about here mate?' I enquired cautiously.

He gave me a skewed look like I was insane. 'Kurt Cobain, who do you think I'm talking about?'

'Sorry, bud,' I said shaking my head, 'never heard of him.'

He took a few steps back in obvious disgust. 'Never heard of him? Never heard of him? Are you taking the piss, or what?'

I answered him with a shrug

'Who's that for then?' he nodded towards my arm.

'Lee Brilleaux – Dr. Feelgood.'

The look on his face confirmed that he thought I was insane. 'Who?'

Dean Newsome – Deano, was ten years my junior, a Salford lad who in nineteen-ninety was just coming to the end of an eighteen month stretch in Strangeways on drugs charges when the riots broke out. Two years later he's a lifer, a triple murderer and a nice kid when you got to know him.

He'd been a dealer for much of his teenage and adult life; knifed a bloke to death, in self-defence, so he said, over some dispute. Inevitably, two of the dead man's associates came looking for him tooled up to the eyeballs. He ended up dispatching the pair of them in much the same way. Three lives in three days didn't look good on the witness stand and the self-defence plea didn't stand a chance, so this Nirvana fan and menace to society was put safely out of the way for a very long time.

Perversely, Kurt Cobain and Lee Brilleaux passing within a couple of days of each other, like they did, meant Deano and I became good mates for the rest of my stay in Wakefield. He told me all about the grunge phenomenon that grew out of Seattle in the late eighties, and from me, whether he liked it or not, got to hear about all things rhythm and blues.

I couldn't seem to equate the images I conjured in my head of this young Mancunian sinking a blade into his adversaries, and the guy who talked so eloquently, passionately about this latter day philanthropist he still worshiped unto death and his angst-ridden, emotionally charged take on life.

Over the next weeks, months, years, we would bat the word genius back and forth as we extolled one another about our respective heroes. We would speak about that divine gift certain souls are blessed with and that almost inevitable inability to cope with the trappings such genius drags along in its wake. Naturally I told him all about Stevie, but the guy I was most able to draw parallels to this Cobain fella with was Hendrix, not least because they both hailed from in or around Seattle,

Washington. And they were both lefties. Around now I was beginning to think that all left- handed guitarists were ill fated.

I'd been in *the bush*, so called because of the mulberry bush around which prisoners used to take their daily exercise, and apparently where the nursery rhyme comes from, for just less than a month, getting used to the surroundings, keeping my head down. Up to that point I'd thought I'd done a pretty good job at staying anonymous. Apart from one or two stare-outs and stand-offs no one took that much notice of the new lag, until one particular meal time in the canteen, that is.

The force of the blow to my back almost sent my fork, which was full of mashed potato at the time, sailing down the back of my throat...

"The fuck...!" I just about managed to choke.

"Nah then, you fackin' norvern cant...!" boomed a familiar voice behind me.

"Gert..." I jumped up, turned round and spluttered all in one movement. "...What the fuck are *you* doing here?"

My star guitar pupil stood over me as bold as brass beaming from ear to ear, flanked by his three faithful goons Johnny, Shergar, and Big Mick.

"How...?" I shook my head in disbelief.

"What? You didn't fink you'd get rid of me that easily, did you my son?"

I didn't realise it at the time but this wasn't Gertrude simply seeking out his prodigal tutor; this was the Baron of Parkhurst announcing his arrival to all and sundry, staking claim to his new manor, directed specifically to the special category lags who resided on F wing, and, unbeknown to me, in particular to a small band of IRA bombers known to everyone else as The Fenians.

Despite Gertrude's arrival, things were never quite as relaxed as they were in Parkhurst; the regime at Wakefield was far more draconian, but, I suppose given the notoriety of the inmates there, that really came as no surprise.

However much of a front they were, old Gert still got his lessons. They were no longer held in the relaxed comfort of his cell but in the corner of a games room where a watch could be kept on the proceedings. And it's only now, as those everyday trifling incidences of the time crystallise, that Caroline's revelation starts to make perfect sense.

Some wise old lags, those in the know who'd heard all about Gertrude and his betrayals, were brave, or daft enough to chance their arm and let him know his secrets weren't safe up there.

"Tweet-tweet, little bird..." I remember one particular jibe from an open cell as we all walked past on our way to a lesson about a week after he'd arrived.

"Mark that nonce," ordered Gertrude calmly as he sauntered along the landing.

"Marked him, Guv," announced Johnny in the same casual manner.

Within a month no less than four inmates who thought they held sway enough to risk a chelp, found themselves in the prison infirmary with varying degrees of mysterious injury. Not such wise old lags after all.

I can't say I miss the old weirdo. Our relationship was just a bizarre diorama of some never-ending bad acid trip that all seems so unreal now. And it's probably just as well I was never fully aware of that invisible, protective, satin gloved arm that kept me out of any major trouble for all those years.

Twelve months before my term was up I was downgraded to category B and got to share a cell. I wasn't too happy about the move, as I'd kind of got used to my own company. Less happy were the procession of cell mates who came and went who, to a man, begged to be moved because of my nightmares and the frequent visits from the heavy metal demons.

"I'll come and visit you Gert, I promise," I'd said about a week before my release.

"Don't be a fucking muppet. Watcha wanna come back here for?" he said with zero sentiment. "Listen my son; as soon as you're aht of it I'll be hot on your heels."

"Oh?"

"Yeah, got me another transfer in the offing; back dahn sarf. Too many villains in this 'ere gaff," he said totally without irony.

"What about your lessons?"

"Ah, I fink it's abaht time the old Man in Black went into retirement."

"You serious?"

"Come off it you little cunt, stop pissing up my back. You know I was never any good wiv the fucking thing. I got myself a new hobby now," he said, producing a small, circular framed tapestry type thing with a half-finished, colourfully embroidered bunch of what looked like chrysanthemums. "Needlepoint," he stated triumphantly. "Whatcha fink?"

"Very nice, Gert. You've obviously got an eye for it," I said, trying to keep the patronisation to a minimum.

"Yeah, well – cest la vie my son, cest la vie," he said slapping a shovel sized hand on my shoulder and almost dislocating it. "So, whatcha gonna do when you get aht then?"

"Find out who set me up; clear my name."

Gertrude nodded solemnly and squeezed my shoulder, almost compassionately, but not quite.

"One word of advice from your auntie Gert," he rasped seriously. "Whatever happens, don't let it eat you up, Jack..."

$* * *$

'...Jack – Jack...'

'Yeah?'

'Why do you do this whenever I'm in your company?'

I look up at Caroline nonplussed.

'You've just done it again; drifting off in your own little world. Where is it exactly you go?'

'I'm sorry,' I say, not having a clue as to how long I'd been gone this time and hoping I'd not missed any important information. 'I was revisiting events. It's just something I do. I don't mean to, it's just that the images are still strong and they tend to come easily.' She cocks her head on one side in that sympathetic way of hers and I heave a heavy sigh. 'Perhaps there might come a time when we don't have to talk about this stuff, a time when I can leave it all in the past where it belongs. It would be nice to talk about other things, wouldn't it?'

Again her eyes scour my features. It's obvious she can't weigh me up, this contradictory man. I know I've asked her to back off, but really, it's the last thing I want her to do. I look back at her while desperately trying to unscramble my emotions, wondering how to convey to her what it is I'm feeling, all the while trying to figure what it is those feelings are.

'Yes... yes, it would,' she says softly. 'I shall look forward to that time.' She wistfully gazes into her empty wine glass and twiddles the stem between thumb and forefinger.

'I'm sorry you had to cancel your date. You didn't need to, you know; we could have rearranged.'

'No, I told you it was okay; she was fine about it.'

'She...?'

There I go again, making assumptions, jumping to conclusions – *dead giveaway, you twat.*

'Yes,' she smiles. 'I was only going to the cinema with a girlfriend – no big deal.'

At this point the lawyer is reading my stupid, possessive, insecure mind, I can see it in that smile of hers, but she doesn't push it. She could have a bit of fun here if she liked, indulge in a spot of teasing, but she decides to spare me seeing as my supposition has coloured me up.

'Oh...' I say trying to hide my embarrassment behind a peevish grin.

We beam at each other across the cluttered table that documents a huge chunk of my life thus far.

'...Erm – is that glass of wine still on offer...?

Twenty Seven

I OFTEN THINK about what normal people think about in the course of a regular humdrum day in the life. I try to think back to what I thought about way back when I was normal. I'm using the word *normal* ambiguously because I've long since forgotten its literal meaning. It's just a lazy word I use to simply describe people other than myself. Try as I might I can't think what notions flitted through my head twenty-four-seven back then, except maybe the memory of the previous night's lay, the prospect of the next lay, or getting a new number down pat. I long to have musings that are wistful; where thoughts bearing no cause or consequence float across my mind on fluffy clouds to disperse into a stratosphere of trivia. I long to be like the boys in the band, carefree, content; living lives devoid of stress, responsibility or commitment. Billy: briefly wed, saw the light early doors, cast off the baggage, followed his muse but turned his back on the bullshit of fame. Digweed: same as. Had his fair share of women knocking at his door, but remained the confirmed bachelor. Free spirit; does just enough within the grind of the rat race to afford him his flash motor and the modern trappings of his state-of-the-art penthouse apartment, shuns the rest. Jed: selfish to a fault, but perversely, the nicest grisly bear of a guy you could wish to meet. Determined to live life to the full and nothing or nobody is going to stop him, but again his wants are simple: beer, food and a healthy dollop of R&B.

I've never been any good at telling porkies, as is evident from the pathetic stories and excuses I used to make back in my philandering days – just ask Liz. And Digweed wasn't convinced with the tale I spun him about what I was going to do with the old wagon curtain I asked him to get from his place, but he didn't pursue it.

I join the queue at the butchers and soon start to attract the attention of a little old lady sporting one of those transparent plastic headscarves that protects her new perm and blue rinse. I try hard not to turn towards her gaze but when I do her eyes are boring holes in me. I give her a little nod and an unsure smile.

'Ee, don't I know you, lad?'

'I don't know, love – do you?'

'I know that face, I definitely know that face.'

I know hers too. It's old Mrs Ramskill who used to live two doors down from Mam and Dad's. I turn away and place my order: two fillet steaks.

A long time ago I would have been the topic of gossip around these parts, what with my innocent, bewildered looking mush all over the news, and banner headlines proclaiming: *The Scrapyard Killer - Exclusive. Marsden man convicted of horrific slaying – read the gruesome details here.* On every street corner, in every shop, at every bus stop, a pandemic of Chinese whispers cultivating hate and malediction on the name Smith; Mam, Dad and poor Jeanie trying to pick up the pieces of their shattered lives, having to deal daily with the hostile stares and the pointing fingers.

People move on, people get old, people die, memories fade, but as I feel Mrs. Ramskill's eyes continue to burn into the back of my head, it would seem twenty-five years has failed to dim this old girl's recollection of the past.

I take a couple of sharp pokes to the ribs. I half turn, reluctantly.

'What's your name?' she demands.

'Why, who wants to know?' I demand back.

Her eyes narrow and the old semi-senile cogs start to whirr. I turn away again.

'Didn't you used to live on Woods Terrace?' she persists, getting warmer by the second.

'No love, I'm not from round here,' I lie and start to colour up as I hand a ten pound note over the counter – never been any good at telling porkies.

The butcher hands me my steaks and change, and in my fumbling haste to get away before the penny drops, that's exactly what I do. Pennies, silver, and an odd pound coin bounce onto the quarry-tiled floor. With the discordant pings ringing in my ears I make for the door, almost losing the steaks in the process. I head out into the street and dodge cars, zig-zagging across the road towards the sanctuary of the van.

'Hey...!' shouts the bonneted, blue-rinsed old bag from the butcher's door. '...You've dropped your change.'

Like I hadn't fucking noticed.

'Keep it!' I half turn and shout.

It was bound to happen sometime, I suppose. I'd been out for months and up to now had gotten away without being noticed. But it only took one nosey old crow to get the rumour mill going again, and in the eyes of the law and the moral majority I'm still as guilty as hell.

After seeing Caroline the other night I'd begun to have doubts about what I'd decided to do. I'd been in a bit of a quandary. I was risking a lot for potentially nothing. But after that little incident back there the resolve just got cranked up again. If I wanted to walk the streets without stigma I'd just convinced myself I was doing the right thing.

With my heart pounding in my chest, like Digweed beating his bass drum, I lean over and open the glove compartment. An avalanche of blues CD's spills forth. I sling the steaks into the vacated hole and start the engine.

* * *

'Penny for 'em.' Digweed stands over me twiddling his sticks and chewing his gum, jaw going ten-to-the-dozen.

'I'd be ripping you off. My head occupies a Zen-like state of emptiness at this moment in time.'

'Fuck, you don't say,' he says, dropping down next to me on the edge of the little plinth that serves as a drum riser here at The Melbourne. He props his sticks out in front of him and leans on them like he always does, looking out at the still half empty old boozer, like some country squire leaning on his shooting stick surveying his land. 'So, are you proper into all this Maharaji Yogi shit then?'

'No, you dipstick, I was joking.'

'Hmm,' he mutters and starts to hum some indiscernible out-of-tune tune. He interrupts the discordant ditty with occasional cracks of his gum, and I can tell he's dying to ask about any developments. But for me, tonight isn't the night to impart what I know. It'll all come out in time. Tonight I have to stay focused.

'So, what's the sexy solicitor had to say, then?'

He just couldn't resist.

'What about?'

His eyes dart about uncomprehendingly in their sockets. 'About Wiggy, you daft pillock,' he hisses. 'What do you

253

think?'

I blow air from my cheeks. 'Not tonight, eh, mate; can't we talk about it some other time?'

'You all right?' enquires Billy, pausing briefly on his way past with an armful of gear.

'Yeah, fine...'

This is the first time I've stepped foot inside The Melbourne since that fateful night; the last place any of us saw Lauren Feeney alive. And although Billy's concerns sound like they're for me and the potential psychological effect playing here tonight might have on me, it's more about making sure my head's together and I don't fuck up again like I did in Colne. Besides, it's not the past I'll be dwelling on this evening, but the future.

He looks down at me for more reassurance.

'...Fine, honestly.'

He nods his head and goes off to set up. Digweed looks at me askance.

'What? – Gimme a break – some other time, yeah?'

The drummer cracks his gum at me by way of reply, gets up and heads in the direction of the bar. Seconds later a shadow looms large, like someone just turned out the lights.

'So, how's the shandy man?' Jed asks, towering over me clutching the obligatory pint.

'I'd be better if people wouldn't keep asking me how I am.'

'A bit touchy tonight, aren't we? – Sorry I asked.'

He ambles away and all light returns to the room.

Touchy, nervy, unsure; I'm all of these things; not because of the approaching gig, not because of the ghosts of the past, but because of the half-baked plan I'll soon be putting into action. I'm doing my best to keep the doubts at bay. I need to have my convictions confirmed, my gut feelings realised, and these considerations have to rise above all others. My resolve can't be seen to fail now. Whatever the consequences, there's no turning back.

The pub is busy and noisy and only about two thirds of the punters are really interested in the music, but we still play a half decent set. Halfway through Black Cat Bone I inadvertently catch a glimpse of a young, short-haired blonde in the audience, and ever so briefly an elusive crab-infested, itinerant, squat-hopping student comes to mind, so I concentrate hard on the quivering, pulsating Titanic rear view of our lead singer as he lurches into his mike and all remains well. I manage to get through the gig without major incident. We perform a couple of well received encores, then, as the applaud fades and the house lights go up I see him amongst a sea of heads, right at the back of the pub. It's the baseball cap that gives him away. As I make the connection, he half turns and sees me looking. By the time I lose the Fender and cowl my eyes with a hand over my brow against the harsh light of the stage spots, he's gone. I hop off the tiny platform and ease my way through the mass of noisy punters that are still milling around. At the entrance I peer into the night, but he's vanished into thin air. I am certain it was him.

I mingle with the throng who have come out for a fag or to wait for taxis. I find a low wall and build a smoke, observing the drunken chatter of couples and groups, hoping no female will venture home alone tonight. Inside my baccy pouch I push to one side the flattened pack of Diazepam that survived being flushed down the lav. I perform a few neck rolls to dissipate the guitar strap stiffness, gaze up at the ink-black night sky and breathe in the relative balminess of the late summer evening air, psyching myself up for the task that lies ahead. The hour is late, but the evening is far from over.

We drop off Jed and Billy, and then drive over to the studios to unload the amps and stacks. It's only a short journey but by the time we get there Digweed has nattered me to death. I cave in and tell him everything I've been told about their ex-roadie.

'I always thought he was a bit dodgy in an Arthur Daley kind of way, but I never knew he'd been inside. He told us he'd been to see his brother in Australia.'

'Yeah, the only down under he ever did was down. Look, you're going to have to keep all this under your hat. You can't tell anyone, not even Billy and Jed. Caroline's given me all this stuff in confidence, and if any of it gets out before I get my case re-opened, I'm fucked.'

'So, when do they re-open your case?'

'Could be months, if at all.'

My mate sighs frustrated on my behalf. He doesn't know the half of it.

'What are you going to do?'

I fix him a stare. 'What would *you* do?'

He looks at me clueless before shaking his head. 'I'm fucked if I know – it's got to be him though, hasn't it?'

'Certain.'

I'm half tempted to let him in on my little plan, but I manage to resist, I know he'll say I'm mad, try to talk me out of it, and I can't take the risk of him thwarting what I'm about to do.

We unload the van empty, save for the folded tarpaulin sheet I asked Digweed to get for me, that he now eyes suspiciously. I quickly close the back doors and jump into the driver's seat. I start the engine and lean out the window. 'As soon as I get to find out anything else for certain, you'll be the first to know – I'll see you later.'

'Hey – promise me you won't do anything stupid in the

meantime.'

I respond with a faint smile and nod while revving the engine impatiently. He looks at me oddly and walks away unconvinced. I watch him head towards his Audi, wait until he starts up and roars off into the night.

Twenty Eight

I DON'T NORMALLY take the van. I made some excuse about needing it to shift a load of rubbish to the tip for Jeanie in the morning, but Digweed knows I'm up to something; he can tell by my caginess.

In the dark, soulless, foreboding heart of Blackmoor that is Ludlam Street, I pull in hearse-like to the spot where I parked Jeanie's Micra a few weeks ago. Same ritual: kill the engine and lights, check the time and wait about for a bit. After five minutes I see headlights in the mirror. I freeze a little and try to make myself chameleon in my seat. The taxi coasts by and I catch a quick glimpse of its semi-comatose occupants: clubbers, spent up and sozzled, and the fare clicks on as they're unwittingly taken the picturesque route home.

I wait another five then reach into the glove compartment and fish out the steaks. I take a razor blade and score deep into the meat in a criss-cross pattern. I take out my baccy pouch and pop open the foil strips of the entire packet of Diazepam. I carefully take apart each capsule rubbing the contents deep into the fillets, this I do under torchlight, as I don't want to waste a gram. I calculate there's enough tranq here to fell an African elephant. I'm not taking any chances.

Somewhere in a remote corner of my head common sense and reason are trying to fight their way out. Trust and a promise can't compete with twenty-five years of injustice. I'll betray the trust; the promise was a false one. Common sense and reason can stay put.

My Casio reads 2:35am. It's now or never. I gather up the steaks and go for it. At the gates I shine my beam in search of the hounds from hell, and in an instant it's met with four startled spots of luminous yellow. The low, ominous growls of warning build to snarls of intent. They shift from shapes of slumber to snap alert readiness. I call them for their supper and they react like bullets from a gun. With the familiar sound of chain on concrete the dogs race to defend their domain. At just the right moment I hurl the meat high into the air. It sails over the metal gates and lands with a dull slap in the path of the oncoming beasts. It manages to halt, silence and confuse them all in one go. The savage sound of barking goes from incessant to intermittent, intentions divided and unclear. They smell food. One of them decides to investigate and begins to sniff curiously at this sudden appearance of manna from heaven, the other emits a low growl of warning at the light source while trying to keep an untrustworthy eye on what its mate is up to. An exploratory lick and a final cautionary look around is all it takes before they both decide to get stuck in to this torch-lit dinner for two. The banquet is over in bolt down seconds. I satisfy myself they've devoured the lot before killing the light and leave them licking their lips. I decide to take a drive around the dark, deserted streets while the dogs digest the consequences of their actions.

At 3:15am I park up and venture over to the gates. I shine my beam at the two great dark lumps of fur lying still on the ground. One half-open eye in its unconscious state reflects back at me. The Diazepam looks to have done its job. I fetch the tarp from the van; it's heavy and awkward. This is the difficult bit. I'm no spring chicken. With the canvas slung over one shoulder I manage to scale the gate in a slow, cling-on-for-dear-life, spastic fashion. With one hand hooked desperately round metal mesh and no real foothold for the rest of my weight, I heave the truck curtain onto the razor wire. The effort pulls something in my neck and pain flashes down my shoulder. With my lungs panting fit to burst and my hang-on fingers cramping up, I try to adjust my precarious position and take a breather. Caroline and Digweed pop into the frame, shaking their heads. I curse them away and go for the summit. After a few abandoned attempts and a couple of near falls I somehow manage to straddle the canvas. The wire is strung out across its metal frame at an overhanging angle, which means I won't be able to descend by the gate on the other side. I would have to drop the twelve-foot or so onto concrete. I fumble for the torch and shine it on the ground below to assess the task. It doesn't really help. To add to my dilemma the gate decides to put in a few shifts and wobbles, and under my weight my protective blanket begins to give way to an uncomfortable sharpness. It's shit or bust time. With my heart in my mouth I start to un-straddle. As my leg comes over my weight shifts, and with nothing to cling to I slowly slither off the canvas and fall into mid-air.

Although I'm expecting it, the ground still meets me with shock and surprise and my right ankle buckles under me. I let out a short, sharp cry of pain and roll and writhe like a striker going down in the penalty area. I grit my teeth and wait for the sickly feeling to go away. I heard nothing snap, so after a few moments I gingerly get to my feet and hope nothing's broken. The pain is excruciating and I reason I must have torn tendons, ligaments or something. Trying to keep the weight off it, I hobble past the pair of sleeping hounds, still giving them a wide berth just in case.

As I approach the building I set off a security light which floods the yard, catching me like a startled rabbit. I hurriedly limp into the shadows out of its range and wait for it to click off. My beleaguered ticker thumps away in protest inside my chest. I'd better start thinking how a burglar would, and fast. I take a route weaving between the stacks of scrap vehicles, limping my way forward like a wounded commando. Reaching the corner of the building I edge my way along its stone wall SAS fashion, keeping an eye out for any other hidden-away security measures. At the office window I take a furtive look around me before shining the torch through the glass. The beam reflects back at me making it impossible to make out what's inside. Further on, the large garage doors are heavily padlocked, so I decide to take a look around the back. I carefully walk an obstacle course of oil drums, old tyres and discarded bits of vehicle until I come to a small window and the top sash is slightly open. Too small to crawl through, I scour the graveyard of rusting iron for something I could fashion into a tool. I manage to rive a car aerial off an old Ford Escort and, in doing so, am reminded of the damage I've inflicted on my neck and shoulder to accompany my now throbbing ankle. I bend the aerial into a hook shape, pile some tyres together and painfully climb the wobbly platform until I reach the open sash. I flick the catch easily enough, and then feed my improvised tool down inside until I reach the handle on the main window. I hook the aerial into position and pull upwards. It moves a degree but is too heavy and stiff for my implement. I fish it back out and re-shape it four or five times before my perseverance finally pays off and I feel the catch relax. I pull at the frame; it feels like it hasn't been opened in years. Again, amidst the sweating, cursing and discomfort, my persistence pays off and the window parts from its frame, groaning and squeaking in protest – I'm in.

It's a toilet. I nurse myself down onto the cistern, the seat and finally the floor. Effort and pain combine to leave me wringing wet with sweat. Inside my chest the thing that pumps the blood around is playing merry hell. Keeping an eye out for beams and sensors I cautiously venture out to an area that has row after row of shelving filled with motor spares. Batteries, alternators, starter motors, petrol pumps. You name it; Wiggy would appear to have it.

In the office on a greasy looking, well-worn old desk sits a computer and its peripherals. I wonder if its hard drive could tell a tale or two, but I'm not about to take the chance of turning it on and have its light illuminate the place; besides, I'm technologically illiterate and wouldn't begin to know where to start looking for stuff. On one wall is a giant map of West Yorkshire dotted with coloured headed pins. On another is a large wipe-clean board with numbers and figures that I assume to be spare part code references and the like. On the third wall sits a clock and a girlie calendar, nothing untoward there. The two grey metal filing cabinets reveal nothing that has relevance to anything other than the trade, drawers and cupboards likewise. In one corner, on the floor, sits a small green safe. I tentatively try the handle, but of course it's locked. I briefly shine the torch around the room to see if there's anything I might have missed, but there's nothing in here to give the guy away apart from what he does for a living.

Beyond the racks of spares and behind a breeze block wall is the garage, and it's massive. Obviously built for heavy commercial use, you could work on a double-decker bus in here. There are no windows, so I feel easier using the torch. Looking around I see it's well equipped: rigs, jigs, propane, butane, cutting tackle, compressors, spray booth, wings, bonnets, hydraulic hoists, ramps, the whole works. On the walls, amongst the hoses, belts, chains and pressure charts are the occasional titty posters. It's slippery underfoot and the whole place stinks of rubber, oil and grease; a typical working garage – what really did I expect?

I point my beam up to the high vaulted ceiling; it's just a space full of criss-crossing supporting metal beams and joists where a hefty looking block, tackle and pulley arrangement hangs from a vast girder. Again I scour each corner, every nook and cranny in the hope I might find something. As to what that something would be and what I'd do with it if I ever found it is a thing I haven't really thought about, and any way, with every passing adrenalin filled second, that prospect is looking more and more unlikely. Just another crazy notion, another mad plan fuelled by desperation.

Wiggy is obviously no idiot, but he's certainly ridden his luck over the years. Maybe it was the thought, the hope that he'd become complacent, over confident, untouchable, that has made me do this, I don't know. It seems I make a habit of clutching at straws. I could find out where he lives; maybe his home is where he hides away his secrets. He can't be too meticulous or the law wouldn't have had him in so many times.

It seems I've drawn a blank here. Save another attempt at burglary, I'm back to relying on The Home Office and the hope that Brian Wiggington hasn't the nous to have destroyed all connection to his wrongdoings.

I now have the task of covering my tracks and getting out of here. I need to rescale the gate and luckily my torchlight picks out an aluminium ladder propped against a far wall. I aim the beam at my watch. 3:35am. I pray the dope is still keeping the dogs in la-la land, and move as quick as my dodgy ankle will allow. Unfortunately, in the dark and my half crippled state I fail to pick my feet up. I stub a toe hard against something immovable and I go flying. The torch sails out of my hand and I land flat on my face amongst the grease and the grime. Struggling to my feet I wipe my oily hands down my jeans and go hobbling in search of the torch. Luckily it's still in one piece and I shine its light back to the spot. It's a slightly raised plank, a sleeper actually; in fact, as I move the light around, there are more sleepers covering a whole rectangular area of the floor. With my good foot I stomp over the surface a few times – hollow. There's something underneath here. And then it dawns on me. Of course, it must be an inspection pit, a whopping great commercial sized inspection pit. With no visible sign of an entrance or a trap door of any description, I look around and find a tyre lever that I manage to wedge down the gap of the raised sleeper and eventually lift out of position. I move a second plank without too much trouble and shine my torch into the void. A set of metal steps is set into the wall and two thirds of the way down a light switch. I grit my teeth through the pain and gingerly lower myself. I flick the switch and four wall mounted fluorescent strips ping into life. I turn around and catch my breath. This isn't like any inspection pit I've ever seen.

A mattress, a tripod, a monitor screen and a VCR sit atop a set of drawers. The rest of it is just a cold, dank, bare chamber. I've pulled the handle and dropped three skulls. Icy shards of foreboding spill forth and chill me to the marrow – jackpot.

I move forward slowly, fear and intrigue a sickly combination. On the mattress, stains of indeterminate age and essence bear witness to sordid activity. With animal-like instinct my nose searches for indelible scent; body secretions to linger musk like amongst atoms of damp and inertia, and yet I try not to breathe at all.

264

I stand in front of the three sets of drawers and tuck my hand up inside a sleeve. I pull on the handle of the top most, my heart going like the clappers. It has already been through the mill tonight, it is about to turn summersault.

As I had envisaged in a nightmare come true: panties, knickers; ass holsters of every description, at least a dozen pairs; a mangle of lace and frill, faded fashion; fragile, forlorn and violated; receptacles for an evil seed where gusset encrusted perversions manifest. Caroline was right, the fucking sicko couldn't resist the trophies; a sordid, soiled collection that he could drool, slaver and do Christ knows what else over. And in amongst the mess of cotton, satin and lace, hope of hopes, is some strand, some fibre of what was once Lauren Feeney.

I'm not certain if it's the combination of pain and effort that's catching up with me, or the mix of triumph and disgust at my discovery that starts me feeling nauseous, but it's only a combination of hard swallowing and practised deep breathing that stops me from chucking up. I close the drawer and lean for a moment as beads of sweat pop out all over my forehead.

Still dithery, my morbid curiosity takes control and I go for the next drawer down.

On a bed of different coloured silk sashes, scattered haphazardly amongst blindfolds and handcuffs are packets similar to the one I kept in my baccy pouch. I lean over for a closer inspection and the words gamma hydroxybutyric acid leap out at me – GHB, Rohypnol – the date-rape drug. I glance over at the musty mattress while the images come thick and fast. I close the drawer with a knee and open the bottom one. It's full of video cassettes, and if I were guessing, not of the sort you'd get from Blockbusters. I hesitate, I sweat; I palpitate. Adrenaline rushes through me, producing a sick excitement. Part of me wants to back off; the rest of me, the dark, animal, ghoul-ish-curious, voyeuristic side forces me to fumble for one at random. With my sleeve preventing contact with my fingers I juggle the cassette, offering it hastily into the slot in the VCR. The whole process has a nasty, sexually deviant taste about it and I feel my skin prickle, like I'm infested with roaches or something. I flick on the power and hear the thing whirr into motion.

A tortured female scream rings out around the four walls of the pit as audio kicks in a second before visual. I leap out of my skin and scramble around for the mute button. Before I get chance to silence it I witness the victim's screams reduced to a muffled struggle as her head is held tight and a cock is roughly forced into her mouth. In the foreground two other men pin her legs spread-eagled while a third violently forces objects into her vagina. I fast forward and watch the torture unfold in mi-cro-flashes. Horrific images register subliminally on my retina until it all becomes too much. I hit stop and I retch. It looked like a snuff movie. I'd heard about them in prison but had never seen one. I couldn't tell if this hellhole was the actual location, but it didn't look like the tripod over there was used for portraits. *Oh you bastard – you fucker – you evil fucker,* I breathe to myself as I power off and hurriedly replace the tape.

I remind myself of the time as fear and panic start to take hold. In my haste it takes what seems like an age to set up the camera application on my phone. What young Ben would do in a breath takes me forever. I've never used the thing before and am useless with anything like this. I manically beep around until I eventually hit the right button, then frantically snap away at all I've uncovered before beating a hasty retreat. Halfway up the steps I turn and take one last panoramic snap, hit the light switch and climb out.

266

My phone rings as I'm manoeuvring the first of the sleepers back into position. The shock almost sends me headfirst back into the pit. I don't know how much more my poor heart can take. The odds of me suffering a cardiac arrest tonight are shortening by the minute.

Digweed calling says the illuminated display. What the fuck does he want at five-to-four in the morning? I ignore the demanding chimes and continue to cover my tracks accompanied by the grunts and groans of my fifty-one year old unfit, exhausted and wounded, protesting body. I drop the last sleeper into place. Through the pain, fatigue, sickness and discomfort seeps a relief, a satisfaction; my instincts spot on, my actions justified. I'm closing in on you Wiggy; my time has come. At last I see a light at the end of the tunnel – I see many lights, and then I see no light at all...

Twenty Nine

I COME TO with the mother of all headaches and find myself staring down the twin barrels of a twelve-gauge. A voice, distant, echoing, utters something garbled, as if I am coming round from anaesthetic in a slipper bath. The voice comes from a hazy image at the other end of the cold steel. It isn't at all friendly. I try to lift my head which feels the weight and size of a demolition ball, but a short, sharp jab from the twelve bore into my face puts me back down. I groan, squeeze my eyes shut, open and try to re-focus. Slowly, ever so slowly, my senses creep back to real time. I begin to remember where I am. The baseball cap is the first thing to register, and the magnitude of my predicament begins to dawn.

'What have you done to my fucking dogs?' are the first coherent words I hear.

'Your dogs are gonna be okay,' I croak. 'Not like certain women, eh?'

He reacts by jabbing the gun into my face again. I flinch backwards, my throbbing head hitting the grease-coated floor.

'I don't know what you're talking about,' he says unconvincingly. 'I should call the cops. I'll have you done for trespass, breaking and entering.'

'Feel free,' I manage a feeble laugh. 'In fact, I was just about to call them myself when I got waylaid,' I say, gingerly rubbing the tender lump on the back of my head. 'I'm sure they'll be interested to have a look at your little set up down there.'

He nervously readjusts his grip on the shotgun, but keeps close to my face. 'What the fuck do you want from me?'

'Justice.'

'For what?'

'Come on, Wiggy, stop pretending you don't know who I am and why I'm here. You didn't think you were going to get away with it forever, did you?'

'I never set you up,' he blurts, shy of an admission. 'It wasn't me what got you sent down.'

'I know that now. We were both victims of circumstance. You got lucky. I got unlucky. You weren't to know that the bass player from Blizzard happened to work at Sutherlands, but as it turned out, lucky for you he did. And the business with the finger and the ring... nothing to do with you, but it got you off the hook nicely...' I sense the cogs whirring inside his head. I'm sure he doesn't fully appreciate the machinations that transpired to send me down after all this time, and why should he; the guy was home free without a single suspicion being raised. Some other mug took the rap and he was free to continue slaking his perverted lust on whomever he liked. He was Midas incarnate, untouchable. '...Justice, Wiggy. I served twenty-five long years for you. I'll never get them back; it's too late now. But I'm as sure as hell going to clear my name. I've nothing else to lose.'

'You'll never prove it was me, not after all this time.'

I keep quiet on that one.

'But it was you – wasn't it?' I goad him softly. I try to sit up again. This time he backs away slightly but keeps the gun levelled at me. 'Why, Wiggy – why did she have to die?'

'She asked for it,' he snaps, becoming ultra-agitated in an

instant. 'The little bitch wouldn't keep quiet. If she hadn't fucking struggled – kicking and screaming...'

'Bit too feisty, aren't they, those Irish girls? – Pity there wasn't any Rohypnol around in those days.'

'It was *her* what led *me* on...' he barks, defensive, '...She fucking came on to *me.*'

'This in The Melbourne, was it?'

'Yeah, she was all over me like a fucking rash, the teasing little bitch. Then when it came down to it, she didn't want to know.'

I have him revisiting the past, and I can see it unsettling him. It wasn't something he did too often. He'd blanked it; erased it from memory, just a faded depraved scene from one of his snuff videos.

'So you put her through that machine where she ends up in bits. Did she really deserve that?'

'She was dead before I put her in the car.'

'Some consolation... How?'

Under the baseball cap the eyes become trancelike as he re-visits a time and place he's never had to. The two barrels aimed at my head slowly lower to the region around my feet.

'She wouldn't stop struggling. I couldn't keep her quiet. I put my hand over her mouth. She bit my finger to the bone and my hands went to her throat... I had to shut her up.' He looks into my face, searching for understanding. 'I... I didn't mean to kill her, but she shouldn't have done what she did.'

He's right of course. I can't begin to imagine what forces were at work that night to set in motion so much shit. Fate? A plethora of karma deciding to play itself out? Or merely an accident; a great big coming together of random circumstance? Poor old Lauren couldn't have chosen a worse candidate to use as an instrument for her silly little mind games. Wiggy was just an anonymous face in The Melbourne, a handy tool of jealousy to get at the hapless Fadge, a guy she should never have got involved with. She'd been blinded by a bit of bling, and the sap asking her to marry him, only to regret it the minute the novelty had worn off, which had been barely a week later.

Brian Wiggington was a predator and a woman-hater. A guy without an ounce of the gift I'd been blessed with; a man who couldn't take rejection, who used the built-up and bitter effects of that rejection and turned them into something evil. He'd never had a girl come on to him before. The alchemy that evening in nineteen seventy-nine was consummate.

I keep him talking, hoping that the hammering going on inside my head will subside enough for me to think my way out of this pickle.

What made him stick around? Why stay so close? Did he integrate and ingratiate himself as part of some master psychological strategy, or was it just a way of getting some extra cynical sick kick?

'You stalked the band. You even roadied for them; what was all that about?'

He gives a shrug full of insentience. 'Where there was rock and roll there were women.'

'And you didn't give a shit about Fadge, her fiancé.'

'Ah, that feckless fool didn't hang around for long; his head was fucked.'

I look up into the dark shadows that the peak of his cap creates around his eyes. I sense a soulless void. On many occasions over the years I would have welcomed the notion of death, now its imminence scares me. It's his only route. In his head there won't be options, and I'm in no fit state to win a fight for my life.

'And now?'

The gun comes up to my head again. 'Well, you've gone and buggered it for yourself, haven't you, you nosey bastard?'

'You won't get away with it a second time; nobody's that lucky.'

'This is my property. You broke in here armed with intent. I caught you in the act. There was a struggle. The gun accidently goes off. I was merely acting in self-defence.'

'They won't buy it.'

'I'll take my chances – now get up.'

I stare up at my executioner; don't move.

'Do as I fucking say,' he snarls. 'Get up, now.'

He tucks the gun tightly into his shoulder and I watch his fingers wrap the trigger. I close my eyes and attempt to get to my feet; all pain now a welcome distraction.

'Wiggy...!' I hear a familiar voice scream, accompanied by the rumbling, rolling sound of heavy metal. I open my eyes just in time to see Wiggy's startled expression in profile as he turns into the few hundredweight of steel block, tackle and chain that catches him square on, knocking him off his feet and triggering the gun that explodes with a blue flash. The noise reverberates in shock waves around the building, and spreading shot peppers the air, pinging and zinging off the roof trusses. I instinctively go back the way I'd just come, hitting the oil and grease, playing hide and seek with my fear. I'm not certain if I reach a count of ten, but by the time I dare chance a look Wiggy and Digweed are already wrapped together in a desperately frantic struggle, the gun lying prone on the floor in no-mans-land between me and them. For some reason I freeze and simply stare at the grappling, tangled mass of arms and legs. My head occupies a vacuous space of abstract thought and irrationality – *what the fuck is the drummer doing here?*

'Grag th shlukn gnnn...!'

He has Wiggy's fingers hooked in his mouth trying to rip his face off and he's talking to me in a strange language.

'Thl gnnn, git thl gnnn...!'

His face is the colour of a Belisha beacon and his eyes are popping out of his head. He sinks his teeth into the invasive digits and Wiggy lets out a guttural scream.

'Get the fucking gun!' he manages to scream desperately before Wiggy re-positions an arm around his throat. I watch his face turn from red to purple. I'm used to seeing him thrash about wildly but usually it's from behind a drum kit. Either by design or accident, a swinging leg catches the stock of the gun and sends it skitting in my direction. A number of red cartridge cases spill from Wiggys pockets and scatter across the floor. I stare hard at them, uncomprehending for a moment, until finally my mate's grotesque choking noises send me into action.

Coming, ready or not, says a childlike voice in my head.

Like the slow-mo versions you sometimes get in dreams, I wade through treacle, scramble for the weapon and stagger to my feet. I point the thing loosely at the rucking pair of bodies, haplessly waving it about in time to their thrashing. Wiggy has lost his baseball cap in the melee revealing a partially bald, sweating barnet. It's a striking moment of exposure, a confirming image of nasty, of evil. I can almost smell his perversion. He isn't a big bloke, but he's stocky and Digweed is no real match for him in the physicality stakes. The monster has started to get the upper hand and I continue to hover inertly, useless and pathetic.

'Shoot him!' Digweed manages to splutter.

'I – I can't, I might hit you,' I offer lamely.

'Do something!' he pleads exhausted.

I tentatively move forward, and then back off as the desperate entanglement rolls towards me. My buddy is having the life choked out of him and there's a barrier I can't cross in order to help him. I'm about as much use as a chocolate fireguard.

With my cowardice confirmed I point the twelve bore up at the rafters, squeeze my eyes shut and pull the trigger. The stock kicks back like a mule into my sore shoulder, but the resulting deafening rapport, for the briefest of moments, manages to unlock them from their life or death struggle.

Digweed is the first to suss neither of them had been shot, and brings a knee up swiftly into Wiggy's gonads. He's quickly up onto his feet and delivers a few sharp and vicious kicks, one to the stomach and two to the head.

'Gimme the gun!' he screams while scooping up a couple of cartridges.

'Gimme the fucking gun!' he repeats, when my reactions aren't quick enough. I comply, offering the thing to him like a simpleton, like I'd been on the Diazepam or something. He gives me the briefest look of disgust before snapping open the shotgun, releasing a smoky blue haze of cordite. Lightning-quick he offers the shells into the still smouldering chambers as Wiggy growls to his feet gingerly nursing his bruised nads. Digweed snaps the thing shut and brings it up to his shoulder like he's out up on the moors and it's the glorious twelfth.

Wiggy looks up to see the roles reversed, and he freezes. He sees the twin barrels pointing at his head, and beyond them, the blazing eyes of his adversary. He frantically looks around him as though searching for a saviour, and then starts to side-step his way slowly in an arc, all the time watching the madman and the gun mirror his every move. He says nothing, as if he knows pleading to reason won't do him any good now – and he's right.

'Die, you bastard!' I hear Digweed snarl in a voice I don't recognise. I watch the familiar curl of the finger and only now

274

does something decide to click inside and fire me into action.

Wiggy sets off fleeing for his life. At the same time I make a desperate lunge.

'No!' I scream, crashing into Digweed's shoulder, racking up the pain.

I hear the explosion. I hear the sound of shot thudding like a parradiddle into the breezeblock wall. I look up to see a chrome wheel hub fall from its mount and rattle to silence on the workbench below. A peppered poster of a big- breasted blonde, shot full of holes, smiles back at me provocatively.

Wiggy has disappeared.

'You stupid cunt!' Digweed barks, jumping back to his feet and heading off in pursuit like he'd been on the marching powder.

'Wait...' I call him back, 'Don't...' but he's already vanished behind the wall amongst the racks of spares. Before I get to him I hear another shot ring out. I fear the worst.

In the corridor I find him standing, staring at the hole and the remnants of shattered glass he'd just shot out of the outer office door; the twelve bore hanging spent by his side.

'Digweed...'

He turns to look at me with staring eyes that aren't his own. We stand there, regarding each other, neither saying a word; me and my best friend, a couple of total strangers.

'Come on,' he orders, suddenly snapping out of it, heading for the door.

'Wait, what are you doing?' I call out after him, but he's already on his way, crunching over broken glass and out into the night. The security flood pops on to light his way and I follow on blindly, past where sleeping dogs lie. I painstakingly check the ground for any tell-tale trail of blood; thankfully, I find none. I limp out through the gates as fast as my injured ankle will let me. At the other side of the road Digweed is sitting impatiently, revving his motor.

'Hurry up,' he shouts, 'we're gonna lose him.'

Before my beleaguered arse hits leather he's wheel-spun us away in hot pursuit of the tail lights of a Mercedes that is just turning a corner.

I grit my teeth and secure my seatbelt. I'm breathless, I'm dizzy, I'm confused, and I still feel like I could throw up, while beside me sits a guy wearing a manic stare and a steely resolve that has surpassed my own, tearing round the back streets of Huddersfield like some half crazed rally driver.

'What the fuck are you playing at?' I chance taking my eyes off the road for a second to confront the nutter.

'No, what the fuck are *you* playing at?' He turns to me with the madness still in his eyes, spittle flecking the corners of his mouth. 'I save your life and you almost cost me mine – you twat!' he adds for good measure.

My arms involuntarily brace out rigid to anything I can hold on to as he handbrake-turns the car, slewing it screeching round a corner. Adding to my discomfort is something sharp and rough digging into my behind. I lift a cheek and come up with a hacksaw blade. I stare at it uncomprehendingly for a moment before slinging it into the back alongside the shotgun.

'Why have you brought the gun? You're going to kill us. Why are you doing this?' I demand without getting a reply. 'We should go to the police.'

'The police?' he snaps, taking his eyes off the road to glower at me. 'And what the hell are you gonna tell them?' He shouts me down to a petrified silence while I give it some thought.

He's right, of course. What garbled story would I want to impart to the boys in blue in my head-scrambled state? At the same time, I can't imagine what this suicidal car chase is going to achieve. Even if we catch him, what does Digweed intend to do, what does he expect me to do? If we survive this madness, and the red light we've just jumped points to that being unlikely, what's the outcome? I can't help but see it all ending in tears; and it's all my stupid, impatient, impulsive fault. What was I thinking? Why didn't I take Caroline's advice? Why couldn't I listen?

We traverse a roundabout the wrong way, and then shoot up the A640 towards the district of Salendine Nook. Thankfully the roads are still empty save the Mercedes that remains a good three or four hundred yards ahead of us. Digweed's sporty motor is faster than the Merc and we begin to eat up the yards as we fly along deserted dual carriageway. Wiggy tries to shake us off, hanging the big silver saloon right towards Lindley and Birkby.

'He's heading for the motorway,' says Digweed, his voice taking on a husky tone due to the throttling he endured.

'What are you going to do?' I venture with trepidation in my voice.

He turns to me just like Arnie would in one of his Terminator films, his left eye starting to swell and close, making this normally mild-mannered percussionist appear otherworld scary. 'Wait and see.' He drops the RS4 through the gears and roars on.

I groan inwardly. I don't know what's going on here. I half wish all this was the twisted work of the heavy metal demons and I would soon wake bathed in sweat but within the sanctified four walls of my prison cell. This is so fucking unreal.

We hit the big roundabout at Ainley Top doing seventy-five miles an hour. The brake lights of the Mercedes flash on and off and his back end twitches a few times, but he recovers.

We're so close now I can see the whites of his eyes in his mirror. Under the motorway, up to the top roundabout, Digweed audaciously closes up on his rear and gives him a nudge. He twitches again. Digweed backs off then accelerates. He's playing with him. Like a cat with a mouse he's teasing, terrorising. The predator becomes the prey. He could run him off the road, but he doesn't. He allows him to escape up the slip road and on to the motorway – the M62 eastbound.

Apart from a solitary artic grinding its way slowly westbound up the long incline of the opposite carriageway, preempting the morning traffic, the motorway is empty. Dawn has yet to break and Digweed continues to stalk and unnerve; up his arse, full beam on.

I want to close my eyes to it all, but I daren't. Rigid in my seat, fear factor into the red, I begin to smell death for the second time within the hour. My best mate has turned into the Grim Reaper. The speedometer needle is coasting past 110 mph, and I've turned into some amoebic blancmange.

We tear down the long decline towards junction 25, the Brighouse – Cooper Bridge exit, my old section headquarters. There's a sign warning of road works a mile ahead, crash barrier repairs on the Kirklees viaduct, the bridge my old engineer and I surveyed many times while under construction, somewhere back in another dimension.

Motorway lights flash by as a strobe then meld together. Certain we are about to die, the mechanics of my mind kick in and take over only to be immediately hijacked by my old tormentor and his wailing groupies.

'Thought you'd got rid of us, Jack? – Shame on you. And still praying I see...'

I shut my eyes for escape, but like some fairground workers of the absurd, the banshees spin my waltzer mind distorted...

In a snuff movie I'm being anally raped by a giant Cockney dressed as The Man in Black. In the background his three goons roar him on approvingly. In a sideshow my sister is being kicked and punched black and blue by the father of her only child. She begs, she pleads for help. No one comes to her aid. I snap myself free of the image only to be confronted by a raging cuckolded man in chef whites bearing down on me with meat cleaver held aloft. The waltzer spins, the Banshees wail.

I look across at the madman in the driving seat. He's mouthing something at me.

'What?'

'I said he's gonna fuckin' lose it,' he barks, nodding at the scene unfolding before us.

Wiggy has gone for the Junction 25 exit at a suicidal speed. He enters the slip road contra flow clipping and scattering red and white cones in his meandering wake; brake lights flashing on and off like some schizoid semaphore. Digweed decelerates but mystifyingly Wiggy fails to slow. He mounts the bridge kerb with a bang and takes to the air. The front wheels clear the barrier, but the back axle catches it, flipping the car into a somersault and a finale of showering sparks. As if in slow motion the saloon becomes a coupe, breaking itself perfectly in two before vanishing silently into the void.

Sensing a kill, the dark angels vacate my head and fritter themselves away into the sub-ether, merging as one with the carbon and carcinogens that permeate the hidden underbelly of the mammoth concrete and steel structure that is Kirklees viaduct, celebrating death, whistling and wailing as the wind between its giant supports.

We abandon the car at the top of the slip and race to peer over the parapet. Almost two hundred feet below us a soup of mist and murk rises up from river and canal, enveloping vegetation, creeping its way up the steeply rising slopes of Bradley Wood.

The viaduct was built over the river Calder, the Calder and Hebble navigation canal, and the Mirfield to Brighouse railway line, and from the small flames that are beginning to rise up out of the gloom, it looks as if the Mercedes, or at least some of it, has smashed into the land between canal and rail track.

'Fuck,' Digweed exclaims softly to himself, almost as a sigh of relief, his breath vaporising instantly in the pre-dawn air. The mask of madness seems to have left him and he begins to look human again. 'How do we get down there?'

'I think I know a way – come on.'

We race back to the car and I guide us down the slip road and onto the A644. The land I remember as site offices and plant depot now has a sprawling industrial estate on it, but it doesn't take me long to find the utilities road that services the waterways and rail network that will take us under the viaduct.

We take the car as far as Digweed is happy with. He kills the lights and the engine and leans over to grab the shotgun off the back seat. 'There should be a cloth in the glove box.'

'What the hell are you going to do with that?' I look at him and the gun in dismay. 'You don't think he'll have survived that, do you?'

'Just get me the cloth.'

I fish around amongst his CDs and hand him a duster. He proceeds to wipe the weapon clean like a seasoned pro. I watch him, slightly awed, partially bewildered, his thought process working far in advance of my own.

'C'mon,' he commands. We vacate the car and take to foot, Digweed clutching the twelve-bore via the rag he's wrapped around it.

The vista has changed beyond recall since my day. The land between canal, rail and river is now overgrown scrub, but I do remember this as the place I first witnessed a Johnny-The-Mole creation, as a naive seventeen year old; the turd steaming away to itself in the middle of a culvert chamber, and the ritual rain dance that followed, along with the inevitable opening of the skies.

Digweed turns and urges me along as I limp pathetically after him, imagining the ghosts of Irish navvies long gone. What crazy mind would have predicted my return and foretold this particular scenario thirty-odd years ago?

We scramble down dew-soaked banking and over the line. Coarse bramble demarks railway and canal. My ankle and head throb and pulse in time to my racing heart; my grease and oil-stained threads, now snagged and torn.

Digweed reaches the scene way ahead of me, his outline silhouetted against the curling smoke and increasing flames that lick out of what is left of the back half of the upturned Mercedes. It's a shot Tarrantino would have killed for. By the time I reach the now blazing wreckage, he's moved on, looking for the other half and its occupant. I smell petrol and stand back, wary of the heat and mindful of the tank that could blow any second.

Twenty yards away, about three or four feet from the canal bank, lies the smashed and battered front end of the car. Digweed has already managed to prise open the twisted remains of the passenger door and is messing about inside.

'Don't look,' he warns as he hears me approach, but that's exactly what I do.

The headless body of Brian Wiggington lies frozen in a macabre diving pose on the crumpled bonnet of what is left of the vehicle. Most of his clothing has been shredded from him

281

as he's come through what was the windscreen, his bare, lacerated arse invidiously invasive; a final fetid *fuck you* to all and sundry. Blood and glass shimmer ruby and quartz and I immediately add to the show with the matt, but no less colourful, contents of my stomach. I stagger to the canal bank to finish what had been threatening for the last hour. I hurl, spit, slaver and retch, and when, in the near distance, the petrol tank explodes, I nearly add to the indignity by almost shitting my pants. It's only when the flare of the ignited fuel illuminates the gloomy murk of canal water and Wiggy's severed head and frozen, startled features bob to the surface, do I finally loose my bowels.

Thirty

CAROLINE GIVES ME a withered headmistress to naughty schoolboy kind of look as she flits busily from one room to another here down at the Bridewell. The clock on the wall says almost 2pm. We've been here nearly nine hours now. I've been through this sort of scenario before, a long time ago, but that doesn't make the experience any easier. Digweed doesn't look in too good a shape, especially now that his left eye has swollen completely shut. And my head and ankle continue to give me hell. Neither of us has had any sleep, nor have we had much sympathy. I don't suppose anyone likes having their Sunday disrupted, particularly busy lawyers and senior detectives, especially at such an early hour. Up to now we've been interviewed separately three times by three different grim faced, officers, and I can only hope and pray that our stories tally down to the last minute detail, because they'll have to. The scrutiny and observation we'll both be under as they try and unravel this sorry mess will be intense, and, as my experience will testify, it has only just begun.

With his good eye, Digweed stares blankly down at the floor in front of him. We haven't spoken for over half an hour. It's funny how you think you know someone, and then you get to find out that you don't at all really. I've known this guy sat next to me, my best mate, for almost thirty-five years, but I suppose in real terms, barely eight. You should never take things in life for granted, not even the little things.

"Derek? – Fucking Derek?" I hissed in his ear as he gave the desk sergeant his details.

"Yeah, it's my name, what's wrong with that?"

It turns out Digweed was plain old Derek Weedon, a fact that had eluded me all the time I'd known him. I never assumed he'd have a proper name. But, then again, like his name it turns out there were a lot of things that I didn't know about Derek Weedon...

* * *

Digweed had let me clean myself up with the rag he'd used to wipe away our prints. I ditched my soiled trollies and in a daze staggered back to the car in his wake feeling wretched. It could only have been about five in the morning, but no doubt the sound of the exploding petrol tank would have gotten someone out of bed in the hillside village of Clifton as it reverberated up their sleepy end of the valley. I couldn't begin to think how we'd be able to explain it all, but I needn't have worried on that score; Digweed had it all thought through, and I wasn't in any fit state to either consider or argue against what he'd come up with.

We were to tell the truth, exactly as it all happened, right up to the moment Wiggy took the pivotal blow to his nads. We were to leave that bit out. Wiggy was the one with the upper hand. He was the one who fired the shots; he was the pursuer, we were the pursued. We were fleeing for our lives from the madman who'd had his seedy operations uncovered. We'd desperately tried to shake him off. He lost control in the contra flow and had careered over the edge of the viaduct.

We hurriedly went over it a few times until we were confident we had our stories straight. Digweed had planted the gun next to his grotesque, headless body and had made sure his prints were all over it. I don't know how he dared do it, but he had. Confident, we might have been, whether we would be convincing or not was another matter. Either way, I still feared we were in deep shit, and in my case, I guess I must have smelled like it.

"Why didn't the crazy bastard just slow down?" I had mused to myself.

"He couldn't," Digweed said in his new husky-hoarse voice.

"What do you mean?"

He reached onto the back seat and picked up the hacksaw blade I had slung there earlier. He held it out in front of him and ran a thumb over the jagged teeth. He looked at me sideways, his sinister Arnie persona taking over again.

"I cut his brake pipes." He pressed a button that wound down his window and then slung the thing into some nearby bushes. He pressed the button again. *Shhhhp* went the window. He said no more, just turned his head and stared out in front of him – expressionless.

I must have stuttered and spluttered for a second or two before he shut me up.

"I knew you were up to something," he said in a calm, measured sort of way. "I pulled up and waited for you at Slaithwaite. Half an hour went and you never came by. You wouldn't have gone home any other way, so I doubled back. I went back to the studios but you weren't there. Then I got to thinking about what you'd said, how all the stuff stacked up against Wiggy, but you couldn't gather fresh evidence until the police re-opened your case. I sensed how frustrated you were. I guessed you might do something daft, so I put myself in your shoes and ended up driving over to Blackmoor. When I turned onto Ludlam Street I could see the van parked up. I also saw Wiggy getting out of the Mercedes. I pulled in sharp, switched off and watched from the top of the road. I watched him unlock and take the chain off the gates. Then he goes to the boot of the car, takes a quick look around and pulls out the shotgun. I'm thinking, if you're in there you're fucked, so I ring your mobile but you don't answer; it goes to voice mail. By now he's gone into the yard, so I wait a couple of minutes then I drive slowly down the street thinking what the hell I'm going to do. I've got the spare set of keys to the van, so I park up and open up the back thinking I might find something I could use as a weapon, but it's empty. I already knew it was empty; I'd cleared the fucking thing out with you an hour earlier. Then I see the hacksaw blade just lying there on the van floor. I think about creeping up on the bastard from behind and drawing it across his throat, but that's all I do. So instead I saw through his brake pipes. I figure whatever happens in there at least the cunt won't get so far afterwards – you know the rest..."

"You know if they decide to try and piece what's left of that mess together, they could find out that the brakes had been cut."

He shrugged resigned. "I'll have to take my chances, won't I?"

"Jesus Christ man, why did you do all this? Why didn't you just ring the police?"

"Because if I had it might have been too late for you – anyway, I wanted that bastard dead, didn't I?"

I turned to look at him open mouthed. I didn't get it. What had Wiggy ever done to him to arouse such hatred? Reservoirs of tears had started to form and spill down his bruised and battered face. I'd never seen him like this; he was alien to me. Apart from those tell-tale signs his expression and voice betrayed no emotion. He continued to stare ahead. I'm not sure if he could somehow tell I was struggling to make sense of it all, but at that moment, out of the blue, without any prompting, he dropped the bombshell...

"Me and Lauren were in love..." The words stirred more sudden movement in the lower colon. I instinctively nipped together cheeks as a caution. "... At least I was in love with her. I'm certain she felt the same way. She never actually said it – never got the chance to – but I knew she wanted to be with me. She wasn't in love with Fadge, I knew that much. She said she'd only gone with him in the first place to get me going, and like an idiot, I'd pretended I wasn't interested. Y'see, I was trying to be too much like you: Mister Smooth, acting all cool, playing hard-to-get. I thought, if I could emulate the legendary JD Smith, I'd have her falling at my feet. By the time I realised I'd been acting like a dick, it was too late. Fadge had got his claws in and I realised I'd lost my chance. Once I'd gathered enough courage to tell her how I really felt it was too late, she already had the ring on her finger. She wouldn't break it off. She wanted him to be the one to finish it. That's why she acted like she did, hoping he'd get fed up of her flirting and flaunting and eventually walk away. I deliberately kept out of it. I didn't want to be seen to be the one to come between them, partly because of the band, partly because I suppose he was a mate, even though he could be an annoying twat sometimes..."

The words continued to tumble out of him, hoarse and heartfelt, and things, as they do, started to fall into perspective. He was still in love with her, I could tell that much. Could that explain his confirmed bachelor status still all these years later? He'd been a good-looking kid, and up to last evening had been wearing well for a bloke about to turn fifty, yet he'd stoically remained single. She'd been snatched away from him before the love could be reciprocated, before it had time to nurture and grow, and the resulting anger from his loss had been festering away inside him all these years. And last night he'd let it all out. Brian Wiggington was never going to face a jury. All Digweed had needed was the confirmation and Wiggy's days were numbered. I'm certain his contingency plan would have come into operation sooner or later. My own resolve transpired to make it sooner, that's all.

I watched the salt tracks streak his face. It seems I wasn't the only one left to cry alone at night way back then. He told me how he would lay in his darkened bedroom playing Son House's Death Letter Blues constantly, over and over, *I didn't feel so bad till the sun went down – then I didn't have a soul to throw my arms around.* I pictured him in his lonely agony having to temper his grief alongside his band mate, storing away his secret sorrow from the world. Digweed: the laconic, laid back kid dude who didn't have a care – how wrong you can be.

His revelation had totally floored me. I would never have guessed in a million years. And what about Billy, did he have any skeletons in the closet? Had she been through the whole band?

"Did you ever... you know... did you...?"

He slowly turned his head to look at me for the first time. "No, I didn't," he said indignantly, "and I know what you're thinking, but you're wrong. I would never do that to a mate, not you, not even Fadge." He turned back to his straight ahead stare. "I won't deny that I fancied her when you two were an item, I think we all did, but I didn't love her back then, that grew long after you'd split up."

I thought back on those past crazy few hours; the essentially honourable, gentle spirited, yet oft demented drummer, the guy I loved like a brother, transformed into the murderous madman he became, and got to thinking some more...

"Let's say, if I'd have confessed to killing Lauren in order to get early release, like I'd been pressured to do... let's say, let's say I had actually done it – like you must have thought over the years – I mean, you must have had your doubts..."

"The thought did cross my mind occasionally, but deep down I knew you hadn't done it, despite the scrapyard and the ring and everything."

"How could you have been so sure?"

"Look, you treat your women like shit for most of the time, but you would never lift a finger to harm anyone physically – I knew you better than that. You were never capable of doing what that bastard did to Lauren."

"Okay, but let's say either of those things came to pass, hypothetically kind of – I'd be a dead man now, wouldn't I?"

He turned to me with his terminator stare once again. "Most probably..."

As dawn finally broke we heard the first of the sirens and saw the flashing blue lights high up on the Kirklees viaduct.

We sat in silence to await our fate.

* * *

'Okay Jack, let's go again.' The detective holds open the interview room door and waits patiently as I grunt to my feet and limp across the way, maybe a little too dramatically. Still failing to garner any sympathy, he looks at me like I was being pathetic.

The other two detectives await my presence; one of them is recording the time and date into a machine. I've survived their solo efforts; this looks as if it's going to be a group grilling. I hobble over and take a seat next to the cavalry. I give my solicitor a weak smile. She remains stern faced.

'You look gorgeous when you're angry,' I whisper out the side of my mouth.

'Don't push it,' she manages through clenched teeth like an apprentice ventriloquist. Under the table I slide a hand over her skirted thigh, feeling the outline of denier as it connects to her suspender. 'You stink,' she hisses while brusquely removing my hand. I let out a wry chuckle to myself. Of course I fucking stink: dehydrated breath, sweat, oil, grease, cordite, vomit and faeces, all on top of a two hour gig almost twenty-four hours ago, without a sniff of soap, water or toothpaste– top rank, I'd say.

Post trauma, sleep deprivation; delirium brought on by extreme fatigue; call it what you will, like emerging from a black hole into daylight, I begin to feel light-headed, almost giddy, like somebody's slipped me an anti-knock-me-down pill. I've been here before. I know the script, and the fact is my bloodied CV will make whatever the outcome here seem pale. All I ever wanted was justice; now in the cold sobering light of day it would seem I have it in spades. At best my hopes were for retribution via the state, the same flawed, monolithic system that put me away, and through my rashness and impatience, the old game of consequences played its part again. Justice has been served, not as I would ever have envisaged, maybe not exactly how Digweed would ever have planned, but now it's beginning to seem to me that the end-game played out perfect, fitting; savagely satisfying, and somehow I get the sense that Derek Weedon with his mangled features is sat outside feeling the same way.

The Home Office will have to re-open my case now;

they've no other fucking choice. I've opened the proverbial can of worms. Caroline can do her stuff and these boys will have to knit soup.

Did I hear someone once say that the truth was just a crock of shit? – Merely a perception?

My grim faced inquisitors close in. The button clicks. The red light says record. I give Caroline's thigh a tender squeeze – *well guys, here's my perception...*

Thirty One

I SIT QUIET in a corner of the taproom at The Melbourne listening to Robert Petway on the I-pod. My eyes open to the occasional external intruding noise or movement, Billy shifting gear, a barmaid stocking shelves. I half take in the faded, jaded Edwardian interior of this old boozer; the frosted, brewery-etched windows, the high dingy ceiling and yellowing ana-glyptic walls; decades of engrained nicotine seeping to the fore despite the recent smoking ban; sleepy old room, taking short respite from the expectant throng of noisy revellers and an on-slaught of down home dirty R&B reverberating from next door. Tired old room with its seasoned, beleaguered floor-boards, tarnished brass and ale soaked oak bar, providing nigh on a hundred years of recreation and refreshment for succes-sive generations, and, for almost four decades of that time, be-ing resident host to a British beat combo peddling their bas-tardised, electric versions of black American music to anyone who cared to listen – but for how much longer I wonder? I came back into this world to see the traditional ale houses and music venues being systematically closed down, boarded up, demolished, and I fear for the time this old place goes the same way, as it inevitably will, its history, stories and ghosts crum-bling to dust at the hands of developers, to be replaced by something new and shiny, but ultimately shallow, sterile, tran-sient and soulless.

I close my eyes and turn hypocrite, cranking up the volume of my wafer thin slither of technology to *take a stroll out west,* back to the delta to get me some Catfish Blues. I do this all the time now before a gig; play all the originals of our set-list to myself. It's become something of a ritual, I suppose, a nod in homage to our heroes, a lot of who never got the recognition they deserved when they were alive.

Jed's favourite, Hound Dog Taylor, plays Give Me Back My Wig. I go to forward it because me and Digweed refuse to include it in the set, too close to home and too many connotations we figured at the time, but it's such a great tune I allow it to play. Apparently this guy had eleven fingers and you can feel them all over the fuzzy tininess of his cheap Teisco guitar, belting it out and some, like he's stuck knitting needles in his speaker cones or something – awesome.

Speaking of the overweight devil, Jed slams his bottle down on the table snapping me out of my toe-tapping trance. He mimes his question to me by raising his eyebrows and cocking his hand back and forth near to his mouth. From this I deduce he's asking if I want a drink. I respond with thumbs up and a grateful grin. I've graduated from shandies now, much to the big guy's relief. He could never get his head around a man of the blues drinking watered down alcohol, and he still can't quite understand why I had to have ice in my Magners, but I was only being a sheep, drinking the stuff in the way everybody else did, making an effort of sorts, trying to fit in. I was still fairly new to the twenty-first century.

I put the I-pod away as the band gather in dribs and drabs, Billy the perfectionist the last to muster, having meticulously gone through his techy-setup ritual. And before long the table is full of empty and half empty glasses and bottles as we execute our own approximation of a pre-gig huddle. In between

293

the jokes, the wisecracks and the piss-takes, the talk is casually small. I use the practised art of stepping out of myself to muse over this ensemble of mature musicians. Jed, the rough but cuddly bruin who I've got to know and like so well, the Guinness residue frothing and settling amongst God knows what other crustaceans dwelling in and amongst his beard; his chesty chuckle and don't-give-a-fuck attitude guaranteed to bring out a smile in all who fail to be intimidated by the size and sight of him.

Billy's taken to wearing a black homburg of late, which is cool. It doesn't make him any less gnarly looking, but I guess it hides the massive recede of hair on his head, where once there was a mane as sharp and as flowing as his riffs. Curiously, he remained uncurious, never delving, seldom asking the questions anyone, let alone a close mate might have, given his drummer and bass player's circumstances. His only genuine concern seemed to be around the possibility of either or both of us getting sent down, and the decimation of his beloved Blizzard. Billy was so single-minded even recent seismic events merely served as an irritant in his closed shop of a world. To him the blues were paramount; anything else was a sideshow. Don't get me wrong, he cared for our well-being, and was forever asking how we were, but it was all in relation to how we were likely to perform rather than the actual traumatic, life or death shit we'd both been through.

'Why don't we try out that other Hound Dog Taylor number tonight?' I throw into the melting pot.

'Give Me Back My Wig? Great idea,' enthuses Jed working his tongue around his whiskers.

Now that he is able to, Digweed raises an eyebrow at the suggestion. I offer him a resigned shrug; we needed to move on. He turns to our unelected leader.

'Billy?'

'Okay,' he says easily. 'Let's chuck it in at the end of the set, see how it goes.'

'Now you're talking, *ever 'body know th' hound,*' whines Jed in a mimicking southern drawl before tipping a large amount of the black stuff down the sluice that is his open mouth.

Digweed looks at me and nods like he knows where I'm coming from. I hear the word closure banded about a lot these days. He's achieved it in the most satisfyingly vengeful way possible and got away with it; it's just his head taking the time to catch up to the fact. Me? I'm almost there but not quite. I still have a degree of fallout from the past twenty-odd years to deal with and I can't say when, if ever, that will get resolved, but little by little I begin to resemble a human again, and a better specimen of the species than I ever was back then. I've even changed my persona. Me and Digweed are the only two members of Blizzard who are clean shaven, well, when I say clean shaven I mean I'm no longer bearded, but I only take a blade to my face when I see Caroline – oh, yeah, put in young Ben's parlance, I suppose you could say we're a bit of an item these days. You see it turns out my whiskers brought her out in a bit of a rash, so now, whenever we get intimate, I go in baby faced smooth. Shit, I've even cut my hair, not conventionally acceptable, not even fashionable, but I've ditched the ponytail. It was kind of strange venturing near a mirror and uncovering the new me: Stevie Marriott at fifty-two, ha, scary. I still don't know what it is Miss Dupree sees in me, but hey, there you go.

I still can't get my head around the drummer. I'll never look at him in the same light ever again. He's almost taken on hero status in my eyes, but of course I'd never tell him that. As long as I live I'll never forget the way he performed in that garage while I stood there like a rabbit caught in the head-lights. And in the aftermath, the way he took control while my head was in bits. Even more astonishing is the fact that his quick thinking worked. We got away with it, and it was an-other of Wiggy's misdemeanours that proved pivotal.

The Merc Wiggy had been driving was one of his ringers. He'd been up to his old tricks, readying dodgy motors for ex-port. The thing he'd been driving was in fact two cars spot-welded together with the chassis number and plates changed. On impact with the kerb and barrier the two halves had parted company as easily as a bitter divorce. It had taken away further scrutiny of what was left of the two snide vehicles. Digweed and his deadly hacksaw blade had successfully pulled a flanker.

Even with that, of course, we still weren't out of the shit, what with the breaking and entering and the rest of it, but with that part we'd held our hands up and told the truth, the rest of our story held firm, and after they re-discovered Brian Wig-gington's nasty little secrets, even the hardest bitten coppers were on our side. Caroline got the bit between her teeth. My case was swiftly re-opened. On a rainy day in Monaghan, the remains of Lauren Feeney, my ex-girlfriend, Fadge's ex fiancé, and Digweed's would be lover, were exhumed. DNA was matched with a solitary item taken from Wiggy's trophy drawer, Caroline's immaculately presented evidence regarding the ring and the misguiding of the original jury finally got my conviction quashed. What me and Derek Weedon did on the night never got to court. Caroline kicked ass and pulled strokes all over the place until charges were finally dropped. Twenty-six years and nine months after the event I was a free man – free, but not complete.

I put jack to socket with that familiar snug click and immediately feel an epicurean sense of calm and contentment, of the sort you get when nearly all is well with the world. The slight hum from the Marshall as its valves warm to a glow, giving life to the Fender that I strap on, to meld as one; and with it that sensation, that surge of something that hits you inside, without fail, no matter how many times, a feeling that mere words could never do justice: indescribable. On a par with sex; better than some sex, less messy, emotions clear and reciprocated. Love? – I'd probably say so, although I'm still unclear about the notion, but if this is what love is, I'm settling for it. Tonight I'm a Voodoo Chile – untouchable. The blues is my Gris-Gris, my talisman; my snake and potion, rhythm and groove swamp offering to the spirits – Gris-Gris Gumbo Ya-Ya – Tonight there's magic in the air. The Melbourne buzzes with unconcealed expectancy and we're ready to deliver.

'Helloo...' Jed croons low into his mike by way of testing it. '...I think most of you in here know who we are by now...'

'I don't,' shouts a young wag from the audience.

'Yeah? – Well, you're gonna know us,' he promises, while stomping Billy in with a foot-to-stage count of four.

Billy starts up a double-eight bar staccato A-chord riff before Digweed drops in with a machine-gun volley on the snare and I finally fall into the mix as we open with a blistering version of The Feelgoods' Goin' Back Home.

Jed snarls in a voice that sounds as if he's been gargling razorblades. It sets the tone for the evening. To a man we're on our mettle; tight yet free flowing; drum and bass laying down mile after mile of groove-track for the guitar, harp and vocal express to ride on; a night train with its Mojo fully working, fuelled with a collective energy that reeks primordial.

There exists a zone, a place certain musicians talk about in hushed reverential tones, a place not of this Earth where on occasion, if the planets are aligned and all that malarkey, you get privileged to go. It doesn't happen too often, but when it does it's like you're taken out of yourself, and someone, or something else, is doing the performing and all the Gods conspire and come together to make love. More rare, but better still, is when this phenomenon occurs collectively. There must be a comet passing over The Melbourne tonight because judging by the suspended looks of mystery we are giving each other, this is one such occasion.

Like a recurring dream, a scene hung on frozen time, familiar, yet neither from the past nor the future, visited a million times as to turn a corner and instinctively know what's about to happen next, but as mysterious and as baffling as if it was happening for the first time. I've been here before; astral or by association, I can't say, but as satisfyingly normal and as it should be in the grand scheme of things, as it is scary and surreal.

I should be used to picking out blonds in a crowd now; I seemed to make a habit of it. Like a lost soul gazing on a beacon out to sea amongst bobbing heads that are waves, I lose it momentarily in the swell only for it to reappear, steadfast, resolute, guiding. Fixated, I home in on eyes of sparkling emerald and liquid jade. Disparate stuff floods my senses, a mash of words and images: *Things will happen as and when they're supposed to...* a cheeky laugh, and a bottle of brown sauce – It is Maggie, my Maggie.

In the sea of hope I also see the beaming faces of two Tall Dutchmen and the wild and sexy features of my woman. Caroline had been threatening to come and watch me play and I've warned her it wouldn't be like an evening at Ronnie Scott's, but it's unbelievable to see her, and Jordi and Edgar – and of course, my little butterfly.

Like some giant conspiracy coming together, Jed, totally unrehearsed, segues from She's Gone, into Talk To Your Daughter: *'I lay down last night and she called me in my dreams – I begin to wonder, what does she want with me? – Man please talk to your daughter for me...'*

I look around the old Melbourne stage totally shocked and bemused. Jed, Billy and Digweed grin inanely at me in turn. I guess it's all shaping up to be a day to remember. *Life is just a bowl of All-Bran* – as Stevie would've said.

CODA

I STAND AMONGST delicately scented jasmine and vibrant bougainvillea on this gloriously bright, hot and sunny December day. My Doshas and Vata have been serviced. My Pitta and Kapha fine-tuned. My good friend Kerin gives me a hug, a peck on the cheek and a flirty squeeze of my bum to send me on my way. With a reciprocal wave I tear up the track out of Chakras on my Bullet leaving a familiar cloud of red dust in my wake. I ride the mazy jungle roads of Apora towards Mapusa with the wind in my silver streaked hair and my mind, body and spirit freshly serviced for another month.

It's been more than three years since John Daniel Smith started life anew. It seems a lot longer when I think back to the day Jeanie was yelling at the more persistent newspaper hacks to *get off her fucking doorstep*! Not that I think back much these days mind. It's funny really; I'd always envisaged myself screaming from the rooftops on the day I finally proved my innocence. I'd be on TV punching the air live to the world like the Guilford Four, on the news giving interviews galore with my sexy lawyer at my side berating the establishment for their incompetence and wrongdoing. I did none of that; no party, no wild celebration. The whole thing happened quietly, with an air of anti-climax. The day Caroline phoned me with the news, I'd been sat in my room practicing scales, and at that moment all I wanted to do, all I wanted to be was curled up with her and a bottle of wine on a sofa listening to some old Billie Holiday tunes. (I get to do that quite a lot now whenever I'm back in England). After I'd told Jeanie and phoned the guys I went back and spent the rest of the afternoon with the Fender and some gentle blues.

I received my compensation around eighteen months ago, and I sunk most of the money into Vis guitars. I was keen to learn the luthierian craft, and the two Dutchmen were as keen to teach me, especially since I invested a sizeable wedge into their business. Since then we've expanded the premises here in Mapusa. In addition to the acoustic range of instruments, we now build solid bodied electric guitars that I have helped design and develop, and thanks to our whizz-kid marketing expert, who has come back to the fold, the order books are full and our reputation continues to grow. Away from the blues, our man Jed worked as an electrical engineer. He enthusiastically agreed to become part of the team, and I'll be collecting him from the airport later today when he jets in from England with a new prototype pickup he's developed.

Nina, my gorgeous granddaughter, now goes to school in England and stays with her Auntie Jean whenever her mum is away on one of her business trips. She has Ben's old room now that he's at University, in his penultimate year. It's funny how time flies when you don't need it to.

Liz and I have spoken on the phone, just the once; slightly awkward but we both managed to keep it civil, neither of us wanting or feeling the need to backtrack. We stopped short of apologies pertaining to our past and wished each other well in our new lives, as it should be.

I guess the time I was re-united with Maggie still remains the best day of my life. After the gig we stayed on in The Melbourne long after the place had shut and the punters had gone home. Billy and me played improvised blues on two beautiful guitars Jordi and Edgar had brought over with them, jamming well into the early hours.

I try not to think too much about fate; it's a notion that still has the ability to scare me a little; for good, for bad, a toss of the coin, a roll of the dice. I'm never too sure where its path crosses with karma, if ever it does at all, and Kerin's mystical explanations relating to the phenomena often leave me just that – mystified.

Mukteshwar is a remote village in the Himalayas. It's here that Nina, contracted meningitis. I don't recall the sequence of events as they were told to me later, except to know that it took four days to organise a helicopter to airlift her the four hundred kilometres for urgent treatment in Delhi, by which time she was near to death. She spent a month in intensive care, where, for much of the time, it was touch and go. Now on a daily basis I offer up a silent prayer to whoever or whatever it was that spared her life. As soon as she was deemed fit enough to travel, Maggie took her to Goa, where they stayed with Kerin at Chakras to recuperate. As well as the people in that Delhi hospital, I'm sure it's no small thanks to our wonderful white witch that Nina is now a robust, healthy five-year old.

It was during their stay at Chakras that Maggie and Jordi were finally re-united and in the course of the reconciliation she heard all about me and my story – the funny, sunburnt English guy and his brown sauce – her old man.

Like I say, I don't like to think too much about how the fallout from a near tragedy can end in forgiveness, reunion and ultimate happiness, not with my life's tapestry of consequences; you never know what's around the next corner. That's why I live one day at a time, thankful of each and every bright new dawn.

I spend the winter months here in Goa, and the summer back in England gigging with the band. Caroline usually manages a couple of trips out here during the course of the season amongst her busy schedule, and we use the time eating, drinking, playing music and generally relaxing in our rented villa by the Arabian Sea. It's our little piece of paradise. Here, at last, I get to define heaven on Earth, and I can be with the woman I love.

And of the twenty-five years that were taken from me? *C'est la vie*, as old Gertrude would have said. I certainly wouldn't be the guy I am today if all that shit hadn't happened to me. Bitter? – I suppose I've a right to be, but nah, life's too short and sweet for any of that. I reckon JD Smith is the luckiest, happiest man alive, but of course, that is only my perception.

I slow and swerve to avoid a wandering bullock, drop the Bullet through the gears and roar off into the heat of the day.

END

About the Author

DERRYL FLYNN GREW up in a northern coal mining town in England during the fifties and sixties. He studied Film-Theatre & TV at Bradford College of Art in the early seventies where he developed a passion for writing drama for screenplay and radio. His debut novel *The Albion* was first published in 2008. *Scrapyard Blues,* is his second novel.

Derryl lives with his wife, on the edge of the moors and just a spit away from Bronte country (not a good idea if the wind's in the wrong direction) where he continues to work on his third MS.

GRINNING BANDIT BOOKS

A word from our sponsors…

If you enjoyed *Scrapyard Blues*, please check out these other brilliant books:

Rupee Millionaires, Kevin and I in India, Ginger the Gangster Cat, and *Ginger the Buddha Cat* –by Frank Kusy (Grinning Bandit Books).

Weekend in Weighton by Terry Murphy (Grinning Bandit Books).

The Ultimate Inferior Beings by Mark Roman (Cogwheel Press).